Twice in a Lifetime

by Clare Lydon

custard books

First Edition October 2017
Published by Custard Books
Copyright © 2017 Clare Lydon
ISBN: 978-1-912019-52-6

Cover Design: Rachel Lawston
Story Editor: Laura Kingsley
Copy Editor: Gabriella West
Typesetting: Adrian McLaughlin

Find out more at: www.clarelydon.co.uk
Follow me on Twitter: @clarelydon
Follow me on Instagram: @clarefic

Also by Clare Lydon

London Romance Novels
London Calling

This London Love

A Girl Called London

Other Novels
The Long Weekend

Nothing To Lose: A Lesbian Romance

The All I Want Series
All I Want For Christmas (Book 1)

All I Want For Valentine's (Book 2)

All I Want For Spring (Book 3)

All I Want For Summer (Book 4)

All I Want For Autumn (Book 5)

All I Want Forever (Book 6)

Boxsets
All I Want Series Boxset, Books 1-3

All I Want Series Boxset, Books 4-6

All I Want Series Boxset, Books 1-6

ACKNOWLEDGEMENTS

There are a ton of people to thank for getting this book out the door!

First, thanks to Richard Evans for graciously letting us stay in his lovely apartment overlooking Lake Michigan for a week — seven days in which the inspiration for this book was born. I fell in love with Chicago then and I hope to go back soon! Thanks also to Anna Hodapp for being on the end of emails to answer all my queries about Chicago chocolate brands and department stores. Finally, thanks to Jason Hill for his Lake Paw Paw inspiration and information — that was a well-timed weekend away, Jason!

Many thanks to my early-reading team for sweeping your eyes over this one and catching all the typos before they skidded through — you're the best. Particular thanks to my super-early reader Iris Faulkner, and also my US authenticity team: Diana Augustoni and Katie O'Neil — you're all brill!

Huge thanks to my cover designer Rachel Lawston for making this a standout success; thanks to my story editor Laura Kingsley for telling me what to fix. Also, a tip of the hat to my typesetter Adrian McLaughlin for his silky skills with words and pages.

As always, huge props to my wife Yvonne for reading this late at night and giving it the thumbs-up — she really is the best.

And last but not least, thanks to you for reading and supporting. I get to call myself a writer because you bought this book, and that means more than you'll ever know. Now, go and buy copies for all your friends, too!

I didn't meet her when I was 17.
She was worth the wait.

Chapter One

Sally McCall had a fear of water, and that was mainly her Aunt Paula's fault.

Scratch that, it was solely her fault.

Sally was a scant five years old when her aunt, then 20, picked her up and threw her into the hotel swimming pool — unfortunately before checking if the young Sally could swim. She still remembered the shiny blue tiles of the swimming pool wall as she was rudely plunged underwater, the muffled shouts from above, along with the fizzing panic as her tiny limbs worked overtime to save her.

When Sally's dad, Rick, dragged her to the surface, his strong arms clamped firmly around her waist and Sally flapping like a sardine, she recalled her mom gesticulating wildly at Paula, her pistachio-green swimsuit clinging to her slender frame. After coughing up her excess water, Sally sat wrapped in a soft towel on her mom's lap, the sky bright blue as if it were illuminated, the thud of her mom's heartbeat in her ear. Sally's mom had smelled like cigarettes and sunshine.

One of the other memorable times Sally met her aunt was ten years later, when Sally was sitting with her dad's family in a fancy restaurant to celebrate his birthday. At the awkward age of 15, Sally was shy, and dealing with only her third-ever period, still not believing this was due to happen to her *every* month for the next 40 years: surely some cruel mistake?

That day, Aunt Paula had barreled in late and given her a crushing hug, before asking, in a voice that could have carried right across Lake Michigan, whether or not she'd had sex yet. Sally had died on the spot.

So now, sitting opposite her dad in her favorite New York City steakhouse nearly 20 years later, Sally was understandably hesitant about his news. All around her, servers rushed by balancing eye-level silver trays stacked with New York striploins and skirt steaks, the air seared with the smell of roasted meat and silky gravy.

"She wants to meet me for lunch. The woman who tried to drown me before my life had even begun?"

Sally was still scared of water to this day, which had affected her life and relationships, too. The Hawaiian vacation with Casey; Mexico with her friend Taylor; even the lake house all those years ago with Harriet. She blew out a long breath, tasting Harriet's sunscreen on her lips, before shaking her head, bringing herself back to the moment. With Harriet, the memories were *so* vivid, the feelings called up as if on speed dial.

"You know Paula — she's excitable," her dad replied,

swishing his red wine around his tall glass. He took a sip and nodded his head in approval.

"She's an excitable menace."

"Try being her brother, you got off easy."

Sally smiled at that. Her dad was laidback to the point of being horizontal, and she couldn't imagine what he'd gone through having a sister like her. Even though he was 12 years older, Paula had been born a crazy whirlwind, kicking up a storm that had never died down.

"Why does she want to see me? She's been living abroad for so long now." As soon as Paula was old enough, she'd fled her home to work on cruise ships, returning on a very irregular basis. Sally had heard muttered tales of her investing in property, but nothing more.

"From what she told me, she's got a business proposition for you, so it might be worth taking this meeting, honey. It sounds like she's got money burning a hole in her pocket. She's coming back to the US for good and wants to settle in Chicago and get to know her family. That includes you, her beloved niece."

Beloved niece? Sally was pretty sure she'd never been that to Paula, because Paula had never really stuck around long enough to get to know her. Where her friends had aunts that were present, Paula had always been a mystery to Sally.

"That sounds ominous. Plus, I live in New York, in case you hadn't noticed." As if emphasizing the point, a Yellow Cab slammed on its brakes to the right of the leather booth they were seated at, the driver honking his horn and gesturing out the car window. You didn't get that in Chicago.

Her dad smiled, rubbing his hand over his gray stubble. They both shared the same strawberry-blonde hair, the subject of much teasing when she was in school, but now a color she'd embraced. Her dad's hairline was receding, but he still had a good covering approaching his 61st year.

"I'm not sure anybody's ever told Paula no, but you could try." He gave her a grin. "I'm picking her up from O'Hare when she flies in next month. I did offer to come along to break your fall, but she was insistent. She wants to get to know you without me being there, so I have to respect that."

Their steaks arrived, garnished with Béarnaise and fries, their waiter topping up their wine before leaving them to it with a smile. Sally's stomach growled as she picked up her knife and made the first incision: it was perfectly pink, just the way she liked it.

"You think she's going to try to drown me again?" Sally asked.

"Make a reservation somewhere pool-free, that cuts your odds," her dad replied. "What have you got to lose? She's offering to help you out, and you've always turned down offers of help from me and your mom. But if Paula gives you some money, look at it as payback for all that childhood trauma she put you through." He paused.

"Speaking of which, maybe she should reimburse me for all the trauma she put me through."

Sally laughed, chewing her steak before replying. "I'll get her to write two checks." She put down her knife and fork. "Next month?"

"That's what she said. Can I give her your email address? Then it's in your hands, I'll leave you both to sort it all out — just don't shoot the messenger, okay?" Her dad licked his lips, catching some stray meat juice.

"I'll try not to," Sally said. "You know Mom's going to go crazy, though, right?"

"Only if you tell her," her dad replied.

Sally chuckled, thinking of all the times her mom had berated her dad. He hated confrontation, so he'd always backed down. Of course, it wasn't an issue anymore now they were divorced.

"So I'll tell Paula it's a yes?"

Sally nodded, resisting her need to be independent. Maybe her dad was right: Paula owed her, and god knows, she could use the money. This steak was the first decent meal she'd had all week, and she was enjoying it twice as much knowing she wasn't paying.

"Tell her it's a yes, just name the time and place. And preferably in New York. Some of us have work to do."

Chapter Two

"So it went well?" her business partner Joanna asked, her voice faint at the other end of the line.

"It went *really* well," Harriet replied, shuffling forward in the queue, her feet still swollen even from the short flight. The fluorescent lights screamed overhead, the AC turned up to chiller cabinet-efficiency. Someone nearby was eating beef-flavored chips, and the smell was making her stomach churn.

"The woman who owns the company was really cool, and we both think we're a good fit." Harriet stifled a yawn — it'd been an early start this morning, with her breakfast meeting at 7am. "We talked financials and distribution, she loves our roster of clients and wants to be a part of it. Their designs are amazing, too — you should see the executive toys and gadgets I've come back with, along with some gorgeous stationery. Apparently, we could be the gateway for them to go into orbit. Her words, not mine."

"Perfect, I love orbit. And I love my beach house, have I mentioned that?"

"Once or twice."

Joanna continued. "We need to get big clients so that I can fulfil my dreams of retiring by 40 to my beach house in the sun. Remember our promise?"

Harriet laughed softly, this being a speech she'd heard before. "This deal could take us one step forward to your beach house."

She paused, moving forward a little more, stooping to wheel her black carry-on suitcase. She shouldn't have to stoop, but the plastic pop-up handle wasn't obeying orders, just as it hadn't ever since she bought it. She should have returned it right away, but life had taken over and she'd forgotten.

A woman dressed in a black, official-looking immigration uniform leaned over the barrier, waving a dry hand in front of Harriet's face. "Excuse me, ma'am – no cell phones allowed in here."

Harriet gave her a nod. "Listen, I gotta go," she told Joanna. "No cell phones in immigration. I'll see you later on — I've got to drop my stuff at home and swing by my parents' house, but then I'll be in, okay?"

"Okay, see you then." Pause. "And remember, beach house, baby!" Joanna signed off, as was now customary.

Harriet pocketed her phone in her green pants and kicked the bag forward with her foot, watching as it slid to the left. The queue for immigration at Chicago's smaller Midway airport wasn't too bad — she'd had a lot worse during her many days of travel to and from New York, especially when she flew into O'Hare.

Fifteen minutes later she was at baggage claim, the overhead lights reflecting on her screen as she checked her phone, waiting for her larger suitcase.

She rolled her shoulders and yawned as she waited, her breath tasting sour, her stomach rumbling. She'd skipped lunch and just had a coffee on the plane, so she should remember to pick up some food on the way to visit her dad, who was still recovering after his "episode", as her mom was calling it. Her mom was having trouble coming to terms with her dad not being the robust man he'd always been, burying her head under the hood of her beloved Mustang, not wanting to face the real world.

She glanced up to the baggage screen, double-checking she had the right carousel: she did, but there was still no baggage in sight. On the other side of the carousel, she spotted a woman in a Cubs cap, and a white T-shirt with denim cut-offs. When the woman glanced up at the screen, there was something familiar about the shape of her mouth, her hair the color of roasted golden sunsets. She looked like… Harriet's heart began to race, the protruding vein on her right hand pulsing like crazy.

The woman looked a bit like Sally.

Could it be Sally?

Harriet bent her head and squinted, but before she could assess the woman, the carousel jerked to life. Harriet straightened up as suitcases began spilling onto the scuffed gray slatted belt. She saw her suitcase with its distinctive orange ribbon right away; she grabbed it, before looking back over toward the woman, but she was nowhere to be seen.

Harriet wheeled her suitcases a few feet away from the belt, looking around, but the woman was gone. Her heartbeat slowed to almost normal and she ground her teeth together, breathing deeply.

It probably wasn't Sally.

And what would she say to her if it was?

She sent a text to her brother Daniel, who was already at her parents' house, to see if they'd eaten. He replied almost instantly, telling her to pick up Chinese food for lunch, Dad's favorite. She had her instructions.

Harriet glanced around the baggage hall one last time before gripping both suitcases and heading to the airport car park, and her waiting silver Prius.

Chapter Three

" I am freaking out here!" Sally looked up to the ceiling of the airport baggage hall, its square ceiling tiles leaking an off-yellow light, the color of soured milk. The space smelt musty, too, like laundry that had been left in the machine too long.

"Slow down, tell me again what happened."

It was good to hear Taylor's voice, even down the phone: it was calming her down, which was what she needed. Taylor was a wallpaper designer who worked in the same creative co-op as Sally in Queens, and they'd been close friends ever since Sally took the workspace down the hall from her nearly three years ago. They'd bonded immediately over color choices and beer brands, the two most important discussions designers can have.

"Somebody has taken my suitcase." She paused. "Correction, some idiot has taken my suitcase."

One month on from meeting her dad, her Aunt Paula had arranged a dinner in Chicago, paying for Sally's flight and accommodation. So here she was, hauling her butt from La Guardia to Midway on a Thursday morning, flying into her home city for the first time this year. Only, just a few hours into her trip, it wasn't quite going to plan.

"I thought you had that orange ribbon on your suitcase that you saw on that show? You were very proud of that orange ribbon."

"I did! But it didn't stop someone taking it."

Taylor had told her she should tie a rainbow ribbon, just to be a bit different and gayer, but Sally had told her she didn't want to be a walking cliché. Now, she wished she'd listened to Taylor's advice.

She sighed loudly as a man and woman wheeled a trolley of suitcases past her, oblivious to her pain. She spotted an orange ribbon on one of them, and shook her head. It seemed like everyone had taken the advice of that travel show and put an orange ribbon on their luggage, thereby negating its original purpose.

"So, you've got nothing? Did you pack anything in your carry-on luggage?"

Sally frowned. "No, smart-ass, I didn't."

"So you overpacked for a weekend away when you could have just taken a carry-on, and now you've lost your suitcase?"

Sally heard the amusement in Taylor's voice, which made her smile at the absurdity of her situation. She rolled her eyes and fingered the peak of her Cubs cap, lying in her lap. "Yes, that is correct, and yeah, I might have overpacked."

"You're screwed then — at least until whoever took

it brings it back. Assuming it was accidental." Taylor paused. "You didn't have anything incriminating in there, did you?"

Sally sucked on her top lip. "Like what?"

"I don't know — a bright pink dildo, some bondage gear?"

"I left that at home this time," Sally replied, deadpan. "No, nothing weird, just all my clothes, my shoes, my journal." She paused. "I knew I should have put my journal in my bag." Her stomach clenched as she thought of all her private thoughts dropping into a stranger's hands.

"Is there anything with your name in it? Your address?"

Sally shook her head. "No, the woman at the baggage desk asked that. I don't know whether to wait here or go to the hotel. This is not how I anticipated my long weekend starting."

Taylor cleared her throat. "Fingers crossed whoever opens it brings it back — chances are, they will. Especially when they see the state of your underwear."

Sally cupped her palm around her face, laughing despite herself.

"Look on the bright side — it's all replaceable. You've got your passport, phone and wallet?"

Sally tapped her black bag, all her worldly goods inside. "Yes, all here."

"Then look on it as an opportunity. Go to the hotel, live it up in the fancy facilities, then do some shopping in Chicago. You're about to get a bunch of money, so you can afford it. Buy some new clothes, you'll impress your aunt and then you can persuade her to invest in me, too."

Sally laughed again. Taylor always had a knack of saying the right thing, making her feel better, even when she was in a frankly lousy situation. She stared ahead to the baggage desk, where the woman she'd spoken to gave her a sympathetic smile.

"You know what, you're right. I'll get a cab to the hotel, and hopefully by the time I've rolled around on my luxury kingsize bed, my suitcase will have turned up."

"Do it," Taylor said. "And don't forget to ask your rich aunt if she needs any custom wallpaper."

Chapter Four

The wheels of Harriet's silver Prius rolled smoothly up her parent's driveway, coming to a stop in front of their white-doored double garage. The door was open, too, which meant her mom must be tinkering with her beloved bottle-green Ford Mustang '68, affectionately named Muzzy.

Harriet climbed out of her black leather seat, yawning as she moved her black sunglasses to her forehead, pinching the ridge of her nose where she knew there would be a red mark. She stretched her arms above her head, glad to stop traveling for five minutes — she'd done enough of that already today.

The lunchtime sun sat high over the top of her parents' gray-and-white two-storey home, which also boasted a freshly painted front porch that ran the width of the house, along with a gigantic Sugar Maple in the middle of the manicured front lawn. Her parents lived in the northern Chicago suburb of Winnetka, which was around a half-hour drive from her apartment on a good commute day. Luckily, the drive from the airport had been traffic-free, which meant she was in a good mood. Harriet's powder-keg patience in traffic was the stuff of legend.

She walked into the garage, its walls stacked with shelves holding car parts, old paint cans, and miscellaneous white plastic storage boxes. At the end of the shelves, there were three ladders propped against the bare brick wall. Harriet had fallen off one of those when she was nine, breaking her arm. She hadn't been up a ladder since, instead employing people who were more skilled at such endeavors.

Her mom was under the hood of Muzzy, exactly where Harriet had expected to find her, her oil-stained hand resting on the car's green paintwork.

"Hey, Mom," Harriet said, in a voice loud enough for her mom to hear and not be startled. She'd done that one too many times and earned her mom's wrath, especially when it meant she was surprised and cracked her head on the hood. Harriet didn't want that look of disdain again.

Her mom looked up, wiping her hands on a dirty rag, still the most put-together mechanic Harriet had ever seen. Her auburn hair was stacked on top of her head in a bun, her pink shirt unsullied, her "work" jeans pristine. Harriet bet if she did a close inspection, even her painted nails would be oil-free.

Her mom might be older than her dad, but you'd never guess it because she looked after herself far better. She'd been a runner all her life, but in later years she'd switched to hiking, which had less impact on the joints. Harriet, by some fluke, had inherited her mom's slim, athletic genes, without putting in any of the work.

"Hello, you," she said, flashing her daughter a tired smile. "You're here early. I thought Daniel said you were in New York?"

"I was, I got an early flight back." Harriet paused. "How are you?"

"Keeping sane in here," her mom said. "It's all a bit stressful, but we're surviving. Your dad looks better today, got a bit more color in his cheeks."

"That's good."

Her mom was approaching 63 and had been retired two years, following a career in corporate banking. Her dad's heart trouble and near-death experience had shaken the whole family, which was evident as this was the fourth time Harriet had visited this week, whereas she and her mom normally caught up every other week.

Perhaps she should make it a more regular occurrence — maybe then their conversation would flow more freely.

"I brought Chinese food; are you joining us?"

Her mom shook her head. "I won't, I'm on a roll here. Plus, I'm not that hungry."

Harriet gave her a look. "Are you eating? This is hard on all of us, but you need to eat." Her mom had always been conscious of her weight, always skipped meals. It was a habit Harriet had carried into adulthood, too, even though she loved food.

"I'm eating, don't worry. Just get the food to your dad, he's the one who needs it most. Are you staying a while?"

Harriet shook her head. "I can't. I have to drop my stuff off and get back to work; it's just a flying visit."

Her mom held her gaze for a moment, then nodded. "Of course, work comes first," she said, turning back to the car's innards. "Make sure you say goodbye before you leave, okay?"

Harriet nodded, unsure of her footing in this emotional maze she and her mom always seemed to construct by accident.

"Will do," she said, wondering if she disappointed her mom. Was it because she hadn't followed her career path and gone into finance? Because she wasn't married with children? Because they didn't have a Hallmark mother-daughter friendship? She'd love to move the needle of her and her mom's relationship, but she wouldn't have a clue where to start.

She rolled her newly tensed shoulders, expelling air as she walked back to her car and opened the trunk.

The gray front door sprang open as she turned, and her brother Daniel came bounding out like an over-sized black Labrador, his arms encasing her before she had time to think about it. His dark hair was hanging in front of his eyes, his stubble two days thicker than when she'd last seen him. He was going for the hipster look, but right now he just looked a little unkempt.

"Get off me, you great lunk," Harriet said, smiling. "And get a haircut while you're at it."

"You jealous of my flow?" he said, flicking his locks in an exaggerated manner.

"I know you're only here to get the food, it's got nothing to do with me."

"Of course I'm here for the food, shorty," he replied, before scooping up the brown paper bags in both hands. "Come on, we're all starving."

The smell of fresh-cut flowers and paint drifted into her nostrils as she followed Daniel across the brightly lit square hallway, her feet light on the polished wooden floor. They walked past the family portrait that hung on the newly painted white wall facing them. Harriet tried to ignore how strong their dad looked back then: powerful, upright, in control. In years past, she'd always focused on how gawky she or Daniel looked, on their mom's bouffant '80s hair.

But now, all she saw was Dad.

She had to remember the prognosis was good.

When they reached the gleaming kitchen, all granite worktops, low lights and white gloss cabinets, Daniel dropped the food onto the pristine counter-top. Four plates already stood on the kitchen island, along with four sterling-silver knives and forks.

"You're very prepared," Harriet said, impressed. Sometimes, when her brother wasn't goofing around, he surprised her.

"I'm fully house-trained," Daniel replied. "I'll make someone a lovely husband." He pushed some hair behind his ear and gave her a wink as he spoke.

"No doubt about it," Harriet said. "No news from that woman you were after last week?"

He gave her a shy smile. "We're going out this weekend."

Harriet held up her palm and her brother gave her a high-five. "I expect good things from this one, you've been going on about her long enough."

"We'll see — I don't want to jump the gun like normal." Daniel leaned a hip on the counter and smiled. "But I really do like her, she's got an air about her. She seems… like she has her act together."

Harriet gave him a warm smile. "That would make a change from the usual women you go for."

"I know, right? You might actually get to meet one."

"She has to be better than the last one I met."

"She is, hopefully you'll meet her soon. And who knows, maybe even Mom and Dad."

Harriet raised an eyebrow as she opened a carton of rice. "The parents? Hold your horses, cowboy, you haven't even been on a single date yet."

He shrugged. "I live in hope."

"Speaking of the parents — how's he been today?" Harriet took the rest of the cartons from the bag, setting them out on the counter.

Daniel's shoulders went up, then down, a sigh punctuating

his actions. "No change," he said. "One minute he's awake and almost smiling, the next he's asleep. He seems to be in a lot of pain when he's awake, so I don't know. He's clutching his chest pillow like his life depends on it, but apparently that's normal. It was open-heart surgery, after all. But when I mentioned Chinese food, he perked up visibly, so I hope he eats some of it."

"Me, too," she replied. "And how does Mom seem? I just went to see her and she was… Well, she was Mom." Harriet gave a little chuckle and rolled her eyes as she spoke.

Daniel stopped spooning rice onto a plate and looked up at her through dark lashes. "She's okay, it's just a shock. She's spending time with Dad as well as Muzzy — the jury's still out on which one she prefers." He gave his sister a wide grin. "You think she loves Muzzy because she doesn't answer back?"

"Or drink her booze?"

"Or spend years slinking in late, trying to disguise her preference for women?"

"Maybe she's got a point," Harriet said, laughing, taking a plate of food in either hand: her stomach growled at the sweet smell of fried rice and chow mein. All she'd had all day was a mini-pastry at her meeting this morning. "Shall we take these up to Dad and eat in his bedroom?"

Daniel nodded. "He'd like that. And you can tell us all about your New York trip and all the women you seduced overnight."

Harriet spluttered at that. "My trips are all work and no play."

"Which makes Harriet a very dull girl," Daniel replied.

Chapter Five

It was after 3:30pm by the time Harriet left her parents, so she was seriously running behind schedule. Still, she'd got to spend a little time with her dad, who'd quizzed her about her New York trip. She could count on one hand the number of times he'd seriously taken an interest in her business, so this was a new turn of events — but maybe this was what nearly dying did to a person, made them try different topics of conversation.

The fact that she ran her own business hooking up incredible designers with retail outlets had always baffled both her parents, not being the steady sort of job they both favored. Whenever they mentioned Harriet being an entrepreneur, they always winced slightly, as if it were a disease they might catch.

She was driving down the highway, tapping her thumb on the steering wheel as the latest Drake track blared from the car radio. Daniel had picked the station, and he had his right leg crossed over his left, so that every time he tapped his foot, it left a mark on her dashboard.

"You wanna not do that?" Harriet said, pointing to the mark.

"Sorry," Daniel replied, moving his foot to the ground before glancing at his sister. "Are you seriously going back to the office now? After you got up at stupid o'clock this morning to get to an even stupider early meeting?"

Harriet rolled her eyes. "I am. Are you not going back to work?"

The AC in the car had kicked in, and she was beginning to cool down, although the air was still thick and stale.

He shook his head, keeping his eyes facing forward. "I took this week off as family leave — somebody needed to be there for them."

"Ouch!" Harriet replied, slapping his arm. "I've been over a couple of times."

"It wasn't a dig, it's just my work is more flexible than yours," he said, shrugging. "Even though you're your own boss and you *own* the business."

This was a conversation they'd had before and they'd probably have again, so Harriet shut it down. Daniel didn't understand the pressures of running your own business, being the free spirit that he was.

"Change the record" she said, the corners of her mouth curving into a smile as she pulled up at the side of the road, in front of the blue-and-white house Daniel shared with two other women. Daniel loved women and he surrounded himself with them in every area of his life.

He unbuckled his seat belt and pushed it aside before turning his body to Harriet. "I just think there are better things you could be doing with your time on a Thursday night than sitting in your office and working, don't you?"

"Not really." Of course, before she'd gotten into the groove of working all the time, there were plenty of things she'd have preferred to do, involving women, drinking, and dancing. But these days, they were never the thing that made it to the top of her list.

"You know, like going out, hitting a gay club, meeting some women." Daniel put a finger to his chest. "If I can meet one, and I'm a humble gardener, you can meet one, Ms Hotshot Entrepreneur. Women would be all over you like a rash. Don't forget, I've seen it happen."

Harriet smiled at all the times the duo had gone out together, first to a bar for Daniel, then to a bar for Harriet. She'd had her fair share of triumphs with Daniel in tow, only none of them had ever lasted more than three dates. Her batting average was usually have a drink, have sex, have sex once more, then never see them again.

It was a record she was keen to change, although lately she'd found herself thinking that if love didn't happen for her, she would be at peace with that. Daniel was always chasing it, but it wasn't a given for everyone, was it? Maybe love and her just weren't compatible, and that's where work stepped in to fill the void.

She gave her brother a tired smile. "Dear Daniel, I

know you're only looking out for me, but if I don't get this work done, Joanna will kill me."

Daniel let out a bark of laughter. "Joanna is a pussycat — and I bet Joanna's out tonight with her hot lady. What's her name?"

"Viv."

"The lovely Viv."

"Don't be so sure: from what I hear, there's trouble in paradise."

Daniel pouted. "Don't say that, I like happy endings, you know that."

"I know, I'm sure they swapped our gender chromosomes at birth," she replied, only half-joking. "Now get out of my car — I need to go home, get changed, then go to work."

"You used to be so much more fun, you know that? I know that girl is still in there somewhere and I'll get her out, just you wait."

* * *

Harriet's apartment door gave a satisfying clunk as she pushed it shut with her butt, dragging her suitcases inside. She strolled through to the living room with her open-plan kitchen at one end, glad she'd remembered to close her wooden blinds before she left — otherwise her apartment would have been a cauldron.

She switched on the AC and grabbed a glass of water, downing it before turning her attention to her luggage. It was only when she went to pick up the larger suitcase with the company samples inside that she noticed the lock was missing. Dammit — how had that come off in the flight? A sense of dread filled her as she wondered if any of the samples had been stolen.

Please let the lock have just fallen off and not been taken off purposely.

Harriet got down on her knees, frowning at the orange ribbon attached to the handle. Now she was up close and concentrating, it didn't look like *her* orange ribbon.

Oh shit.

Did she even have the right suitcase?

She took hold of the black metal zipper and trailed it round its track, the whirr of metal on metal filling the air, along with her accelerated breathing. She did the same on the other side and then flipped the lid open.

And then she stared at what was laid out before her, her eyes not quite believing what she was seeing.

Plus, it smelt of… what was that smell? Harriet recognized it: sweet, musky, sexy.

And then it hit her: Hugo Boss Red perfume. One of her short-lived conquests had worn it.

And clearly, so did whoever this suitcase belonged to.

She wrinkled her nose.

Hair dryer. Make-up bag. Navy blazer. Jeans. T-shirts, one red, one blue. A shirt with bright yellow bees. A single white Nike sneaker — she assumed that somewhere, there was another. An old JoJo Moyes novel Harriet had read a few years ago.

There were none of the carefully packed samples.

Mainly because this wasn't her suitcase.

"Shit," she said, sitting back on her heels and cupping her chin. "Shit, shit, shit…"

What was she going to do? She needed those samples to show Joanna, but also to show she was a capable businesswoman, not someone who grabbed the wrong suitcase and didn't notice for four goddamn hours.

Where the hell was her suitcase now? She had no idea. It could be halfway across the country for all she knew.

Shit, shit, shit.

She stood up and began to pace her living room, reaching its picture window, opening the blinds and staring out at Lake Michigan ahead of her, sunlight bouncing off its surface. Its mere presence usually soothed her, but not this afternoon.

She turned sharply and grabbed her phone from her bag, finger poised over the keypad. Should she call Joanna to let her know? Not much point in that.

She should call the airline first, or perhaps the airport. Maybe whoever had her suitcase had handed it in and was sitting in the airport, nursing a beer, wondering when she was going to see her make-up bag again.

Yes, she should call the airport.

Or maybe there was something in the suitcase? Some clue to the mystery woman's identity?

Harriet dropped her phone, ran over to the suitcase and began piling the clothes on her beige carpet, finding the other white Nike underneath. The shoes were worn, showing that whoever this suitcase belonged to was into exercise.

Harriet had a brief flash of guilt for not using the gym in her building more. She'd sworn she would when she moved in, but then, work had overtaken everything and she'd only made it a handful of times. When the gym overlooked the city from the 45th floor of her building, that was criminal.

Underneath the clothes were some sketch pads, which she flicked through: whoever she was, this woman could draw. There was also a pack of colored pencils, and a journal. Aha! This could be what she'd been looking for. She flicked open the front cover, and sure enough, written in a pencil that clearly needed to be sharpened, was a name.

Sally.

And after that, a phone number.

She exhaled, sitting down on the floor, journal in hand. It was one of those fancy ones with a hard cover and a Japanese-style design on the front. Harriet flicked to the back of the book, seeing that the last entry had only been written yesterday.

And the owner was called Sally.

A memory of *her* Sally flicked through her mind, sitting on the balcony of her family's lake house, writing her journal — but that was all a very long time ago.

Her eyes flicked over the handwriting, surprisingly neat and legible. The woman was talking about meeting up with someone called Ben and another person called Taylor.

They'd met at a bar and hadn't got as much done as they were meant to, but they'd got the ball rolling on the new project, and the woman had drawn a thumbs-up.

What project were they working on?

But then Harriet blushed, guilt spreading through her. She shouldn't be prying into this woman's life: she should be calling her and asking if they could meet to trade suitcases and sort this mishap out.

She scrambled to her feet, picking up her phone from her light oak dining table.

She grabbed the journal and dialed the number.

Outside, she heard a siren wail down below; the only sound in her apartment was the hum of her AC and the boom of her heartbeat in her ears.

"If this is you again, Taylor, calling from a friend's phone, I don't appreciate it," said a silken voice in her ear. "I've already lost my bag today, I'd hate to add a friend to that list."

"It's not Taylor," Harriet said, flexing her shoulders and clearing her throat. "Is that Sally?"

"It is." Beat. "Who's this?"

"My name's Harriet and I'm not sure if you've realized yet, but I think we switched suitcases at the airport."

"Wait, you've got my case? It hasn't been stolen or lost?"

"No, I took it by mistake, and only realized that when I opened it up. I'm really sorry."

"Thank fuck," Sally said. "I've just been on the phone with my friend wondering what the hell I'm going to do in Chicago for four days with no clothes or make-up. I hung around the airport, but they said all the bags had been picked up."

"So you don't have my bag?"

"No, the airport does. I didn't take it, as I could see it wasn't mine because it had a lock on it. Although I did have it in my hand to take, because it had an orange ribbon on it, like my suitcase." She paused. "You didn't happen to watch a show on the travel channel the other week which mentioned tying a ribbon around your suitcase handles so they were more recognizable, did you?"

Harriet let out a scorched laugh. "I did. But I guess it doesn't work if everyone does it, right?" She shook her head at her own stupidity. "Especially not if we all use the same color ribbon as on the show."

"Not so much," Sally said. "So, how did you get this number?"

Harriet felt a blush invade her cheeks. Even though she'd had to do it and she wasn't sorry, she was still embarrassed to tell a complete stranger she'd gone through her stuff. Although, Harriet felt like she knew her a little already: she liked to exercise, to draw, to journal, to wear casual clothes.

"I unpacked your suitcase to see if I could find out who it belonged to — I found your journal at the bottom and it had your name and number in it." She winced. "Sorry, that sounds bad, but I wanted to return your suitcase to you."

"No problem," Sally said, sounding a little less sure than she had been a few moments ago.

"I didn't read anything other than your name and number, I promise," Harriet lied. "Anyway, getting it back to you. Where are you — in Chicago?"

"I am," Sally replied. "I'm here to see my aunt for the weekend, it's a flying visit."

"You're not a light packer, then," Harriet replied.

Sally laughed. "You sound like my friend Taylor, who was just admonishing me for packing so much, and then losing it."

"Where are you staying? I can drop it off on my way to work, it's the least I can do."

"I'm at the Kimpton Gray Hotel in the Loop. Are you anywhere near there?" Sally said. "I've got dinner tonight with my dad, and it'd be good to have my stuff so I can look presentable."

"I'm sure it would," Harriet said, looking over at Sally's Nike sneakers on her carpet. At her journal on the table in front of her. At her clothes piled beside her suitcase. And feeling like there was something familiar about her voice.

Sally. It couldn't be her Sally, could it?

No, that would be ridiculous.

"I could get to you in an hour?"

"Perfect — I appreciate it."

Harriet smiled, glad to be able to fix her mistake so soon. "Maybe you'll let me buy you a coffee as an apology."

There was a beat of silence before Sally spoke. "A coffee sounds good. It was an early start from New York this morning, so it's needed." She yawned on the other end of the line. "Thanks for taking the time to track me down."

Harriet put her phone on the table, staring out at the lake. Her bay window covered almost the entire width of her living room and its floor-to-ceiling presence allowed her a 360-degree lake view, something her visitors always commented on. To her right she could make out some of the buildings from downtown, including Willis Tower and the John Hancock Center. And every night, the Navy Pier fireworks lit up the sky, and she often drank a cup of herbal tea as she looked out at them.

She blew out a breath as she crossed the living room and began to repack Sally's suitcase. She'd sounded upbeat and not too pissed with Harriet, which she was grateful for.

Hadn't Daniel just told her she should get out more and meet new people? Here she was, doing just that.

She zipped up the suitcase and shook her head at the orange ribbon that had caused the confusion in the first place. Then she picked up her phone and searched for the airport's baggage reclaim number, crossing her fingers they still had her suitcase. In all the excitement of chatting to Sally, she'd forgotten she still didn't have it yet.

She dialed the number and took a deep breath.

Chapter Six

What was her name again? Had she really said Harriet? Sally hadn't met any other Harriets since *the* Harriet.

The Harriet who'd changed everything and made her whole body sit up and take notice.

If only she'd listened and followed that path to its logical conclusion, without marrying Todd and putting herself and him through all of that pain. If only she'd listened to what every inch of her was screaming when she walked down the aisle: that she preferred women to men.

This Harriet had asked her to have coffee with her — a bit weird, and Sally hoped it wouldn't be *too* awkward. Her voice had sounded soothing and assured, so that was a start. Plus, she had her suitcase, so maybe it was polite to do so.

The elevator reached the lobby and Sally strolled down the impressive marbled hallway, and then across the main entrance hall, the whole space awash with candied sunshine from the front windows. She walked past the sharp, sleek reception desks and the hotel's Japanese-inspired dark wood backdrop, with low-slung leather and metal chairs, stone-colored tables and high-gloss polished floors.

She spotted her suitcase first, with a chestnut-haired woman sitting beside it, her shoulders slightly hunched, the sole of her silver Oxfords tapping on the floor. She was facing in the opposite direction, and as Sally approached, she could see the woman had her phone in her hand, the familiar Facebook screen being scrolled through.

When Sally drew up behind her, she cleared her throat and put on her best smile. "Harriet?" she said, a weird feeling flowing through her body.

Because all of a sudden, she knew who this was. Even before she turned around, Sally knew this was not just any Harriet, but *her* Harriet. She knew, because she'd never forget those hands, or the way she smelt. She was still wearing the same perfume 17 years later, and every time Sally had smelt it in the intervening years, she'd always thought of her. How could she not?

Sally held out a hand as Harriet turned, staring back at her with those piercing green eyes. Eyes that Sally knew. A mouth she knew. A face that was so familiar, Sally felt like she'd traced it with her heart a million times.

And now, here she was, the suitcase thief.

"Harriet?" Sally repeated, taking Harriet's hand in hers: it was warm, just like she remembered. And despite the intervening years, a shiver ran through her. She shook her head slightly, reminding herself she wasn't 17 anymore.

Only, around Harriet, she'd only ever been 17.

"Harriet Locke?" Sally had to say her full name, just to be sure she wasn't making this up on the spot. She glanced down at their intertwined fingers, neither of them letting go.

Harriet nodded, an incredulous smile on her face. "Sally McCall?" she replied, her voice a whisper. "What the hell?"

All around them, the hotel lobby buzzed with activity, but all Sally could see was Harriet. All Sally could feel was Harriet.

It was like she'd been transported back to her 17-year-old self in the blink of an eye, rendering her speechless.

Like nothing had changed at all.

Only, it had.

Sally was pleased to see Harriet looked just as freaked as she was, too.

"What are you doing here?" Sally asked, her mouth dry, a throbbing in her head.

Meeting Harriet again was giving her a headache.

"I'm bringing back your suitcase."

Sally dropped Harriet's hand before replying. She still couldn't quite wrap her head around this situation. "I can see that," she said. "But… it's *you*. What are you doing here?"

Harriet laughed, breaking the tension. "I live here."

"You do?"

Harriet lived in Chicago. She'd always thought of Harriet living in New York or LA, not Chicago.

"And you picked up my suitcase. What are the chances?"

Harriet blinked rapidly. "A million to one?" she replied, sweeping her bangs off her face. "I thought you sounded familiar on the phone, but then I thought it was just me being stupid."

Harriet Locke was standing in front of her. Gone was the teenage attitude, the messy hair; this Harriet's shoulder-length bronzed hair was streaked on one side, her smile undimmed. And she'd filled out, too, in a good way, her green pants and white shirt hugging her body in all the right places, her skin tanned against the bright white fabric. Harriet looked hip and beautiful, just like always.

"It's great to see you, Sally," Harriet said, flashing Sally her smile, coupled with her dimple.

Sally's stomach flip-flopped, just like always.

Harriet Locke.

Damn, she looked good.

"It's great to see you, too," Sally replied. But was it great to see her? She had no idea.

The last time they'd seen each other she'd been in so much pain, she'd gone to ground for weeks after. She and Harriet had tried to carry on when Harriet had gone to college, but it hadn't worked out.

Okay, that was the understatement of the year. It had exploded spectacularly, splattering Sally's heart all over town, leaving her a gibbering wreck. When they split up, the pain had been so real, Sally still recalled its texture and its taste: it was gnarly, gristled.

She'd rehearsed this scene in her mind so many times: how she'd puff her chest out and tell Harriet just what she thought of her.

But now, here she was, doing none of that, like none of it mattered.

In a way, after 17 years, that was true.

Then again, as Sally knew from her elevated heartbeat, it was a big fat lie.

All of it mattered, *so very much*.

"So what happened?" Sally asked, before realizing that question could be taken in a myriad of ways. "With the suitcase, I mean?"

If she just stuck to talking about the suitcase, she could keep her thoughts clear, straight. Although, when it came to Harriet, her thoughts had never been all that straight.

Harriet was staring up at her with those emerald eyes. Sally steadied her nerves, remembering those up close, staring into them, never wanting to let them go. But Harriet had forced her hand.

"Well, I took it by mistake." Harriet held up her hands in apology. "And it was totally my fault — blame my early start and the extended nap I took on the plane."

So many thoughts were racing through Sally's head, but she put them to one side. "So you live in Chicago," she said. "What were you doing in New York?"

"Business meeting," Harriet replied. "Flew in last night, it was a quick visit."

Sally nodded. Of course she had a business meeting. Business meetings and Harriet Locke were made for each other. She was probably some hotshot lawyer by now, Sally had no doubt.

"What about you?" Harriet asked, her eyes searching Sally's face, making Sally unsteady on her feet.

"Me?"

"Yes — what were you doing in New York?"

"I live there, in Queens," Sally replied. "I'm an artistic cliché."

Harriet's face lit up at that. "You've done something with your crazy talent?"

Sally smiled. Harriet thought she had crazy talent? "I'm trying. But my luck might be about to turn: it's sort of why I'm here in Chicago."

Harriet furrowed her brow. "How so?"

Sally shook her head: that was a story for another day. "I'll tell you another time."

She paused. She was talking to Harriet Locke; this really was too surreal.

Harriet checked her phone. "I've got to get to my office, but I'd love to grab a coffee with you, at least."

Sally assessed her. "Sure," she replied. "You know, when you called, I wondered if going for a coffee with a stranger was going to be awkward."

"And what do you think now?"

"I'm not sure what to think now," Sally replied, shaking her head. "Harriet Locke." Her stomach flip-flopped again, closely followed by a nudge of confusion.

Harriet grinned. "Sally McCall."

Chapter Seven

"So, what have you been up to for the past 17 years?" Harriet asked. Her voice was coming out clear, but inside, her heart was racing. Not that she was surprised: she was having coffee with Sally McCall, which was totally preposterous.

They were sitting in the hotel's ground-floor café on padded white seats, their earthenware mugs sitting atop solid wooden tables, their spoons brass and heavy. The café was full of people enjoying afternoon coffee and snacks, the air pregnant with the smell of melted cheese and sweet baked goods.

"Not much," Sally replied, sipping her coffee before adding a little more milk. "The usual: went to college, met my husband, got married, got divorced, came out, that sort of thing."

Harriet's stomach plunged. "You got married?"

Sally nodded. "Got married, yes. Took part in being actively married? Not so much." She paused, eyeing Harriet's hands. "What about you? I don't see a ring."

Harriet shook her head: there had never been anyone to

call her own, not in the married sense. Not in most senses, if she was honest. "No, never done it," she said, trying to come across as breezy as she could manage. "I mean, there have been people, but nobody I wanted to hang my hat on, you know?"

Nobody since she'd fucked it up with Sally.

Sally nodded, averting her gaze. "Sensible — that's a tag I never would have slapped on you."

Harriet smiled. "It has been 17 years," she replied, exhaling as if she'd just run a marathon. Which, in her mind, she had. "But can I just say, you don't look 17 years older. You almost don't look any different at all."

Sally spluttered. "I hope I do — do you remember the hair cut I had back then?"

Harriet smiled. All she remembered was that Sally was the most amazing person she'd ever met, and Harriet had steamrollered her heart. Did Sally still remember as much as she did? She was trying to gauge her reaction, but she couldn't quite pinpoint it. She seemed pleased to see her, but also a little defensive? Harriet wouldn't blame her if both were true.

"I mean, your face hasn't changed, your eyes haven't changed, they're still beautiful." Then she stopped, the blood rushing to her cheeks. "And I'm going to shut up now before I embarrass myself even more."

Sally gave her a slow smile. "If I didn't know better, I'd say you were flirting with me, Harriet Locke."

Harriet put a finger to her chest. "Me? Never. This

is just a coffee to say sorry for switching suitcases." She paused, getting the gift out of her bag, wrapped in purple tissue paper. "Oh, and this is for you, by way of apology. And now I know it's you — not just any Sally — it makes it even more wildly appropriate." But she'd be lying if she said she wasn't also nervous about it.

Sally took the present and turned it over in her hands, glancing up at Harriet. "You didn't have to get me a gift."

"I know, but I did," Harriet said. "It's to apologize for the suitcase mix-up. Plus, you haven't opened it yet, you might hate it."

Sally sighed. "I remember your gifts, Harriet. I doubt that a lot." She ripped open the tissue paper, to reveal a stone-colored journal, bound in soft leather with tan leather ties. Sally bit her lip as she looked up at her. "It's just perfect," she said. "I need a new one, too." She turned the journal over in her hands, stroking the soft exterior with her elegant hands.

Harriet had missed those hands.

"I know — it was your journal that gave me your number, and I saw it was full."

Sally's face clouded over when she heard that.

Understanding, Harriet shook her head. "Don't worry, I swear I didn't read it. I was just looking to see if you'd written your number in it." She reached over and touched Sally's leg with her hand, and Sally's warmth flowed up and into her, making her heart pump that little bit faster. Harriet steadied her breathing before continuing.

"I wouldn't read your journal — I learned my lesson a long time ago." A stab of regret shot through her — it was still one of the worst mornings of her life, the one where she thought she'd lost Sally. But as it turned out, that had been a few months down the line.

Sally's cheeks flushed, and she gave her a faltering smile. "Glad to hear it," she said, regaining her composure a little, putting the journal on the table. She gave Harriet a look she couldn't quite decipher, before changing the subject. "How's Daniel?"

Harriet relaxed a little. "He's great — Daniel doesn't change. He's still Mr Happy-Go-Lucky, which in this day and age you've got to admire. I just dropped him off before I came here."

"He lives here, too?"

She nodded. "He does — you say that like we should have moved away."

Sally shook her head. "No, I guess I just thought you might, after going to Boston for college. You didn't stay there?"

"I dropped out," Harriet replied. "Harvard wasn't for me, which thrilled my parents, as you can imagine. But I made it work."

"You dropped out of Harvard? You rebel."

Harriet laughed. "That's me," she said. "All the Lockes are just where you left them: Mom and Dad still live in Winnetka in the same house, and Dan's a gardener now, would you believe? He found his calling and now he sculpts gardens for Chicago's great and good. And because he's outdoors all the time, his skin's so tanned it's unreal." She shrugged. "He's happy, though — it's a talent he was born with."

"Tell him I said hi," Sally replied.

"I will. He'd love to see you."

Sally raised one eyebrow. "Perhaps he would now, but I'm not sure he was all that thrilled about us hooking up all those years ago."

Harriet gave an uncertain smile. "Water under the bridge — we've all moved on since then, haven't we?"

But even as she said the words, she wondered how true they were. Harriet cast her mind back to that summer, to her and Sally, to the moonlight on Sally's soft, pale skin. The actual details were fuzzy now, like so many things that happened in the past, her mind only recalling some details and forgetting others.

But the feelings she'd had for Sally were still crystal-clear, and they were swamping her body now, pressing into every pore of her skin, every inch of her soul. She hadn't put a name to them back then, because she hadn't wanted to believe it. She'd never told Sally she loved her, that she would lay down her life for her, because she hadn't realized until it was too late.

Until Sally was gone.

But now, Sally McCall was sitting opposite her in a café, the same beautiful smile on her lips, the same eyes the color of the ocean.

Sally McCall could never be water under the bridge for her. Sally McCall was part of her history.

Scrap that, she was a part of *her*.

She was the reason Harriet believed in love, as well as being the reason she'd given up on love, too.

Harriet glanced down at her hands before looking back up at Sally, hoping her thoughts weren't written all over her face.

"Do you want to meet up again while you're here? For a drink, or dinner?"

Sally drained her coffee and eyed Harriet hesitantly. "I'd like that."

She didn't sound convinced, but Harriet didn't want Sally to run off again without knowing how she was, what she was up to.

And perhaps knowing if she had a girlfriend or not.

"I'm having dinner with my dad tonight, then lunch with my aunt tomorrow," Sally said. "Are you free tomorrow night?"

Harriet was nodding even before she scanned her diary in her head. It was only then she remembered she had plans already: work plans. She was due to meet some clients for dinner tomorrow night. Could she get out of it? She'd have to talk to Joanna.

"I'm meant to be working tomorrow night, but I'll try to get out of it."

"You're working?" Sally said. "It's Friday night."

Harriet gave her a rueful smile. "And that's the state

of my life right now — I've got dinner with some clients, but I'd much rather spend it with you," she said, holding Sally's gaze, a long-lost memory of Sally deep inside her beginning to play in her head. Harriet let a slight shudder rattle through her, styling it out. "How long are you in town for?"

"Till Sunday," Sally replied, licking her lips. "I've got lunch with Mom, then I fly back Sunday night. But I kept Saturday free to do some shopping. If Friday doesn't work, Saturday could, too."

Harriet winced: she really needed to sort out her work-life balance. "Leave it with me and I'll let you know." Harriet leaned forward. "But I'd love to have a proper catch-up," she said, her heart racing as she stared into Sally's oh-so-familiar eyes.

Sally held her gaze before replying. "Me, too," she said. "It's been a very long time."

"It sure has," Harriet replied.

Chapter Eight

Their office was the top floor of a converted house on a sleepy, leafy street in Logan Square, and it looked out over the 606, Chicago's converted old train line that was now a recreational trail and running track. At 6pm, the amount of runners' heads passing by their window was increasing, as the sun set and workers knocked off. Harriet's desk had the large, picture window on her right, and she loved watching the 606 activity every day. Joanna said it distracted her, so she sat with her back to it.

Harriet slid into her slate-gray Aeron office chair, giving Joanna a breezy smile. She cracked her knee on the filing cabinet under her desk as she had done every day since she moved it there three weeks ago, letting out a gasp of pain.

"Goddammit!"

Joanna simply rolled her eyes with a smirk, seeing as this was an occurrence she witnessed every day. "And what time do you call this?" she asked, running a hand over her perfectly shaved head.

Joanna was one of those people who'd shaved her

head a few years ago and immediately, everyone swooned and asked why she hadn't done it years ago. She had a perfect scalp, enormous brown eyes to match her skin, and dark lashes that went on for days.

They'd met at a networking event for professional women and hit it off right away, before eventually going into business together five years ago. Now, they ran Panache, a business that linked designers with top retailers and special clients, helping them get their products into the right hands and onto the right shelves around the world.

"Bite me," Harriet said, clutching her knee, staring at her computer like she'd never used one before. Her head was so scattered right now, it was all she could do to walk, talk and function like a human being.

She'd just met Sally McCall for the first time in forever, and Sally had agreed to have dinner with her tomorrow night. That thought sent a shockwave to her system once more, and she had to hold her breath to regain control of herself.

Get a grip.

Joanna raised one perfectly sculpted eyebrow. "But you're never late — I mean, never. I've always thought it was some weird setting in your DNA, because we've worked together for five years and I can count on my hands the times you've been late. I'm not complaining, it's fine, but you said you'd be here by 4.30 and it's now nearly six."

Harriet blew out a raspberry and shook her head. "Something came up, okay?" she said. "But I'm here now, so is there anything that needs my urgent attention, or do you have it all under control?"

"Of course, so you can just get your coffee, say hello to Nathan and Kristy before they leave, then fill me in on your meeting. Because you seem a little weird today." She paused, frowning at Harriet. "Everything go okay yesterday? Apart from the suitcase debacle?"

"Everything went fine. The designers loved us, now it's just a matter of ironing out some minor details. I'll show you their stuff — did the suitcase arrive?"

Joanna shook her head. "Not yet."

Harriet sighed. "It's on its way — some of their stuff is absolutely gorgeous, I think our clients are going to love it." She grinned. "Talking of wowing our clients," she added. "You know I've got that dinner tomorrow with Bruce and Val from Macy's?"

Joanna nodded, picking up a pen and twisting in it her fingers.

"Something's come up and I was wondering — d'you think you'll be able to step in and cover this one?" Harriet said it as nonchalantly as possible, as if switching a dinner engagement was something she did all the time. Instead of never once in their entire business relationship.

"What's come up? Is your dad okay?" Joanna sat up, looking concerned.

"Yeah, he's fine," Harriet replied, blushing despite

herself. "It's just, I ran into an old friend today. She's only in town for the weekend, and she wants to have dinner tomorrow night."

"Which old friend is this?"

"Nobody you know," Harriet said, spinning round in her chair, but not managing to escape Joanna's curious stare. "Sally, a friend from high school, a long, long time ago." She said it as off-handedly as she could manage, but when she looked at Joanna's face, she knew she wasn't fooling her.

They'd been friends *far* too long for that.

"Sally," Joanna repeated. "And is Sally an old friend or an old flame? Because you've got a look on your face I haven't seen much before." She sat forward, staring at Harriet with a smile playing around her lips. "Is it bashful? I don't think I've ever seen you do bashful, but I think that's what it is. Am I right?"

Harriet rolled her neck from one side to the other, then folded her arms across her chest, clearing her throat as she sat up. "No, I'm not bashful. She's just an old friend." She paused. "And she might be an old flame, too."

"I knew it!" Joanna said, triumph in her voice. "So let me get this straight, you're ducking out of a client meeting to meet up with an old girlfriend? And judging by your body language, someone you still have the hots for."

Harriet glanced down at her feet, then at her desk, her cheeks flaming anew.

Damn Joanna and her detective work.

"I do not have the hots for her," she replied, putting the word "hots" in finger quotes. "I'm 35, for chrissake — I'm too old to have the hots for someone."

"Bullshit," Joanna said, pointing a finger at Harriet. "You've got the hots for her, you're blushing, and you're avoiding my eyes. If this were a poker game, you'd be toast, my friend." She let out another throaty laugh as Harriet squirmed. "Anyway, whatever, you've cheered me up no end. Harriet the ice queen has been melted, and then some."

Harriet gave her a look. "I'm hardly an ice queen."

"You're hardly Mrs Hallmark either."

"Pot. Kettle."

Joanna's face clouded over at that; her jaw twitched and she swiveled in her chair, turning her attention to the runners bouncing by their window. The sky outside was still clear blue, with not a cloud in sight.

Harriet knew she'd hit a nerve. "Jo, I'm sorry, I didn't mean that how it came out. I wasn't meaning it to apply to your current situation per se."

Joanna spun in her chair, her face now arranged in a way that told Harriet it didn't matter, even though Harriet knew it did. She sighed and shook her head. "I know I can't really be a relationship judge and jury right now, not with where my relationship is at the moment."

"Things still no better?"

Joanna's cheeks filled with air, before she expelled it. "Not really. We've lost our way somewhere along the line, and Viv's got a whole new set of friends from the theater." She shrugged. "It all starts out great, doesn't it, and then it always seems to go downhill at some point." She shrugged. "But I'm not talking about your old flame."

Now it was Harriet's turn to shake her head. "It's just dinner. She lives in New York, too, so it's not like anything can happen."

"If Viv lived in New York, things would be so much easier," Joanna said, almost to herself. When she realized she'd said it out loud, she winced. "Anyway, I can cover for you, no problem. We're supposed to be going to Viv's friend's bachelorette party, but I've only met her once and I'm sure Viv will have a better time without me."

"Are you sure?" Harriet said. "I don't want to cause more drama than you already have."

Joanna nodded. "I'm sure. I didn't want to go anyway, and this gives me the perfect excuse." Joanna sighed. "It's not like our romance is setting the world alight right now."

Harriet gave her friend a sympathetic glance. "Maybe it's just a phase you need to go through."

"Maybe," Joanna said, not sounding convinced. "Anyway, back to you," she said, getting up and walking over to Harriet's desk. "Sally. I don't think I've heard about Sally before, have I?"

"She's a girl from school, we had a thing when we were young, but then we went to college and it fizzled out."

Joanna frowned, staring at Harriet as if trying to locate the rest of the story. "How did you meet up again?"

"Would you believe it was her case I took by mistake?"

Joanna clasped both hands to her chest, leaning back on Harriet's desk, eyes wide. "Oh my god, that's so romantic! You didn't tell me that part. All these years, and then an accidental meeting like that? This is something!"

Harriet waved a hand, rolling her eyes at Joanna. "It's a coincidence, that's all. But it'll be nice to meet up tomorrow — there's a lot to catch up on."

Joanna narrowed her eyes. "Was she your first love?"

Harriet glanced down at the carpet again. Had her cheeks turned even more crimson? It felt like they had.

"Holy shit, you're going to dinner with your first love!" Joanna said, poking Harriet in the shoulder. "And what did she look like? Is she still hot?"

There was that word again. "What are we, 12?" Harriet said, trying to steer the conversation in a different direction.

But Joanna was having none of it. "She was, wasn't she? Was she hotter than she was before?"

No matter how hard she tried, Harriet couldn't stop the widescreen smile that crossed her face and stayed put in answer to that. She nodded her head ever so slightly, before shaking it at Joanna. "You're terrible, you know that?"

Joanna bumped her chair with her hip. "And you're going on a date with your first love and she's still a hottie!"

"It is not a date," Harriet replied. Even she wouldn't hope that, not after what had gone before. Harriet had no idea how Sally's life was going and what she thought of meeting her again. Sally might have gone home and stabbed pins into a Harriet voodoo doll for all she knew. But despite that, Harriet couldn't deny there was still a tiny bit of her that longed for tomorrow to be a date.

Because deep down, despite the fact she fucked it up, she'd always wanted another date with Sally.

"It so is!" Joanna said. "And I think it's amazing. One of us should have some romance in her life, and that person is you!"

"It's not a date, Joanna."

Joanna grabbed both the arms of Harriet's office chair and swung it around, leaning down so their faces were now only inches from each other. "Sure, it's not a date," she said. "You keep telling yourself that. But my spidey senses are tingling and they tell me date." She paused. "Have you even thought about what you're going to wear yet?"

Shit, she hadn't at all. Mainly because it wasn't a date, right?

Seeing her body tense, Joanna laughed and stood up, running a hand over her head again, as was her habit. "I'm going to leave you to ponder that and go get us both a coffee, okay?" she said, walking out of the door.

Harriet watched her go, her heart racing, her mind blank.

It wasn't a date; she was just having dinner with an old friend.

Harriet got out her phone and started to text Sally to let her know she could do dinner.

She tried to ignore the fact her hand was shaking.

Chapter Nine

Sally arrived at the hotel's restaurant at 1pm as instructed, its slanted glass roof meaning sunshine flooded the space, the scent of garlic and herbs filling her nostrils. The modern white upholstered chairs and minimalist naked wooden tables told Sally this was a hip space, and the mustachioed bartender shaking a Manhattan behind the glinting art deco bar only confirmed it.

Her dad had shown her a recent photo of his sister when Sally had met him for dinner the night before, but she wasn't difficult to pick out. Her aunt's rash of copper hair announced itself in a room way before she did, and the fact she already had a martini in front of her when it was only one in the afternoon told Sally certain things about her long-lost relative: she was either an eccentric or a drunk. Or perhaps an eccentric drunk.

Still, she reckoned this lunch might just take her mind off Harriet Locke for a few hours, which was exactly what she needed. Meeting Harriet yesterday had been a jolt to the system, and she still wasn't sure where she stood. Was she happy they'd reconnected or would she prefer to leave Harriet in the past? It was a tug of war between her heart and her mind, just like always with Harriet.

She took a deep breath, pulled down her black shirt, and walked up to her aunt's table.

"Aunt Paula?" she said, an annoying waver in her voice.

Be confident, pull your shoulders back.

Aunt Paula looked up, producing a rasping hack of a cough before she spoke, her voice sounding like one of Marge's sisters from *The Simpsons*. "Aunt? Nobody calls me that," Paula said, getting up and grabbing Sally into a bear hug. "So if we're going to be friends, you've got to promise to just call me Paula, okay?"

Sally nodded, winded, as Paula let go and held her at arm's length.

"Good to see you got the McCall gene with the hair and the eyes, although that mouth is all your mother." Paula grinned. "How is she these days?"

Sally sat down on the white chair, pulling it under her. "She's good, she sends her love."

Paula's laughter lit up the room like a siren, making more than one head turn. "She does not, but good try. Your mom and I always rubbed each other the wrong way, but I always liked her. She had spunk, which is all a woman needs for me. Don't you agree?"

Sally nodded, wondering briefly if she needed to answer, but her aunt — rather, Paula — seemed to be waiting till she did.

"Totally. Spunky gets me every time."

Paula gave her a wicked grin. "Is that so?" she said, taking a sip of her martini. "First things first, you want a drink?"

"Sure," Sally replied. "I'll have a Manhattan."

"Classy," Paula said. "Don't drink martinis, they get you drunk far too quickly." With that, she downed what was left of hers, then flagged down a passing waitress to order herself another, along with Sally's Manhattan. "We'll order food soon, too, but let's get to know each other a little first.

"Tell me, what have you been up to for the past 20 years, apart from figuring out you're a lesbian?"

Sally choked on her glass of water, spilling it on her lap, convulsing like she was about to die. What was it about water and Paula that always seemed to end with her choking?

A passing waiter offered her a glass of water, along with an extra napkin, clearly afraid she was going to vomit, pass out, or both. Sally waved him away, standing up and leaning over, eventually regaining her breath and her equilibrium.

Across from her, Paula grinned. "Sorry, was that a little too forward?"

Sally smiled, still coughing, her eyes streaming, her face, she imagined, the color of eggplant. "I just wasn't quite expecting that to come out of your mouth."

"And I wasn't quite expecting you to come out, but you did. Not after little Miss Goody-Two-Shoes got married at 24. When Rick told me, I thought you had your whole life mapped out: kids, mortgage, suburbia, the works. But then you dumped your husband and got a girlfriend and I thought: my niece has got spunk."

There was that word again. Sally hadn't even been aware her aunt had been keeping such track of her life, assuming that on the few brief meetings they'd had, she'd made zero impression. Apparently not.

"That may be true, but your niece was also an emotional wreck."

"Yes, but you took charge of your life, steered your own destiny. Not easy to do, ask all the other housewives who are closeted and fucking their best friend, their cleaner, any woman they can get their hands on."

Sally sat back as the waitress brought their drinks, her ears still ringing, not just from her coughing fit but also from the words falling from Paula's lips.

When she'd imagined this conversation in her head, she'd had in mind her aunt offering her money for her business in hushed tones, laying out ground rules. Somehow, she doubted this lunch was going to play out that way.

"You sound like you're speaking from experience," Sally replied, taking a large gulp of her cocktail.

Paula nodded. "I am. I've fucked my fair share of women in closets, but now I'm out and proud." She furrowed her brow. "Didn't Rick tell you?"

Sally's mouth dropped open. Paula was a lesbian? No,

her dad had left that pertinent piece of information out of their conversation. Typical Dad. "No, he never did."

Paula shook her head. "Men," she tutted. "What is their use?" She paused. "I mean, I think I've settled on lesbian as a label now. I was polyamorous for a while, but still only with women. I guess that makes me a lesbian still, right? I had three girlfriends at once and don't get me started on that — exhausting, I don't mind saying."

She'd had three girlfriends? All at once? Sally had never felt like a more inadequate lesbian.

Paula sat forward, wiggling her fingers as she did. "Nervous energy," she said, holding up her hands. "I gave up smoking, but my hands are still looking for something to do, especially when I drink. My therapist says it's just a programmed response and I have to fight it, but fuck, I'd give anything for a cigarette right now. And to be able to smoke indoors? Heaven. I went to Japan this year and fuck me if everyone wasn't smoking indoors? It was like, Japan was built for me, and they like to drink. Perfect! But they kept making me take my shoes off, I wasn't so down with that."

She took a breath before continuing. "Did you see the movie *Carol*? I loved that scene where she takes her for lunch and they just drink martinis, smoke, and eat creamed spinach and eggs. I mean, I was born in the wrong era for boozing, clearly. Not sure I would have liked all the other things about the '50s, but you know, if I could pick or choose my era, that'd be the one.

"Anyway, I'm getting sidetracked — it's a speciality of mine, drives Rick crazy, that's why he avoids me. Says I'm embarrassing to be out with in public. But you know what I say? Get over yourself, Rick, take your finger out of your butt and lighten up! He's not so keen on that, but hey. What can I do? I keep him around because he's my only brother and he amuses me. Plus, he can't hold his liquor, so he's always fun to take out and watch him flail after a few drinks. But you know this, I'm sure, he's your dad!"

"He is, but I rarely see him drunk," Sally replied. Her dad liked a glass of decent red or a neat single malt, but that was it. After going out with Paula, he probably took the rest of the week off to get over it.

"That's what I mean, he needs to loosen up! But I digress. I'm not going to beat around the bush — pun intended — but the fact you're family in every sense of the word makes me want to help you. I made a lot of money in real estate and I'm looking to invest in a business. The money's there if you want it, because I'd prefer to back my spunky lesbian niece rather than another white boy from Harvard who wants to build an app. Please, *spare me*." Paula sat back, narrowing her eyes. "So what do you say, would you like some money from me?"

Sally laughed, shaken up in more ways than one. "When you put it like that," she said. "But I have conditions. I don't like taking money, I'm not a trust-fund baby. I want to make it on my own, but I have to admit, a little help would be nice. But if I take the money, it's a loan I'll pay back, okay?"

Sally was serious about this. She'd resisted all help before, from both her parents, because she'd always been very clear she wanted to do this on her own, to achieve the American dream of making it big on her own terms. Somehow, this felt different. She hadn't seen Paula in years, so it was almost the same as borrowing from a bank. Impersonal.

Although she didn't recall the last time she'd had lunch with her bank manager. The last time her bank manager had put her up in a hotel. The last time her bank manager had drunk two martinis in quick succession and was already signaling for the waiter to get a third.

"Loan, schmoan," Paula said, cackling a wicked laugh. "Honey, if it makes you feel better taking my money that way, sure, it's a loan. You can pay me back whenever. But I just want to see you succeed. And I want to make Rick even prouder of you than he already is, which, by the way, would be quite some feat. That man is getting softer with age, don't you think? I've always thought it, but I think I'm the one who really got the balls in the family, if you know what I mean. Still, I digress again, something for another day." Another breath. "So, do we have a deal?"

Sally computed in her head all the things she could do with an investment: advertising, outsourcing, scaling up. All those podcasts she'd listened to on how to run a business, she could finally put their advice into practice and start making some money.

She took a deep breath, looked up, and gave her aunt a grin. She needed this money badly, and like her dad said, this was payback time for nearly drowning her when she was five.

"We have a deal," Sally said, raising her glass to Paula.

"Awesome!" Paula said, clapping her hands together and performing a small whoop. "Did your mom ever tell you about the time I took her to a lesbian strip club? Oh my, you shoulda seen her face, I thought she was going to have a cardiac. But then she had a few drinks and she got into it. Your mom can unwind when she lets herself."

What the actual fuck? "Please, if we're going into business, there are some things I'd rather not know — and that was one of them." Sally closed her eyes and tried not to picture her mom stuffing dollar bills into a dancer's G-string. It half worked.

Paula grinned. "If we're going into business, I'm taking you to a lesbian strip club!"

Sally shook her head, laughing despite herself. "It's more suitable for me than Mom, I'll give you that," she said. "Mom really went to a lesbian strip club?"

"Yes!" Paula said. "I mean, I wasn't even out then, and nobody was catching the clues, not even me. We all thought it was a hoot, sticking money down women's G-strings. Your mom had a few too many tequilas that night, let's just say that."

Sally put up her hand: this was getting a little too much. Surely there was such a thing as over-sharing? "If you tell me she got a lap dance, I might never be able to look at her again."

Paula chuckled at that. "She did not. I, on the other hand, might have gone behind the curtain." A smile crossed her face at the memory. "Those gorgeous, jiggly titties in my face might have been my sexual awakening. I'm definitely taking you."

Sally furrowed her brow: what had she gotten herself into? Then again, she'd never been to a lesbian strip club, so maybe, at the age of 34, it was about time. "I'll look forward to it," she said, raising her drink. "But for now, here's to your loan and to my future success. If I appear on the cover of *Forbes* magazine, I promise to name-check you, okay?"

"You fucking better," Paula replied, tapping her glass to Sally's. "And if you need advice, I'm always on the end of a phone. I'm not just your new investor, I'm *invested*. And I want to hear all about your business over lunch. Your dad told me you design artsy greetings cards, right? 'I love you so much' written in 18-carat gold and all that shit. The ones that cost a fortune?"

"Were those his exact words?"

"I might be paraphrasing," Paula said with a grin.

Sally plowed on. "With your investment, I want to expand from just cards, designing stationery too, maybe umbrellas and bags as well."

"Nice, I like it a lot. Creativity is good, you know? It means there's something inside, which is important. I'm a creative, I understand. Plus, we're dynamite in bed."

Sally wasn't sure how to respond to that, apart from taking another swig of her cocktail, which seemed to please Paula.

"Now, shall we order some food? I'm starving, and then you can tell me about all the beautiful women you're currently seeing."

Paula buried her head in the menu, before lowering it slowly and peering over the top.

"You are seeing multiple women, right? Gorgeous young thing like you, the world at your feet? Because business is good, but when all's said and done, the main things that matter in life are women, wine, and food, am I right?"

Sally blushed, and took another swig of her drink. Multiple women? She didn't even have time for one. In fact, as Taylor had told her before she came, she needed to get back out there.

"If only the world was that simple," she replied. "No, I'm totally single and have been for two years."

Paula looked at her, aghast. "But you've had sex in that time, right?"

Sally blushed anew, fiddling with her napkin. This wasn't the line of questioning she'd imagined with her aunt when she was prepping for today. "I've had the occasional hook-up, but I've been too busy trying to get my business off the ground."

Paula shook her head at that. "If I'd have known, we could have hit up some hotspots later." She paused, knitting her fingers together and resting her chin on her hands. "Are you free tonight?"

Sally shook her head as an image of Harriet Locke dropped into the front of her mind, like a vacation snapshot she'd forgotten taking, all tanned, perky, dimpled. How was it she was so fucking dimpled?

"I'm not, I'm meeting up with an old friend for dinner."

Paula raised an eyebrow. "An old friend or an *old friend*?" she asked, pulsing her forehead as she said the final two words. "Don't worry, you can tell me, I'm not your mom."

Sally took another swig of her Manhattan, assessed the glass, then finished it. The alcohol had already hit her system, and her limbs felt heavier, her burden lighter. She was on vacation after all, and a little lunchtime drinking and celebration was called for today because this was a big deal getting money for her business.

Oh, and going out with Harriet Locke after almost two decades of nothing.

She smiled at her aunt. "She's just a friend, an old school friend," Sally said, feeling her cheeks burn at the lie.

Just an old school friend she'd fucked way back when.

Just an old school friend who made her hair stand on end when she thought of her, as if the intervening years had never happened. As if the catastrophic ending had never happened. Why was her body such a Judas?

"Next time, then," her aunt said, picking up her menu again. "Or maybe we can go on the prowl in New York when I come and visit you?"

Paula was coming to New York? This was a new turn of events.

But like her mom always told her, there was no such thing as a free lunch.

Chapter Ten

Sally checked her watch and squinted as she tried to figure out what it said.

Shit, she couldn't even read her watch. She really shouldn't have tried to keep up with Paula even a little: the woman could drink for America. Whereas Sally had never been a big drinker — she loved whiskey, red wine, and craft beer, but never in huge quantities.

Her phone vibrated in her pocket and she frowned, pulling it out. She was lying flat on her back, on top of her kingsize bed, but she needed to move because the room had begun to spin. She sat up, wondering if she was about to throw up. Daytime drinking was so bad — if she survived this, she was going to be hungover for her first date with Harriet.

First date? Where had that come from? Somewhere deep in the back of her mind clearly, in a box marked "teenage thoughts". Also marked "Too painful. Stay away". She took a deep breath and checked her phone, nausea rising in her.

"Finishing on time today. Shall I pick you up at your hotel at 7:30? X"

She squinted again at the clock at the top of her phone. 5:04. She had a little over two hours to make herself less drunk and presentable. Could she manage that?

"Make it 8. Look forward to seeing you," she texted back before flopping on the bed again. She did it too quick and the room swayed from side to side. She closed her eyes again.

Her phone beeped once more, but this time it was her dad.

'Hi sweetie — you made a terrific impression on Paula, but I had no doubt you would. She just called to say she loves you! I hope she wasn't too much and didn't make you drink too much, I know how she can be. Talk soon, love you. Dad.'

Sally closed her eyes as another wave of nausea rolled through her.

He had no idea.

Then she clicked back up to Harriet's message, reading it again, staring at the kiss she'd left on the end. Was that a bit odd, a little forward? She had no idea because Harriet and her were hardly strangers; but then again, as adults, they were. Their history was made when they were both teenagers, but did they have anything in common now? She guessed they were about to find out.

Chapter Eleven
Seventeen years earlier ...

A horn sounded outside her house and Sally scrambled to squash her clothes and toiletries into her red weekend bag. She'd been trying to do it unsuccessfully for the past 20 minutes, and now Harriet was outside in her blue Chevy, and she still hadn't managed it.

"Dammit!" she said, dragging a brush through the unruly red hair she hated — "it's not red, it's strawberry blonde!" her mother said — and checking her make-up one final time: lipstick unsmudged, eye shadow on-point, mascara shoveled on to achieve the desired effect. She looked as presentable as she was going to manage today, and that was all she could ask for.

Sally grabbed a spare tote bag from her closet, filling it with her stuff, finally managing to drag the zipper of her weekend bag closed. She gave a sigh of relief as she heard the car horn honk one more time.

"Sally!" her mom called up the stairs. "Harriet's outside and she's slamming that damn horn again!"

"Coming!" Sally said, pulling her bedroom door shut

and clomping down the stairs, her mom appraising her every step.

"You look nice," she said, smiling at her. "Is that a new shirt?"

"Got it on the weekend," Sally replied, hating her mom's interrogation — she could never just leave the house without comment. She couldn't wait to leave home and go to college next year.

Harriet was going this year, but she pushed that thought away.

"The green suits you. And it's got some beading on the shoulder, which makes a welcome change — a bit more girly than your usual style." Her mom reached out her hand, touching the side of her cheek.

Sally flinched. "Mom," she said, hitching her tote bag up on her shoulder, gripping her weekend bag, which was heavier than she'd have liked.

Her mom smiled. "You're still my little girl, I'm allowed to touch you."

"I'm 17," Sally countered.

"Exactly." Her mom paused. "So you'll be back on Sunday?"

"Monday," Sally said. "I told you that."

"Right, I forgot."

The horn sounded again, and they both jumped.

"Call me when you get there, and give my love to Harriet's parents, okay?"

Sally nodded, leaning over to kiss her mom's cheek.

"I will." She yanked open the front door and caught a snatch of the music seeping out of Harriet's car. It was their current favorite, Christina Aguilera.

"Drive safe," her mom said as Sally walked out to the car, throwing her bags in the back, before sinking into the passenger seat and slamming the door.

"My mom loves you, despite the honking," Sally said, glancing over at Harriet as she revved the engine and pulled away with a squeal of her tires. Harriet always drove too fast, because Harriet did everything too fast. Which was one of the reasons Sally loved her.

"What can I say, parents love me," Harriet replied, eyes on the road, then on Sally, then back. "I'm like some kind of parental catnip. They should give me out at teenage classes to reassure parents that nothing bad will happen to their precious offspring."

As if to un-illustrate her point, Harriet pumped on the brakes just a little too sharply as they arrived at an intersection and Sally, having not put her seat belt on yet, slammed her hand into the dashboard.

"Sorry," Harriet replied, turning left and heading toward the freeway that would take them to the lake, just the two of them and Harriet's family.

"Try not to kill me before we get there," Sally said.

* * *

They arrived two hours later, the drive pretty clear, just them and a smattering of weekenders all heading for the lakes. As they approached the house, Sally rolled her window down and breathed in the fresh country air, which smelt so clean and sweet. She wasn't a runner, but out here, she always imagined tearing through the fields, the cool wind in her hair. Above them, the sky was a rich blue, while under them, the grass was scorched. It had been a relentless summer so far, and it showed no sign of ending.

Harriet's family's house was on Lake Paw Paw, and Sally had fallen in love with it when she first came last year. It was set at the top of a perfectly manicured lawn that swept down to the lake, with a wide black front door and polished windows to either side. There were two jetties at the front of the house, a covered veranda that wrapped around its vast frontage, and a decking that stretched out to the right.

Sally loved Harriet's lake house, and wished her mom had one, too. But as holding onto their own house after her parents split had been enough of a struggle, she knew it was never going to happen.

Sally had been here twice already last year, the first time as a guest of Daniel who she'd been seeing for a while before they'd fizzled out. But Daniel had led her to Harriet, for which she was forever grateful.

The second time she'd visited, Harriet had taught her to smoke, taken her out on the family speedboat, and later, they'd lain on the front lawn till after midnight, staring at the stars and discussing their futures.

But that was last year. This time around, they were a

year older, a year wiser, a year down the track with their friendship. And they'd been getting closer — something had shifted. With every passing weekend they spent together, their friendship had deepened, for Sally at least. She hoped she wasn't misreading the signs, but she guessed this weekend she'd find out for sure. She hoped they'd get a chance to lay together again, and that this time, the outcome would be slightly altered.

Her cheeks heated up just thinking that, and when she glanced over at Harriet as she pulled into the long, graveled driveway, her friend gave her a grin.

"Ready for the weekend of your life?"

Sally gulped down a nervous smile and nodded. "Ready," she replied.

* * *

No sooner had they arrived at the lake house and said hello to Mr and Mrs Locke in the grand wood-paneled living room, than they were told what time dinner would be and what time they were expected.

Sally winced when she heard it: she wasn't sure she'd brought any clothes that might be deemed formal enough, and she didn't want Harriet's parents looking down on her. Harriet's parents were nothing like Sally's, which fascinated her. They weren't crazy rich, but they were a class above her family, using cutlery that couldn't be put in the dishwasher.

"But we have plans tonight," Harriet replied, her face curling into a snarl. Sally loved that face in particular, it

told people not to fuck with Harriet — even her mother. Sally would never have dared try that at home. "We can't make dinner at that time."

Her mother gave her a steely look. "Fine. But if you're not eating with us, you'll have to eat in the kitchen. I'll have Robert whip you up something first then and leave it on the side or in the fridge, okay?"

Harriet nodded, her attention already shifted, exactly the same as her mother's. "Sure."

She took Sally's hand and tugged her out of the stuffy living room, Sally's attention drawn to her hand in Harriet's, her whole body pulsing with the contact.

She'd spent the last few months battling with her emotions, but she was finally ready to face up to them. Did it mean she was a lesbian or bisexual? She had no idea. But striding up the stairs of the lake house, hand in hand, she knew her feelings for Harriet were real. She wanted to do more than just spend time with Harriet: she wanted to kiss her, to hold her.

She wanted to sleep with her, whatever that meant.

The thought of Harriet's hand between her legs made her go weak. The thought of her mouth on hers? She wasn't sure she'd live through it, because right now, her hand in hers was almost giving her heart failure.

"Did I tell you about Daniel?" Harriet said as they reached the top of the stairs and walked along the magnolia-painted hallway, every surface pristine.

However, if the hallways were neutral, Harriet's bedroom

was anything but. That was a riot of posters and colors, with Blink 182 sneering at them, along with Macy Gray and a very punk-looking Pink.

As soon as they got inside, Harriet lit an incense burner on top of her white dressing table, and the slow release of lavender filled the room. She flung open both the windows of her dual-aspect bedroom, before sinking onto her old-fashioned copper bed, her loose brown hair falling around her, splayed like a fan.

Sally opted for Harriet's red Ikea sofabed — it seemed the safer place to be. "What were you saying about Daniel?" she asked. She knew he was working in New York, which was way cool. She'd love to do that when she was older.

"He's got a boyfriend, says he's bi," Harriet replied, staring up at her ceiling. "It's the one time I thought the dork might be a bit cool."

Sally gripped the sofa's arm, trying hard to remember to breathe. Harriet thought Daniel was cool for being bi?

"Daniel's bi?"

Harriet turned her head now, grinning. "Bi, gay, whatever. I can just imagine Mom's face if she finds out: her golden boy with another man." Harriet laughed. "It'd really put her liberal morals to the test."

Sally was still clinging to the sofa, not trusting her hand not to shake if she didn't. "Has he told them?"

"No, he's too chicken, he wouldn't dare. Plus, he's in New York, so why cause a fuss when you don't have to? He let it slip to me because, well, Dan's not known for his

ability to keep secrets." She grinned at Sally. "But don't you think everyone's a little bit gay? Or bi, even? I mean, I like some girls and some guys, it's no big deal these days, is it? It's not like we're living in the 1960s."

Time stood still as Harriet spoke, Sally watching her mouth intently.

And that mouth: it was full, glossy, and so kissable. And out of it had come some beautiful words.

Harriet thought we were all a bit gay, which was the conclusion Sally was coming to as well. At least, she was definitely a bit gay. And if Daniel could have a boyfriend, did it mean Harriet might consider having a girlfriend? And would she consider her?

Harriet's mouth moved again, her eyes searching Sally's face.

Sally tuned back into the room, the colors refocusing again as she came back to the present from her Harriet daydream. Only, maybe it wasn't such a daydream at all now.

Which only made everything a little more scary.

"Sorry?" Sally said, furrowing her brow.

"I said, what do you think? Are we all a little bit gay?" Harriet's emerald eyes were on her, and she gulped before she answered.

"Maybe we are," she replied, the words coming out far meeker than she meant them to. She gathered herself, trying to appear a little more off the cuff. "Labels are so uncool. I mean, who cares?"

"*Exactly,*" *Harriet said, running a hand through her hair.* "*Did you think my mom was even less interested in us this time around than she was last?*"

Sally shrugged: Harriet and her mother's relationship had long been a mystery to her. At times, she longed for something similar herself; her mom's constant intrusion in her life was a thorn in her side. However, this other extreme didn't seem what she wanted, either.

"*She seemed like normal,*" *Sally said, rubbing her index finger and thumb together.*

"*I heard her talking about the dinner party she was having tomorrow night, which means she's going to be caught up doing that.*" *Harriet cocked her head.* "*So tonight, we could take whatever Robert's made us for dinner down to the lake, have a picnic, and watch the sun set. What do you say?*"

Sally nodded. "*Sounds awesome.*" *Plus, it meant a night with Harriet, who thought everyone was a little bit gay.* "*So what'll we do till then?*"

Sally yawned, stretching her arms above her head, her green top riding up above her belly button. She closed her eyes and blocked out the world, but when she looked back, she could have sworn Harriet's eyes were on her exposed midriff. When she caught her looking, Harriet looked away, then cleared her throat, standing up.

"*We can just hang out here for an hour, listen to some music? There are some dope new tracks on this new CD I bought.*"

Sally nodded. "Sounds good."

Harriet looked at her like she wanted to ask her a question, but then she shook her head, thinking better of it. "I'll run downstairs and get us a soda. What would you like?"

"Sprite would be cool," Sally said, the heat of Harriet's stare still marking her skin.

"Be right back."

Chapter Twelve

"So how much did you drink, exactly?" Harriet asked, a gentle smile creasing her face, her eyes smiling. She always did have kind eyes, even when they'd been telling Sally things she didn't want to know. Like the fact their relationship wasn't working anymore.

Sally shook her head. "I lost count after the first couple, but not as many as her."

"She sounds like quite the character, I'd love to meet her."

"Careful what you wish for," Sally replied. "Let's just say she tried to drown me when I was little, and today she tried to drown me again, but this time with alcohol."

They were walking along Ohio Street Beach, at Sally's request, to get a little fresh air. In preparation, she'd had a shower in the most upmarket bathroom she'd ever encountered, replete with huge mosaic tiles. Then she'd drunk enough weapons-grade coffee to make her hair stand on end, followed by four Advil. Operation Refresh had sort of worked, if you discounted the fact she still felt like she'd just been hit by a truck.

Still, a fresh paint of make-up, some clean clothes, and she was presentable. And the story of her long lunch that had stretched far into the afternoon appeared to have tickled Harriet, too.

"I really do have to stress again, though, this isn't me," Sally said, as they walked, the summer air still warm to the touch. To their left lay Lake Michigan, along with sand, empty sun loungers, umbrellas in the retreat position. To their right, the city's architecture twinkled, some buildings still housing workers chained to their desks. Up ahead, Navy Pier whooped and hollered as tourists rode the illuminated big wheel and ate cotton candy, just as Sally recalled doing as a kid.

And, as a teenager, with Harriet Locke.

Harriet guided Sally over to a wooden bench and they sat side by side, Harriet giving her some more water to drink, along with a smile.

"You know, we don't have to go to this fancy restaurant if you don't want to — I won't be offended. We can just get a hot dog on the pier, or go to a local bar if that's what you'd prefer. Just say the word."

"Would you mind?" Sally asked.

Harriet shook her head. "I'll call to cancel and let's just see where the night takes us. No pressure, okay?"

Sally nodded, glad to be taken care of. "Sounds great."

Harriet made the call.

Sally's shoulders unclenched, and she breathed a sigh of relief.

"Was going to dinner with me such a terrible thought?" Harriet asked, turning to face Sally.

"It's not that," Sally said, as a couple walked by with an empty stroller, the man with a toddler on his shoulders. "It's just I've sat in a restaurant for long enough today. But thanks for understanding."

"Of course."

They were silent for a few moments with their thoughts before Harriet spoke again.

"You know, if you'd told me last week I'd be sitting on a bench with you, I wouldn't have believed you."

"Me neither." Sally shuddered as she spoke: she still remembered the tears when Harriet had come home and told her they couldn't carry on, because long distance was too hard and she didn't want to be tied down at college.

Not even three months of long distance and they'd fallen apart at the seams.

But now, 17 years on, she was sure she could be zen about it, couldn't she?

"It was all a very long time ago."

Harriet nodded, staring out to the lake. "I know, half a lifetime." She paused. "It doesn't mean I haven't thought about you over the years, though."

"I'd be sad if I didn't at least warrant a thought."

"I considered looking you up on Facebook, but wondered if that seemed desperate."

Sally didn't like to admit the amount of times she'd

held her breath, wondering if this new friend request was from Harriet: but it never was.

She laid a hand on Harriet's thigh, and stared at it, as did Harriet. She used to put a hand on her thigh all the time once, but not anymore. She licked her lips, glancing up briefly at Harriet. Was this okay? Could they touch each other casually, like it had never meant anything different? The blood rushing around her body told her it still held something for her, but she ignored it.

"I think slates are wiped after a certain amount of time, aren't they? Some people hold on to emotions for far too long, and they fester and breed." Sally squeezed Harriet's thigh, before moving her hand. "We were young and naive, that's all — it wasn't meant to be."

Harriet glanced up at Sally. "So is there anyone now?"

Sally shook her head. "No, not for a while." She thought back to Casey, to what might have been. She and Casey had been together for three years, having met six months after she split up with Todd.

"There was someone — Casey — my first long-term relationship with a woman. It was good while it lasted, we even moved in together, but we split up a while ago.

"She's the reason I moved to New York, actually. I needed to get away, take a break from Chicago. There's only so much a city can support, and it saw me through my marriage to Todd, and then my first big relationship with a woman, and subsequent break-up." Sally paused, remembering, feeling the hurt all over again.

"Break-ups with women leave you far more scarred than break-ups with men." She fixed Harriet with her gaze as she spoke. "You'd think I'd remember that much, wouldn't you?"

Harriet looked away at her words, and Sally felt bad when she saw that — she hadn't meant that to come out quite as harsh as it had. "I'm sorry," she said. "That wasn't a dig."

Harriet let out a muffled sigh in response. "You don't mince your words, do you?" She paused. "So you ran off to New York with a broken heart?"

"Something like that," Sally replied. "I threw myself into starting my own design start-up and set up base in Queens, seeing as that was the area of New York I could afford. Just." She laughed at the absurdity of that. "Maybe I should have stayed in Chicago, the rents are cheaper and I might have been able to get a foothold quicker in a smaller place.

"But I don't regret it — I've made some great friends in New York, and it was a good change of pace. And now my aunt wants to put money in my business, I might finally be able to give it the push it deserves."

"What do you design?" Harriet asked.

"Greetings cards — not the Hallmark variety, but the bespoke, hand-made style. I don't make up cheesy rhymes, much to my friend Taylor's sadness. I sell them to shops, galleries, gift shops, book stores — anywhere that will take them."

"Sounds awesome," Harriet replied. "I remember how crazy-talented you were."

Sally blushed, looking out to the lake. "I still remember that summer so clearly," she said. "I remember the feelings like they were yesterday."

"It was all so new then. All so... fresh, exciting, unknown." Harriet shook her head. "I've often tried to recapture what I felt that summer at the lake house with you, but I don't think it's possible. I guess it's called being 18."

Sally's head throbbed as she nodded, and she took another slug of her water. "We were both young, it was something so..." Sally shook her head. It was still the most exciting summer of Sally's life.

"So... what?"

Sally swallowed down the old emotions swirling around her body where Harriet was concerned. Every hair on her body stood up, woozy with feeling. Blood zoomed to her cheeks, and there was the familiar tingle in her stomach. She was momentarily dazed, surprised. The old feelings were still there? That couldn't be right, could it? So much had happened since, not least that she was no longer 17, no longer hanging on Harriet's every word.

She blew out a long breath. "It doesn't matter now, does it?" she said, straightening up. "It's a long time ago, and nobody forgets their first, do they?"

She heard Harriet draw a breath at that, then she looked away, her chest rising and falling fast, like she didn't dare look at Sally. "Your first?"

It might be years ago, but Sally still recalled how hard it had been to function when Harriet left, like someone had ripped away a limb and asked her to just carry on as if nothing had happened. She'd tried to, but her best efforts at life had been wonky, haphazard. And back then, she hadn't been able to put a name to what she was feeling, to call out the pain and devastation she'd felt even thinking about Harriet.

Picturing her in her mind. Picturing them both, naked, on the boat, wrapped in each other's arms.

No, back then, it had been far too painful.

Sally nodded. "You knew you were my first, I told you that."

"Right," Harriet replied, her face clouding over. "You mean first sexual encounter."

"Of course," Sally said. "What did you think I meant?"

She knew what Harriet was getting at, she just didn't want to admit it.

Yes, Harriet had been her first love, the grand first love that had marked her for life, made her run screaming back into the closet, made her doubt herself and her feelings for *anyone* who came afterwards.

But she was over that now, wasn't she? She wasn't the type to hold on to feelings; she'd been through enough therapy to know that did no good at all.

"What about you?" Sally asked, changing the subject swiftly.

Harriet chewed her cheek. "Me?"

"Yes, relationship, job, the works. We seem to have been talking about me a lot, but you've said nothing. The great Harriet Locke, have you got a girlfriend hiding at home?"

Harriet snorted at that. "Nope, no girlfriend, I'm very much single. You think I'd be here if I did?"

Sally's heart sank: was she the consolation prize where Harriet was concerned?

Harriet twisted in her seat and took Sally's hand in hers, covering it with both her palms. For a moment, Sally thought she was going to lift it to her lips and kiss it; but if she had been, she thought better of it and took a hand away.

"That didn't come out as I meant it," Harriet said, wincing.

Sally narrowed her eyes, taking her hand back, closing down her body for self-preservation. Her head was still aching and she didn't need Harriet messing with it tonight, too. She pictured her massive kingsize bed and how she was longing to crawl into it, sink into its Egyptian cotton sheets and drag the duvet over her head.

She didn't need any of Harriet's mind games now or ever: she'd survived this long without them just fine.

"Sounds like it came out exactly as you meant it to me."

Harriet shook her head. "It didn't, believe me," she said, squeezing Sally's hand. "What I meant was, there is no-one at home, and I'd be lucky to have someone who could compare to you."

Sally shook her head. "How do you know what I'm

like anymore? We haven't seen each other in half a lifetime. I could have turned into an awful person, be really selfish. I might have treated all my girlfriends terribly."

"I doubt that," she replied. "I don't think the core of anybody changes that much from who they were when they were young to who they are now. And you were always one of the kindest, sweetest, warmest people I'd ever met — you were so open and generous, I'd never met anybody like you. And you're right, I don't know you now, how could I? But I'd lay bets you're still warm, smart, and funny, all the things I loved about you back then. So I'm sorry if I upset you, okay?"

"Just then, or when we were kids?" Sally asked, the hurt from both occasions surging around her like a hurricane. She needed some food, lest she start feeling sick again.

"Both," Harriet replied, fixing Sally with her gaze, and Sally was powerless to move from it. Instead, she immersed herself in it, wanting the warmth it had always bestowed on her, but then shying away from it, knowing its power and its history.

She shook herself and yawned, covering up what she was feeling. "Shall we walk to the pier and get some food?"

* * *

They walked over to the edge of Navy Pier and leaned against the railings, eating their hot dogs, topped with onions and ketchup. As soon as it hit her stomach, Harriet wanted more: turned out she was hungry, and she realized she hadn't eaten all day. She'd been too nervous about tonight — for good reason. If nothing else, even if she never saw Sally again, she wanted to leave her with a good impression of the current-day Harriet Locke.

She knew she'd been at fault for their break-up, but college had just been too distracting — plus there were a lot of girls there. But when Harriet had told Sally she didn't think they should carry on, she could still see the salty tears that had rolled down her flushed cheeks, still see her shaking shoulders, the fault all hers.

Her actions had devastated Sally, but they'd crippled her, too. Yes, they'd been at different stages of their lives, but it had never stopped Harriet wondering what might have been. What if?

Of all her exes, Sally was the one who'd never left Harriet's heart. After they split, Harriet had concluded a clean break would be better for both of them. Better to cut all ties and get on with their lives than stringing it out and prolonging the heartbreak. It was only a few years later, when she was much older, she realized how stupid she'd been.

"I've had three long-term relationships, to answer your earlier question," Harriet said, once her hot dog was done.

Sally was still only halfway through hers, but she wasn't looking nearly as green as she had been an hour ago.

"None of them have lasted more than two years, and none of them have ever resulted in me moving in with someone. Daniel says this makes me a very unattractive prospect now, that I'll be far too set in my ways for the unfortunate woman who has to try to change them."

Sally gave her a sad smile. "Is Daniel right?"

"No, I think he's selling me a little short, but that's brothers for you. I could totally live in harmony if I met the right woman. If that happened, I'd be willing to bend and twist in ways Daniel hasn't even dreamed of." She blushed as she said it, not meaning for it to sound so flirtatious. She hoped she might stop putting her foot in her mouth sometime soon.

She closed her eyes to try to recover her composure, but when she reopened them, Sally's soft gaze was caressing her face, a smile playing around her lips. "Possibly best not to tell him that. If he's anything like he used to be, he'd ask you to spell out exactly what you mean."

Harriet nodded. "Nope, still the same, that's exactly what he'd say," she said, smiling. "Anyway, that's me — I've been focusing more on my business and getting that up and running — it's why I was in New York the day I stole your suitcase."

"What do you do?" Sally said, before eating another bite of hot dog and wiping some ketchup from the side of her mouth.

Harriet's fingers itched to reach up and wipe it away herself, to look after Sally just like always, but she kept her hands right where they were. There came a time and place to be doing things like that, and she was pretty sure this wasn't one of them.

"We're called Panache — mainly because that's what we supply. Big stores and picky clients want something that marks them out from the crowd, and so we showcase cutting-edge and brilliant designs that otherwise wouldn't see the light of day. Stuff like stationery, accessories, gadgets, little items that you didn't know you needed but will make your life infinitely better."

"You don't sell spiralizers, do you?"

Harriet let out a bark of laughter at that. "We try to only market stuff that will survive trends. No spiralizers have crossed my palms, promise. We champion companies and designers who are doing things that little bit differently, but they then don't want to put all their time into trying to market their products. We've got contacts with stores, big and small, all around the world, and we can place those creations where people want to buy them. We also have a list of individual buyers who'll pay a premium to get this stuff before anybody else."

Sally nodded her head, licking a crumb from her index finger.

Harriet watched as she trailed her tongue briefly along its tip, before sucking it slowly into her mouth. A shudder ran down the length of her body, but Sally was blissfully unaware.

Harriet needed to focus, and not let her mind draw back the curtain on when that had happened before.

When Sally had sucked Harriet's finger into her mouth, before sucking Harriet into her mouth completely.

Harriet swallowed and brought her mind back to the present.

"Wow, who knew stuff like that even existed? I work with a ton of artists in New York and they'd kill for a company like yours to come along and discover them."

"Well, you have to have been in business for a certain time and have the capacity to scale up and increase your production by quite a way. We've been burnt before and so now we only deal with clients who are ready. If you've only been used to supplying 40 units of whatever it is you make per month to the market, and then suddenly one of our clients orders 1,000 for their stores around the globe and they need them in two weeks, our suppliers have to be ready. We do our homework." Harriet smiled. "Saying that, your friends might be viable, who knows? What I know is there are so many talented people everywhere looking for a break, and we want to make that happen."

Sally eyed her now as if for the first time, turning up one side of her mouth as she did so. "You've surprised me, Harriet Locke."

"I have? In a good way?" *Please say in a good way.*

"Yes, in a good way."

Phew.

"Your dad's a corporate lawyer, your mom's a financial whiz, and you were brought up to do something traditional, something staid that makes a lot of money. And while I'm sure you make enough money from this — I'm not naive enough to think you do it out of the goodness of your own heart — this business is serving a need, one that means that artists can make enough money from their work, and that's priceless."

Harriet grinned. "I'm glad you get it." She hoped her line of business was gaining brownie points with Sally, which she could clearly do with scoring.

Sally rolled her neck before she spoke again. "You mind if we get a coffee? I think my system could do with a pick-me-up."

"A coffee this late?"

Sally smiled. "I will sleep the sleep of the dead tonight."

They walked away from the pier, leaving the tourists behind them, through the sculptured Polk Bros Park and out into the city's heartbeat, pulsing with lights, people and cars. As they navigated North Lake Shore Drive, Harriet went to take Sally's hand — it was such a natural response, she almost did it without thinking — but she stopped before she connected.

They were different people now, with their own lives. She couldn't just take Sally's hand as if she still had the right to — she'd forfeited that quite some time ago.

Five minutes later, they found a small diner on a side street still open, two metallic stools empty at its white counter. A thick-set middle-aged man near the door was tucking into a plate of meatloaf with gusto, his lips smacking together as he ate. At the back of the diner, a young couple were holding hands across the table as they shared an ice cream sundae.

Their youthful exuberance reminded Harriet of her and Sally before she'd fucked it up.

Behind the counter, a serious-looking coffee machine made a statement in polished chrome, and several fruit pies stood inside a clear cabinet.

Harriet and Sally sat down on the empty stools, their metallic legs making a grating sound on the scratched floor as they shuffled them forward. Harriet ordered two coffees and some cherry pie, insisting Sally could use the sugar, and she didn't argue.

The woman serving gave them their drinks in thick, white mugs, and the pie arrived with steam rising off it, the sweet smell curling into Harriet's senses. The woman dolloped two scoops of vanilla ice cream on the side of the plate and presented them with a fork each, and their cutlery clashed as they dove into the pastry at the same time.

They both grinned, and just as Harriet was about to say something about the cherry pie being "damn fine," Christina Aguilera's *Dirrty* began blaring from the radio, taking her back to *that* summer: the summer of them.

When she looked up, Sally was giving her an intense stare, and Harriet didn't look away.

"This takes me back," Harriet said.

Sally nodded. "Uh-huh." She finished her pie before continuing. "You, me, Robert's food, a bottle of wine, and Christina serenading us." She flicked her gaze away from Harriet, staring at a point over her shoulder.

"Christina was a constant, wasn't she?" Harriet cleared her throat as Sally nodded. Thinking about that summer was making sitting here with Sally feel a little claustrophobic, so she flicked the subject matter back to now.

"Big news with your aunt investing — does that mean your business could really begin to fly soon?"

Relief swept over Sally's face as she toyed with the pie, flicking her gaze back to Harriet. "That's the plan. Right now, it's just me working out of a studio complex in Queens, right around the corner from my apartment. But if things work out, I might expand and think about stepping up my marketing plans. It's scary but exciting."

"It sounds like it," Harriet said. "I'd love to see some of your work sometime."

"I'll mail you a card," Sally replied. "A thank-you for the hot dog and the pie."

Harriet smiled. "Maybe I could stop by the next time I'm in New York and we could do lunch or something."

Sally eyed her thoughtfully. "We'll see."

Harriet nodded, not sure what to make of that sentence.

Sally was silent for a while, a slight frown on her face when she spoke. "But seeing as I've messed up tonight being hungover, we could meet up again tomorrow if you like." She paused. "So long as you're not working."

Harriet cast her mind forward to tomorrow and the mountain of work she'd been planning to do, as well as going to visit her dad. However, she already knew that going out again with Sally McCall trumped both of those. "I'd love to," she replied.

Harriet stared into Sally's eyes and what she saw almost took her breath away. It was as if the intervening 17 years had never happened, and they were teenagers again. Before life got in the way.

"I'll get my work done and we can meet for dinner later? Properly this time, when we can eat dinner sitting at a table. A table is a prerequisite, wouldn't you say?"

"I always said you were the classy one," Sally replied with a renewed smile. "But seeing as we're catching up tomorrow, you mind if I duck out early tonight and get some rest? Daytime drinking and me are not friends."

Harriet shook her head. "No problem. So long as tomorrow is a definite."

"It's a date," Sally replied, before blushing bright red. "I mean not a date, but you know…" she stuttered, before looking at the floor.

"I know what you mean," Harriet replied, putting a hand on her knee.

Sally took an audible intake of breath at that, before looking up at her.

And when she did that, time stood still, and Christina Aguilera faded out. The only sound Harriet could hear was her heartbeat booming in her ears and the distant sound of Chicago traffic outside. But when Sally jumped off her stool, the colors came back, and all of a sudden, everything was too loud.

"I really should be going," Sally said, taking a gulp of her coffee. "Thanks for tonight. Text me about tomorrow. You've got my number." She reached over and squeezed Harriet's hand.

Harriet shuddered.

Another scorching look from Sally McCall, and then she flitted behind her and out the door, leaving Harriet alone to rake over what just happened.

It was a lot to process.

Chapter Thirteen

*T*wo hours later, Harriet led Sally out across the lawn, the sun just beginning to descend over the water, its rays still pink and warm. Harriet was carrying a red checkered woolen blanket and a chilled picnic bag, while Sally had a bottle of contraband Pinot Grigio wrapped in her sweater.

"This place never fails to impress," Sally said, as Harriet spread the blanket over the grass, putting the food on one corner: their chef, Robert, was a sweetheart and had thought of everything. "You don't know how lucky you are."

Harriet loved bringing Sally here, loved seeing the world through her eyes. She often wished she could feel the joy Sally felt at stuff like this: for her, it was all too tied up with her family, a place she couldn't wait to get away from.

"I guess," she replied. "It's pretty at sunset."

Sally gave her a look, her piercing blue eyes vibrant under her long lashes. "It's pretty all the time."

At that look, something stirred deep in Harriet's belly, but she ignored it. "We can go for a swim in the lake tomorrow — did you bring your suit?"

Sally frowned. "I did, but you know me and water. I might dip my toe in, but that's all."

"I thought you took lessons?"

"I did, to please my mom, but I'm still not comfortable."

They settled down side by side, a breeze wafting from the left laced with the smells of the Sugar Maples. Ahead, the lake was silky, and her family's speedboat rocked gently against the larger of the two wooden jetties.

Harriet leaned back on her elbows and closed her eyes, finally away from prying eyes, just she and Sally, relaxed.

She turned her head, to where Sally was watching her.

Sally looked away instinctively, her reddish hair swishing around her pale face.

Harriet wanted to tell her there was no need.

"You know, there were times in this school year I never thought this moment would come, did you?"

"Uh-uh," Sally said, picking lint off the blanket and rolling it in her fingers. "Especially with all the tests we had to take." She paused. "But that's it for you, though — how does it feel?"

Most of Harriet's friends had jetted off to sunnier climes on their parents' expense accounts when school was done, and were now partying in the sunshine, getting wasted. It wasn't that she didn't want to do that, but she was also acutely aware this was the last summer for her and Sally, before Harriet left for Harvard.

Having spent so much time with Sally over the past year, that thought scared Harriet so much. She didn't want to leave her, but she couldn't stay either. However, there was something she could do about the time they had left, and that was to spend as much of it with Sally as possible.

But it didn't stop Boston seeming very, very far away from her best friend.

"It feels… kinda numb. Like I had this whole school experience, and then, that's it, done. I got the grades, I got into college, the next part of my life is just about to begin." She sighed, looking over at Sally. "I want to leave home and go to college, but I kinda still like this part, too."

Sally looked at her with such intent, Harriet's heart began to boom.

"Yeah, I know exactly," she said, before looking down at her fingers.

Harriet's whole body tensed, but she took a deep breath and gave Sally her best smile. "Shall we have some food and wine, and toast to what might come next year?"

Sally shrugged. "I guess we should — make the most of now, right?"

"Exactly," Harriet said. "This time next year it'll be your turn, and you'll be going off to some elite art college, far more exciting than me."

Sally gave her a look. "You're going to Harvard. I think most people would disagree."

Harriet shrugged, grabbing the wine and unscrewing the cap. "I'm studying law, it's hardly sexy or anything I *want to do." She paused. "Thank god for non-corkscrew wine," she said, pouring it into the plastic stemmed glasses Robert had included in her picnic box. "And here's to Robert for the food and glasses."*

"Everybody needs a Robert in their life," Sally agreed.

"Amen," Harriet replied, raising her glass to Sally. "To a fabulous weekend, I'm glad you could come."

"To you and your future. And to us — I wouldn't want to be anywhere else," Sally replied, her gaze burning a hole in Harriet's soul.

All of which made Harriet's insides churn anew, and she gulped down her wine to cover it up. Was she reading this wrong? Just how were you supposed to read girls? She had no fucking idea.

Not for the first time, she wished she could talk about it, open up to Sally, but she couldn't. It wasn't like Sally was a boy and this was what they were supposed to be doing. Her parents weren't concerned about her being on the lawn with Sally because she didn't have a penis.

What they didn't realize was what Sally had was way more dangerous than that: she had beauty, charisma, style, the works. And while Harriet still couldn't put a finger on exactly what she was feeling, it was strong, that's all she knew. And it was brewing, sloshing around inside her, waiting for a release.

But what she was going to do about it, she had no idea.

* * *

Two hours later, they dragged their food debris and blanket back into the house. In the living room, the TV flickered as Harriet's parents watched, but Harriet didn't go in and say hi like Sally would. Rather, she simply put a finger to her lips and took Sally's hand. It was still the same thrill as the first time she'd done it earlier.

Sally's limbs were a little floppy, but she wasn't too drunk: the alcohol had greased her system, allowing her to move freely and not seize up at the slightest touch from Harriet.

They got back to Harriet's room and collapsed on her double bed, which squeaked as they did. They both giggled at the sound, warm skin touching, arms and legs in the air comparing mosquito bites. Even though they'd sprayed before they'd gone down to the lake, the insects had been hungry tonight.

"Stupid things, spoiling a romantic moment," Harriet said, before freezing, glancing at Sally.

A romantic moment? Sally had thought so, but had Harriet too?

If this was a boy, Sally would know she had to wait till he kissed her: that's just how things went. But when you wanted to kiss a girl, to tell a girl you liked her, who made the first move?

She sighed and slumped onto the bed, putting an arm over her eyes. Her insides were tight like a coil and she felt like she couldn't breathe. Why couldn't she just say something, see if Harriet thought the same? And even if she didn't, wouldn't she be cool about it, after what she'd said about Daniel? She shook her head as Harriet wriggled beside her, giving her a quick peck on the cheek.

Sally's mind went blank. She couldn't wait to be older when she'd have it all figured out.

As it was, she was lying beside the most beautiful girl in the world, and she was stuck, with no idea how to change it.

A wave of sleepiness washed over her and she felt herself succumb to it. Maybe going to sleep was the easier option, because she wasn't sure how she was going to survive if she had to put up with much more of this tension that was building a wall inside her.

Sally sighed. "What time is it?" she asked, her body heavy, yet every hair on it standing to attention.

Harriet checked her watch "Nearly ten," she said, glancing at Sally, her breath caressing Sally's cheek.

"I'm tired. You think it's too early to go to bed?"

Harriet shook her head. "No — fresh air does that. You wanna get ready?"

Sally nodded, even though getting into bed with Harriet didn't sound any safer.

Fifteen minutes later, she was shivering under the duvet in her skimpy white cotton T-shirt and boy shorts, even though it was a balmy night and the room had no AC.

Harriet grinned at her as she crossed the room, a streak of toothpaste at one corner of her gorgeous mouth, and the bed squeaked again as she got in.

"You've got toothpaste on your mouth," Sally said, glancing at her.

Harriet sat up on one elbow, facing her. "This side?" she asked, pointing to her right.

Sally's eye was drawn to the skin on her chest that was revealed by Harriet's V-neck T-shirt: tanned, smooth, eminently lickable. As she thought that, her tongue ran across her bottom lip, and when she looked up, she knew she'd been caught.

She waited for Harriet to say something, to admonish her, but Harriet said nothing. Rather, she just held her gaze and then her eyes traveled to the same part of Sally's skin, making her squirm inside, even though her body stayed stock still.

It was all she could do to still breathe.

"No, the other side," Sally replied, her voice coming out an octave lower than usual, not sounding at all like her own. What was going on? Her body was pulsing, her chest heaving, and she could feel herself getting wet, just like when she touched herself. Only this time, it was happening with another live person and in a bed.

Holy sweet mother of god, if she had to do something about this now, she might faint.

At Sally's direction, Harriet poked her tongue out to the left side of her mouth and licked off her toothpaste.

Sally closed her eyes, wondering when this torture might end.

Harriet gave her a final stare, before settling down

under the covers, until all Sally could hear was their breathing, hot and heavy. It was a few moments before Harriet spoke again.

"Sally?" she said, her voice a whisper.

"Yes?"

"I," she began, before pausing. Then Sally heard her head move on the pillow next to her, and she turned to meet the whites of Harriet's eyes. "I just want you to know that we're in a double bed together and you know, we might touch each other tonight. I mean, I might accidentally cuddle you, whatever. But if that happens, we should just go with it, you know? I mean, it's no big deal, we hug anyway, don't we?"

Sally's breathing stalled as she nodded. Was this code? Should she be deciphering something, like they did in World War Two to win the war?

At a loss for something to say, she simply nodded her head.

"Good. I'm glad you think so, too."

She couldn't make out Harriet's facial expression as she said this, but her eyes never left Sally's face, and in turn, Sally never turned away. It was like she was caught in Harriet's headlights, with nowhere to run, and it felt gloriously risky.

Sally had never felt so alive or so vulnerable in her life, and she never wanted to leave this state. Ever.

"Right," she agreed eventually.

She heard Harriet smile then, her cheeks squeaking

just like the bed. "Good," she said, turning onto her side, throwing an arm over Sally and pulling her close, Harriet's bare legs touching the back of hers, her bare arm slung casually over her torso, her hand ending just above Sally's crotch.

Sally breathed in and held it, wanting to feel as small and streamlined as she possibly could in Harriet's arms, to fit perfectly. When Harriet had said she might cuddle her, she'd been lying. That preamble was clearly just a run-up, getting permission to take Sally in her arms.

But she wasn't complaining.

Far from it.

The heat from both their bodies swirled around her head and the feeling of being held in Harriet's arms was intoxicating, like Harriet had just put a spell on her.

But Sally still hadn't moved: it was as if as soon as Harriet had claimed her in the bed, Sally had frozen solid to the spot, unsure how to act, what to do. How did Harriet know? Had she done this before? Had there been other women in her bed, in her arms?

But that thought only made Sally stiffen, which Harriet clearly felt.

"This okay?" she asked into the back of Sally's neck, her words tickling Sally's skin as she said them.

Only if you haven't done it with anyone else, Sally thought. But she didn't say those words out loud; she wasn't an idiot.

Instead, she made a noise that sounded like a grunt,

and then tried to relax. But in doing so, she breathed out and moved her legs, and then Harriet responded by pulling her closer, which made Sally freeze all over again.

"Just relax," Harriet said from behind. "We're just getting comfortable."

Sally breathed her in, the scent of her, the feel of her.

Comfortable? Right, she could do that, of course she could. She took a stuttering breath in, then out, just as Harriet's hand stroked her belly over her T-shirt.

Sally felt it right at her core.

Boom.

Chapter Fourteen

*T*he following morning Harriet woke up in bed alone. *She frowned: where was Sally? They'd fallen asleep last night in each others arms and it was almost perfect, with just that final step to take. The one that Harriet was so worried to, because who knew how Sally would react? She hadn't said no to getting close in bed, and that had felt... just wonderful. Beyond anything Harriet had ever felt with anyone else.*

Her last thought before she'd drifted off was how delicious Sally smelt, and her smell infiltrated Harriet's dreams, crisp and sweet.

When she'd woken up in the middle of the night, Sally had been curled up in a ball on the other side of the bed, but she'd smiled to have her there, anyway. Whenever Sally was around, Harriet felt calmer, more sure of herself, of who she was.

Her parents and her classmates all thought she was this sassy, strong-willed young woman who could get any boy she wanted: and she was. But Harriet was also starting to think boys weren't the only option. Girls were, too.

All girls? She wasn't sure — but definitely a girl named Sally McCall.

Sally McCall was quickly becoming everything Harriet had ever dreamed of.

Harriet shrugged off the duvet, stopping as the scent of Sally rose into her nostrils from her pillow. Harriet allowed herself a brief stoop to take her in, then she shook her head. What was happening to her? She had no idea.

She got some shorts from her white dresser drawer on the left-hand side of her room and walked over to the balcony that faced out to the back of the house, to the Green Mountain Maples behind. And there sat Sally, soaking up the morning sunshine, one leg curled underneath her body, scribbling in what Harriet assumed was a journal.

Sally hadn't heard Harriet behind her, and so she stood for a moment, just taking her in: her creamy white legs, her hand clutched around a chewed ballpoint pen, her shoulders hunched, her hair still messy from sleep. Like Harriet, she'd just added a pair of white shorts to her outfit, and Harriet's gaze settled on the piece of skin just below her neck, the place where her nose had been last night.

Sally turned then, as if sensing her, and jumped when Harriet's presence was confirmed.

She let out a shriek and put a hand to her chest. "Jesus!" she said, her face winding through a gamut of emotions. "You almost gave me a heart attack. How long have you been standing there?"

Harriet sat down beside her, a satisfied grin on her face. "Not long," she replied. "What are you writing?"

Sally looked down at the open page, then hastily shut her journal with a bang. "Nothing, just scribbling," she said.

"Have you been up long?"

Sally looked away, then back to Harriet, gathering herself after the intrusion.

"Not long, about half an hour. You were dead to the world."

"Shall I get us some coffee?" Harriet asked, getting up and yawning again.

Sally's gaze settled on her exposed midriff, before she looked up, nodding her head. "That'd be great. Is it okay if I jump in the shower?"

Harriet's mind went to go somewhere, but she shut it down. Not this early in the morning, not when she had a whole day to get through. "Be my guest," she said. "I'll go and see what Robert's doing for breakfast, too."

When Harriet came back up ten minutes later, the shower was on, and she tried not to think of Sally, naked, just a few feet from her. Instead, her body beating with desire, she made herself walk the other way and back out onto the balcony, setting down the two mugs of coffee.

And that's when she saw Sally's journal on the chair next to where she'd been sitting, an elastic band tied around it, her pen sat neatly on top of it. The journal looked expensive, blue with gold embossing on the cover.

Harriet took a sip of her coffee, then winced: it was too hot. She cast her gaze over to the trees, but then it was immediately drawn back to the journal. Sally had looked so intense when she was writing it earlier. Had she been writing about her, about being here? Did that journal hold the key to what Sally was feeling about her life? Harriet would love to know.

She got up, then sat back down again. She shouldn't read it, she knew that. It was a gross invasion of privacy, and if she kept a journal, she'd be so mad if someone read hers. Which was the reason she didn't write one.

Then again, Harriet was Sally's close friend, and Sally shared most things with her. She would probably know most of the stuff Sally was writing about: school, her family, boys. The usual teenage-girl stuff.

And that thought propelled Harriet to the balcony door once more: the shower was still running.

It was now or never.

Before she could second-guess herself, she was moving the chewed blue pen, slipping off the pink elastic band, and flipping open the journal to the page of the last entry. It took a moment for the words to come into focus for Harriet, but when they did, her hand started to shake, followed by a roaring in her ears and a rhythmic thumping in her chest. Harriet's jaw locked as she took in the words, tripping over them, reading again just to make sure Sally was saying what she thought she was saying.

She was.

"And last night we slept together in the same bed, and when she put her arm around me, I froze — I don't think she knows what that does to me. It's a kind of torture, but one I'd choose every night. I'm not sure what it means or what to do about it, though. What if she slaps me if I try to kiss her? What if I have no idea what I'm doing, because I don't? What if I'm not ready to sleep with her? This place is so idyllic, just like her. But I'm so aware she's going away soon, and this could be the last chance I get to tell her how I feel. I don't know what it is, or if I'm gay or bi or what, but it's there. I can't ignore it. Whenever she's in the same room as me my chest tightens, and I never know if I'll be able to speak."

The creak of a floorboard broke Harriet's reading, and she took a moment to realize where she was, so enthralled had she been by Sally's words. The tips of her fingers were white where she was gripping the journal hard, and her skin prickled as she took it all in.

This was huge news: Sally wanted her, too.

"Are you reading my journal?" Sally's voice shattered Harriet's picture-perfect moment of triumph as her words brought her crashing back to reality and she looked up.

Busted.

And there was Sally wrapped in a white towel, shoulders naked and glistening, clutching the white wooden door frame of the balcony, confusion on her face.

Was that confusion or was it anger? Harriet wasn't sure. She winced, then got sidetracked with Sally's wet hair *that was stuck to the side of her face, forgetting she'd just betrayed her.*

Only, it didn't feel like betrayal to Harriet.

This felt like a moment for them both to share, to rejoice.

"How dare you!" Sally said, reaching for the journal, just as it fell from Harriet's hands, landing on the floor with a slap.

Harriet shuddered with fear as it dawned on her that Sally was not seeing this moment as she was; there was no triumph in her eyes. And that was because she didn't know the other side, what Harriet was feeling.

But that was easily rectified, right?

Harriet just had to explain to Sally.

She stood up to do just that, shaking her head. "It's not what you think," she began, bending down. "I read a tiny bit of your last entry, and it was incredible!"

Sally's hand hit hers as they both reached for her journal at the same time, both getting a hand to it, and both standing together.

Only, as she did, Sally's towel came loose and dropped on one side, revealing Sally's right breast and a whole chunk of body.

Seeing that, Harriet let go of the journal and just stood, transfixed. She was even more beautiful than she'd ever allowed herself to imagine.

Sally grabbed her towel, hoisted it up, and ran into the bedroom. "Just stay where you are!" she said as Harriet went to follow.

Harriet did as she was told.

She stood behind the curtain of the balcony door, giving Sally the privacy she needed, but determined to talk to her, too. "Sally, listen to me. I read a tiny bit, but it was enough—"

"—enough to embarrass me, for you to have a good laugh? I can't believe you'd do that, I trusted you. You're supposed to be my best friend."

Was she crying? She sounded like she was crying.

"Well fuck you, Harriet. Those are my private thoughts." Sally appeared at the doorway, dressed in white shorts and a green T-shirt, drying her hair. "I put an elastic band round it for a reason, or did that escape you?"

"I just—" Harriet began.

"—You just nothing. Everything has to be on your terms, doesn't it? You've always gotten everything you ever wanted, life is easy for you." Sally paused. "It's not easy for me, I don't know if you noticed. I can't control much. But the one thing I can control is my thoughts." She paused. "Well fuck you, and have a nice life."

Sally turned, grabbed her bag and started throwing things in it.

Alarmed, Harriet ran into the room, putting her hand on Sally's arm.

Big mistake.

"Get your hands off me!" Sally screamed, such venom in her words it made Harriet stop in her tracks.

She put both her hands up and stepped backwards.

"Okay, whatever you say," she said. "I'm really sorry about reading your journal, I don't know what came over me. But I hardly read anything, and what I did, I wasn't scared by, if that makes things any better. And you can totally leave and run out, only you won't get far, the nearest bus stop is three miles away and it's the summer. Buses run when they want to."

Sally was still packing her bag, not looking her way, the occasional sob escaping her mouth, wiping her nose with the back of her hand.

"I get it, I shouldn't have done it, and if you want to go, I'll drive you home right now, I promise." She paused. "But please stay — we don't have long together till I go to college, please stay till Monday, just like we planned."

Sally paused, her chest going up and down.

Had her words got through, made a difference? Harriet had no idea. But after what seemed like an eternity, Sally put her bag down and gave a deep sigh. She didn't turn around, but at least she'd stopped packing.

"Do you know what you've done by reading my journal?"

"I do, believe me," Harriet said. "But I wanted to know if you feel the way I do. And I got my answer."

Sally shook her head. "You could have just asked me instead of invading my privacy."

"I know and I'm so sorry. I promise I'll never do it again." Harriet paused. "Will you stay?"

Sally still wasn't looking at her. She walked over to the

bed and sat on the edge, putting her head in her hands. That's when Harriet saw her hands were shaking. She wanted to go over and take her in her arms, just like last night, but she couldn't.

"I don't know," Sally replied. "I need some time to clear my head." She stood up, standing tall, giving Harriet her purposeful stance. "I'm going for a walk."

"You want some breakfast first?" Harriet said, just for something to say. She knew it was a stupid question even as it came out of her mouth.

"I'm not hungry," Sally said, walking past Harriet, giving her a murderous look.

But even as she did, Harriet breathed her in, shower-fresh: she looked and smelt good enough to eat. "I'll be here, waiting."

Sally didn't look back as she slammed the door; then Harriet listened, the only sound the thump of Sally's footsteps on the staircase and the thud of Harriet's heart in her chest.

If Sally didn't come back, she might throw herself in the lake.

She'd really fucked it up this time, hadn't she?

Chapter Fifteen

Sally walked across the lawn, which seemed so different than it had last night. Last night had been more innocent, no bases loaded. Now, as she contemplated what might happen, everything seemed up in the air. She'd spent the day walking round the local village, had lunch in a café, and hadn't known what to think.

She'd thought about calling her mom to get her, but that seemed lame, the sort of thing a little kid would do. But today, she kinda felt like that. Like calling her mom to come figure out her life would be preferable to going back and facing Harriet.

Only, she knew she had to, because she and Harriet had to talk about what had happened, about what Harriet had read, and how they were going to deal with it. Sally really wasn't looking forward to that at all, to Harriet's sympathetic looks as Sally's feelings were laid bare.

She'd tried the bedroom first, but Harriet wasn't there. She'd said a brief hello to Mrs Locke, who'd stared at her as if trying to place her, before remembering she was her daughter's guest. She'd told her Harriet was sunbathing on the boat if she was looking for her, and had followed that up with a long, hard stare at Sally, as if she knew what she wanted to do with her daughter, knew everything about her and wasn't impressed.

Sally walked down the wooden jetty, the boards solid under her feet, her palms clammy as she bunched her fingers together. It was just past 5pm and the lake was still, hardly any breeze unlike yesterday. The sun was still high in the sky and Sally was a hot mess of emotions, her nerves frazzled. If she stopped moving forward she might never start again, so she kept going.

She wrapped her fingers around the ladder that led to the speedboat, the metal hot to touch. Luckily, the boat was tethered tightly, so she had no trouble boarding. And when she did, she gulped at the sight that greeted her: Harriet, in a red bikini, laid out on the boat's deck, book in hand. She looked like she was in some kind of ad for swimwear, her chestnut hair splayed both sides, her other hand up, shielding her eyes despite her yellow sunglasses.

Sally snagged her leg on a piece of metal jutting out and swore under her breath, which alerted Harriet.

When she saw it was Sally, she hastily stood up, putting a hand on her hip, her shades on top of her head. She looked unsure, which was unusual for Harriet.

"Hey," she said. "You're back."

"Looks like it." Sally sounded cool, like she was in one of those '80s teen movies her mom loved. She was *channeling her inner Molly Ringwald, even though she felt anything but inside.*

"Are you staying?"

Sally nodded. "I'm staying."

Harriet gave her an uncertain smile. "Cool," she said, bringing down her sunglasses once more and chewing her lip. "Where have you been all day?"

"I walked to the village, and then back along the lake."

"I drove around, but I couldn't see you." Harriet paused. "I was worried. I'm sorry about this morning."

Sally shrugged like it meant nothing. And while that wasn't the case, Harriet reading her journal was a secondary issue now: the primary one was staring her in the face, almost naked, her red bikini covering barely anything. It was all Sally could do not to gape, but she knew she couldn't do that. Instead, she turned her head and stared out to the lake, avoiding Harriet's intense stare.

She saw movement out of the corner of her eye and looked over, to where Harriet was putting on her blue V-neck shirt: thank god for that. Sally released a breath, and Harriet sat down on the deck again, patting the space beside her.

"Are you going to come and sit next to me?"

Sally nodded, all the rational thought she'd had today flown from her brain. Now, all that was taking up her thoughts was Harriet and her tanned skin, her dimple, her gorgeous green eyes.

"Did you eat today?"

"What are you, my mom?" It came out harsher than Sally had intended, so she followed it up with a smile, before sitting down next to Harriet. Her heart revved as she did. "I had something in the café."

"Maybe that's where you were when I drove in."

"Maybe." Sally stared at her perfect face, her sunkissed hair. This was impossible, wasn't it? "I'm still fucking mad at you." She was trying to grasp the burning injustice she'd held all day, but it was fizzling out in the face of a semi-naked Harriet.

Harriet cast her gaze to the deck. "I don't blame you," she said, almost inaudibly, before glancing up and taking Sally's hand in hers. "But before you run off again, I only read a tiny bit and I know that's not an excuse, but it's true." She paused, staring into Sally's eyes. "But what I read didn't scare me." Harriet ran the pad of her thumb across Sally's palm and Sally's heart stalled.

Was she going to vomit? She was still looking at Harriet's thumb on her, not daring to break the beauty of this moment, to see and hear the inevitable words that would soon come tumbling from Harriet's mouth. "But this isn't what I want…"

Only, they never came.

Instead, Harriet said: "In fact, what I read made me relieved. You said you had feelings for me, and I…" she stalled, just as Sally looked up, unable to stop herself. "I have feelings for you, too."

Harriet's body juddered as the words hit the air, and she gripped Sally's hand whole now, her eyes drilling into her. "Well, say something," Harriet said eventually.

Sally narrowed her eyes. "I'm not sure what to say." Her gaze caressed Harriet's face, before slipping to the patch of skin visible on her chest, then down further. And when she cast it back up, Harriet was leaning in, her lips coming closer to Sally.

Sally froze. Fucking hell, was this really happening? Were her wildest dreams coming true?

But her hesitating was done: if this was her moment, she was going to seize it. She leaned in, too, putting a hand on the deck to steady herself, and then Harriet's lips were inches from hers, the smell of sunscreen wafting under her nose. Harriet smelled like a tropical paradise, which was somehow wildly appropriate.

"Sally, I," Harriet began.

But Sally wasn't going to speak anymore.

Or think.

She'd done enough of both.

Instead, she slowly closed the gap between them and pressed her lips to Harriet's, the slightest touch making them both jerk backwards an inch like they'd just had an electric shock. Her breathing was ragged as she stared into Harriet's swirling depths, before leaning forward once more and this time, her kiss was more sure of itself: she was just doing what felt right, what came naturally.

And this? This felt like the most natural thing in the world.

She lost herself in the kiss, and when Harriet's hands came up and tangled themselves in her hair, she wilted a little more. All the things she'd been worried about all day had simply melted away just because of Harriet's kiss.

This was perfect — it had been this simple all along.

And when Harriet edged her tongue into Sally's mouth, Sally groaned out loud like she'd never done before, ever, in the history of her life.

And then she was grabbing onto Harriet and they were tumbling onto the deck of the speedboat, its floor hard under her body, but Sally didn't mind. She wanted to feel like this was something out of the ordinary: the more memorable, the better. When she'd done this with boys, it'd been in cars, on sofas.

Never on the deck of a speedboat.

By association, girls were sexier.

Eventually Sally broke the kiss, and then they were lying side by side, with Sally's lips parted, her thought processes jumbled. When Harriet looked into her eyes, Sally could have died on the spot. She couldn't move, she couldn't speak, every nerve ending in her body waiting to see what happened next.

She had no idea: she was petrified and deadly excited, all in one go.

She was glad to see Harriet's breathing was ragged, too, and that her focus was completely on Sally.

Sally felt like the luckiest girl in the world.

"I can't believe we just did that," Harriet said, breaking into a slow grin. "We just fucking kissed."

Sally grinned right back. "I know. And it was incredible."

"It was more than that," Harriet replied, her grin stretching to a laugh.

Before Sally knew it, they were both lying on their backs, holding their sides, hysterical giggles taking over. Sally had no idea why, but it was a release, such a relief. Their laughter echoed in her ears, and it lasted a good few minutes, until Sally was clutching her side, fighting to get her breath back.

She was shaking her head when she spoke. "Is your heart beating as fast as mine?"

"More," Harriet replied, propping her head on one elbow, her gaze languidly raking Sally's body.

She reached out and grabbed Sally's hand, pressing it to her chest.

Sally's fingers had never been so close to Harriet's breasts, and Sally shivered.

"But I kinda liked it," Harriet added, edging her whole body closer to Sally again.

Sally nodded. "Me, too."

"Wanna do it again?"

Harriet's glistening lips were inches from hers and Sally didn't answer, just crushed her lips to Harriet's, this time with so much more confidence than before. And holy shit: kissing girls was so much better than kissing boys. Harriet's kisses were exactly what she wanted and needed, gentle and rushed in equal measure.

And then Harriet's hand was under her top, roaming over her naked skin, before it reached her breast and cupped it. Sally let her head fall back, then her gaze came back to Harriet, who was grinning.

"Fucking hell," Sally said, her breath now sliced and diced, her thoughts scattered. All that mattered was Harriet's hand on her breast, her tongue in her mouth.

Was this what all the fuss was about?

Was this what happened to normal girls when they were kissed by boys?

If so, she understood now like she never had before.

Now, she just wanted more.

They kissed some more, slowly, with tongues, feeling breasts through clothing, and then Harriet was stripping off her shirt, quickly followed by Sally's. And then she was pushing aside Sally's bra, her mouth wrapping itself around her nipple and Sally's head fell back, smacking against the deck with a thud.

Harriet sat up, concern on her flushed face. "You okay?"

Sally just grinned up at her. "That's what happens when you do that," she gasped.

"I have the power," Harriet said, crawling on top of Sally in her red bikini, which only made Sally more wet than she already knew she was.

"Yes, you do," Sally said, staring up into her eyes, before looking down at Harriet's small cleavage in front of her and pressing herself to it, licking her way to the top of Harriet's chest, to the piece of skin she'd been obsessed with since she arrived. It tasted just as delicious as she'd imagined.

Moments later, Harriet sat up and unhooked her bikini top — and as it fell away, so did Sally's inhibitions: she'd never seen anything more beautiful. She didn't hesitate, sucking Harriet's breasts into her mouth, her tongue flicking and exploring Harriet's sweet skin as Harriet groaned on top of her.

When Sally wriggled out of her shorts and they were both in their final piece of clothing, Harriet pulled back, wiping Sally's hair from her face, her dark gaze telling Sally so much. And when Harriet put her hand between Sally's legs minutes later, both their breathing stilled.

The sun was still hot on Sally's skin, but it was nothing compared to what was going on inside. She was almost naked and she was about to have sex with Harriet. There was no room left in her brain to process that thought, it was all taken up with heat, desire, and Harriet.

"Is this okay? I don't want to—"

But Sally put a finger to Harriet's lips to stop her speaking. "Yes," she said, simply.

And then Harriet was easing down Sally's underwear, with Sally's brain screaming in fear and delight.

When Sally did the same to Harriet, she heard her breath change gears.

"We're both naked," she said, her voice scratchy, scattered.

Harriet gulped. "I know."

But then Sally's bravado left her, a horn screaming in her head to put the brakes on, but her body wasn't joining in. No, her body wanted to carry right on, full steam ahead.

To drown out the horn, Sally gathered up all her bravery and rolled on top of Harriet, and the feel of her naked body on top of Harriet was on another level: she couldn't help the groan that escaped her lips, and she suspected, neither could Harriet.

It took a moment to gather her thoughts, and when she opened her eyes, Harriet was staring back at her like she hung the moon.

"They don't teach this in sex ed, do they?" Sally said, shaking her head.

Harriet followed suit. "There would be a stampede, that's why." Then she crushed her mouth to Sally's again, and they writhed, Sally pressing her thigh between Harriet's legs, feeling her wetness on her skin as she did.

She pulled back in wonder. "I… I don't know what to do."

"Just touch me," Harriet blurted, her face bright red, her pupils like flying saucers.

Sally reached down, her heart racing, her fingers skating through Harriet's coarse hair.

Harriet gasped.

When they connected with Harriet's wetness, Sally

gasped, and Harriet's eyelids closed as her whole body shuddered.

Sally paused: it had got a good reaction, so she did it again.

Same result. She smiled, kissing Harriet again, getting bolder. This time, she left her hand there, circling Harriet, feeling her passion fully. And then, she slipped a finger inside and Harriet lifted her shoulders off the floor, then slumped back down again with an "oooof!" sound.

"Good?" Sally said, sliding a finger out, then in again. Was this right? She had no idea, but it felt amazing, like she was dipping into Harriet's soul.

Sally could feel herself throbbing as Harriet squirmed underneath her. Then she kissed her again and Harriet moaned as Sally buried another finger in her, then Sally was moaning too, kissing her through the moans, sliding her fingers all over Harriet.

They rolled to one side and Sally lost her bearings.

No matter, Harriet just grinned, and did so even wider when Sally found her again and slipped back inside.

"Oh my god, Sally," Harriet groaned as Sally picked up a rhythm and stayed with it. Sally was lost to this all-encompassing feeling, lost to watching Harriet, lost to this precious moment. She never knew it could be like this; she'd hoped, but this was beyond all expectation.

Harriet's face contorted — with pleasure, Sally hoped — and then she stilled, before her whole body shook and she came with a mighty gasp.

In response, Sally plunged her fingers back in, feeling Harriet's walls shake around her, and just like that everything she thought she knew came undone. She had no words, just kisses, which she rained down on Harriet.

When Harriet reversed their positions moments later, sucking on her nipples, Sally closed her eyes and floated away: from her real life, from the sunlight, from everything she wanted to block out. She felt Harriet's hot breath on her skin, her tongue like velvet, her fingers like silk.

And when Harriet's silk slipped into Sally's core, she couldn't quite believe what was happening, couldn't quite grasp it. But she felt it in every single inch of her body: Harriet was inside her and they were having sex. And she knew then they'd do it again this weekend, and the weekend after, and the one after that. Until Harriet had to leave, but she wasn't going to think about that.

She opened her eyes to see Harriet's gaze on her, her vision hazy as her orgasm built inside. Harriet's fingers were playing a delicious harmony on her, one she recognized from doing it herself. But with Harriet on her, the tune took on a different depth, bringing in new instruments, new melodies, ones she longed to hear again.

Sally began to groan, to writhe under Harriet, just like Harriet had done with her. Sally gripped Harriet's free arm and dug her fingers in, groaning as a wave of ecstasy swept through her, wiping her mind of everything that had gone before.

She felt like her eyes were pulsing in their sockets as a

sensation she'd never felt before whipped through her like a hurricane. She clung on, but she knew it was impossible as another wave swept through her. Sally surrendered and came in a spluttering mess, Harriet's mouth pressing into her, the boat hard beneath her, not able to recall her name, where she was, who she was.

So this was an orgasm with somebody else involved. This was what it was like to be had by Harriet Locke. She didn't think there could be anything finer.

After a few moments, Harriet stopped and Sally's body stilled, as Harriet covered it in kisses. And then there was silence, apart from the gentle ripple of the water around them, the occasional bird flying by, squawking as it did.

Sally lay still, getting her breathing back to normal, as Harriet's fingers curled around her own, sticky and oh so sweet. Eventually, she smiled, and turned her head to Harriet; they were both still naked, and Sally took a moment to take in Harriet's tanned, toned physique. She'd never been shy of showing it off, whereas Sally was feeling a little exposed.

"You know, lying here like this, we look kinda goofy."

"We do?" Harriet replied, smiling.

"Yes — you're all tanned and I'm the opposite." Feeling suddenly self-conscious, Sally sat up, reaching for her T-shirt.

Harriet sat up, too, putting a hand on her arm. "Don't rush to put it back on," she said, her eyes sweeping Sally's body. "I'm kinda enjoying the view."

Sally blushed anew. "Now I'm definitely putting it on," she said, doing just that.

Harriet stayed as naked as the day she was born. "Have you... done that before? I mean, with another girl?"

Sally's heartbeat quickened again as she shook her head, still distracted by Harriet's perfect pale breasts — one of the few parts of her body that wasn't tanned.

"No," she replied, her voice small. "You think we did it okay?"

Harriet laughed gently, kissing Sally's cheek. "Felt okay to me."

"Felt more than okay to me," Sally replied, feeling another rush at Harriet's touch. It restarted the fire in Sally's belly and further below. "Have you done it before?"

She didn't want to look at Harriet, just in case the answer wasn't what she wanted. She didn't know why it mattered, but somehow, it did.

Harriet cleared her throat, before looking down. "No. You're the first."

Sally risked a glance her way, shielding her eyes from the sun. "I'm glad," she replied, leaning back, her arms on the deck behind her. "Have you with a boy?"

Harriet nodded. "Yes, and it was nothing like that." She paused. "Have you?"

Sally chewed her lip before shaking her head.

At that, Harriet hastily pulled on her shirt, before taking Sally in her arms and kissing her cheek. "I'm so glad my first time was with you," she whispered in Sally's ear.

A rush flushed through Sally's body at the words, as she leaned back into Harriet, the sun on her face, the lake all around them, her orgasm still pulsing within. If she'd ever had a more perfect moment in her life, she couldn't remember it.

"I am, too," Sally replied, twisting her head to kiss Harriet's flushed cheek. Then she lay down on the deck, her hand in Harriet's — and Harriet did the same. A sensation of falling overtook her body, and she gripped Harriet's hand tighter, smiling at all these new feelings.

Smiling at making love with Harriet.

She understood the term now, completely.

"My heart's still thumping in my chest. Is yours?"

Sally nodded, not opening her eyes. "Yeah."

Harriet brought Sally's hand up to her chest, placing it on top of her heart. "I never want it to stop."

Sally turned her head, gulping up Harriet. "Me either."

"I never want to let you go." Harriet's words were laced with such sincerity, it made Sally's breathing still.

"Then don't," she replied.

Chapter Sixteen

Sally had spent a fantastic morning reacquainting herself with the city, flexing her fresh memory muscles to erase the old, embracing the town like new. So far, it was working. She'd visited a couple of times since she and Casey imploded, but she hadn't stayed long enough for the grit to get under her skin again — even a long weekend here last year had made her twitchy, which had annoyed her mom no end. Her mom was of the opinion that Sally had to reclaim her city, because it wasn't just somewhere she'd lived with Casey — she'd grown up here, it was her home.

Maybe her mom had a point.

This morning, she'd ridden the L, marveling at the architecture as the metal tracks sizzled beneath her, steam rising up from the streets below. In Andersonville she'd browsed in the vintage stores and tried not to think about how close by Casey lived — assuming she still did. She'd also taken in The Bean at Millennium Park, looking at her reflection in its shiny surface, wondering who she was today.

Because today was different.

Today, she wasn't hungover and she was meeting Harriet Locke for dinner. Today, she was ready to deal with her emotions in an adult fashion, not like last night, where sitting in the diner and listening to their old song had caused all sorts of old emotions to slosh around her body. Today was just catching up with an old friend, one who happened to be gorgeous, single, and a whole lot of fun to be with. Their ease together had warmed her: she and Harriet still fit, Harriet the Locke and Sally the Key.

Now she was sitting in Links Taproom in Wicker Park, waiting for Harriet to arrive, jitters in her stomach. Her aunt had told her about this bar and it wasn't what she expected — but then, Sally didn't really know her aunt, did she? She'd anticipated something classy, but this bar showed Paula liked something more rough and ready, too. It was a hipster hangout, all wood, craft beer, and old-school tunes, the front windows wide open to let the summer in. The Ramones blared out of the speakers, and every guy at the bar wore a beard.

Sally ordered a coffee and was just finishing it when Harriet walked in, black sunglasses covering her electric green eyes, the golden streak in her chestnut hair taking center-stage. She was out of breath, her cheeks showing a hint of pink, her yellow shirt popping against her black jeans. She looked like she wasn't even trying to be effortlessly cool, but she pulled it off with aplomb.

"Hi," Harriet said, approaching the stool Sally was sitting on, not sure how to greet her.

Sally understood: they were on odd terrain here, not knowing where they stood emotionally or physically. The last time they'd spent any significant time with each other, when they were teenagers, they'd mostly spent it naked and in bed, the lock on Harriet's bedroom door securely fastened and checked a million times.

So on days like today, it wasn't a surprise that neither knew quite what to do with their hands, their mouths, their everything.

"Hey — sorry I'm a bit later than I said. Work was hectic, and then my mom wanted me to do some grocery shopping for her."

"I didn't think your mom did the grocery shopping?"

Harriet laughed. "She doesn't normally, but Dad's recovering from surgery and she's gone into super-wife mode. Which mainly involves trying to cook him meals and then hiding under the hood of her beloved Mustang. Plus, getting your children to do the shopping. She's acting weird, too — like she wants to interact and she keeps patting my arm." Harriet shook her head, baffled. "It's very strange."

"Things have changed in the intervening years," Sally said. She still remembered the buttoned-up, staffed household she'd visited all those years ago, when the only reason Harriet's mom had to visit the kitchen was to get Robert to whip her up more food. "What's happened with your dad?"

Harriet ordered a beer from the waiter, who arrived with waters for them both.

Sally ordered a Diet Coke. "Starting off easy today."

"Wise woman," Harriet replied. "Dad went into the doctor's with suspected indigestion and came out being told he needed to go to the hospital. He still didn't think much of it, but when they checked him out they found a bunch of blockages that meant he wasn't allowed to go home. That was nearly two weeks ago — he was admitted, had open heart surgery, and now he's recovering while Mom tries to work out what to do now he's at home all day with her. She's still processing."

"She's retired?"

Harriet nodded. "Yep, two years ago. She's taken up golf like a good retired person, along with a whole slew of other activities."

"And your dad's going to be okay?"

"Fingers crossed, but the doctors say he should make a full recovery. He's young and fit otherwise — just a little overweight but I think that's coming down with every day that passes. So long as he takes up a more active and healthy lifestyle, there's no reason he can't live to see his grandchildren, so the doctors told him."

"Is he getting grandchildren any time soon?" Sally said, giving Harriet a quizzical look.

Harriet coughed, then took a sip of her water. "Don't look at me," she said. "Can you imagine me pregnant?"

Sally squinted, cocking her head at the same time. "We did say last night we don't really know each other that well anymore."

"I don't think I've changed that much since I was 18."

Had she? Sally had no idea. "No, maybe not." She paused. "Sorry to hear about your dad, anyway. I remember him as a very active guy."

"He was — he still is. Hopefully he'll make a full recovery. And I have to say, you clearly made a big impression on him."

Sally was flummoxed. "I did? I thought he'd remember me as that woman who drank his wine and corrupted his daughter."

"Maybe that's why he likes you," Harriet said, laughing. "When I told him I was meeting you, he said to say hi."

"Tell him hi right back."

Sally was enjoying how comfortable she was feeling in this conversation, like they had chats every day, like their banter had never stopped. Maybe it hadn't really, it had just been going on in Sally's subconscious, seeping out of the box marked "Harriet."

"So what's in store tonight, wise city woman? I've done the tourist thing, now I'm at your disposal to do with what you will." And then she blushed as she thought about the impact of her words.

If Harriet noticed, she didn't say. "I was thinking a meal at a bar I've heard a lot about, my treat for ditching you today."

"You didn't ditch me."

"No, but I wasn't available and I should have been. It's the weekend, after all. Everyone keeps telling me I should free up my time a little more, but I've always said what for? I'm single, I don't have many weekend plans. But you've made me see I never will unless I free up the time, correct?"

"Parkinson's law," Sally replied.

"Sorry?"

"Parkinson's law. It means, if you allot a certain amount of time for a task, that's the amount of time it will take you. If you give yourself two hours or ten hours, it will take you that long."

Harriet pointed a finger at her. "Story of my life." She paused. "So today, I'm going to make sure you have a great time in Chicago and I give us," she checked her watch, "around 8 hours to make it happen. You think we can do that?"

"What happens at midnight, do you turn into a pumpkin?" Sally cast her mind forward to still being with Harriet at midnight, after dinner, drinks, and more chat. More time spent studying her face that still held the kindness Sally remembered, her hands that still held promise, her skin, which Sally had never wanted to run her fingers over more than right now.

Her eyes caressed the skin Harriet was showing through the opening of her shirt, and when Sally lifted her eyes to Harriet's face, their gaze met and they both stiffened.

It was still there, she knew it.

All of which made today terribly complex.

"I can't believe you're here!" came a booming voice from behind, breaking Sally's thoughts.

She turned to find her Aunt Paula, arms outstretched, larger than life despite being only 5ft 5.

"How's my favorite niece?" Paula asked, pulling Sally off her stool and into her arms. The fans overhead whirred around as Sally was crushed by Paula, then let go, her aunt grinning at her.

"I had so much fun yesterday, I called your dad right after, asking him where he got such a good, funny kid." She paused, looking at Harriet. "Hi, I'm Paula, Sally's aunt — only she's under strict instructions never to say that in public." Paula stuck out her hand and Harriet shook it.

"Harriet," she said. "Nice to meet you, Sally was telling me all about you last night."

Paula raised an eyebrow at that. "Was she now? All good things?"

"Every last one."

"Good," Paula replied, checking her watch. "I'm meeting a friend here for pre-dinner drinks, but you mind if I join you while I wait?" She indicated their drinks. "Join me?"

They both nodded and Paula pulled up a stool, signaling to the waiter to come and take their order. "It's hot today, right? I'm roasting in here, these fans aren't cutting it."

Sally shook her head, her whole body alight with adrenaline.

It was one thing meeting up again with Harriet when it was just the two of them, but adding someone else to the mix was dangerous, because then they'd have to explain who they were and how they came to be.

And she still wasn't sure of how to answer those questions.

"Harriet, nice name," Paula said, still grinning. She was dressed more casually today, but she still had an air of money about her. Navy pants were paired with a mustard-colored shirt and white slip-on shoes, her pale skin matching Sally's. She took a long pull on her beer when it arrived, just like Sally knew she would. "So how do you two know each other?"

And there it was, that fear coursing through Sally's veins. She couldn't tell the truth, because that was too stark: she was my first love and she broke my heart. No, that would never do.

"We're old friends," Sally replied. "We knew each other from school and we're just catching up." Not really a lie, almost true. She glanced up at Harriet, who was nodding her head, but the fact she too looked like a rabbit trapped in the headlights wasn't lost on Sally.

"Old school friends, how gorgeous." Paula leaned in. "In a time of more innocence, before you realized you preferred Martha to Arthur." She grinned at her own joke, as Sally gave her a rigid smile, and Harriet cast her gaze down to the table.

Paula leaned back, her eyes narrowing. "Or not, as the

vibe I'm picking up tells me." Her face fell. "You know she's gay, right?" she asked Harriet.

Harriet spluttered, nodding her head. "I was aware," she said.

Sally, on the other hand, buried her face in her hands wondering what she was going to do with her aunt. When she came up for air, she shook her head. "Paula! If you're going to be back in my life, we need to have words. You're not going to embarrass me every time we meet, are you?"

"Is every other time okay?" Paula grinned a wide smile, nudging Sally with her arm. "Kidding! You and your dad are so easy to rile up." She paused, resting her chin in her right palm, rocking her index finger back and forth. "But I'm picking something up here, something more between you two. Was there something between you at school, something going on even back then?"

Sally shook her head to deny it, but she couldn't get any words out of her mouth.

Meanwhile, Harriet was just blushing a deep shade of purple.

"I'll take that silence and the color of your cheeks to mean yes." She paused. "Is there something going on now?" She put a hand to her mouth. "Am I crashing a date? Oh god, I am, aren't I? Trust Paula, to wade in with size ten boots. You know, you'd think I'd get this, considering I'm gay too, but sometimes, you're still my niece and not a grown woman with a love life, you know?"

She began to laugh. "Well, you'll have to forgive me.

And you're a dark horse," she said, wagging a finger in Sally's direction. "You said nothing yesterday while I sat and regaled you about my sorry love life. Yet here you were all along with this gorgeous woman waiting in the wings." She stopped, assessing Harriet. "You're very cute when you're embarrassed, you know."

Sally shook her head, a wry smile on her face. She looked over at Harriet, catching her eye and wincing.

Harriet gave her a knowing smile, showing they would ride this out together.

"There's nothing going on, Paula, we're just catching up on old times." Sally tried to put as much conviction into her voice as possible, but she wasn't sure she achieved it.

"Sweetheart, life's too short to be flying under the radar. Go after what you want, grab it by the horns, spread your wings, your legs, whatever," Paula told her. "And you two make *such* a cute couple. I take it this is on the down-low, seeing as your dad didn't think you were seeing anyone."

"You're not crashing a date, believe me," Sally said, questioning now whether that was true.

Paula's face was still set to grin. "You know, when people say the words 'believe me,' it normally means they're lying. It's like when people say 'no offense,' just before they're about to offend you." She smiled broadly. "But don't worry, I'll pretend I've never seen you; your secret's safe with me." She gave Sally an exaggerated wink and sat back on her stool, crossing her arms, very pleased with herself.

"I give up with you," Sally said, shaking her head. "So who are you meeting tonight, *Aunty*?" Sally's use of the term was intentional.

Paula narrowed her eyes. "I see what you're doing," she said, smiling. "I'm meeting up with my ex Jolene — she lives around here, she introduced me to this bar, actually. You like it?"

Sally nodded. "It's cool, I love this area, too."

"I'm renting here, looking to buy." Paula glanced at Harriet. "So you live around here, Harriet?"

Harriet nodded, still coughing. "Lincoln Park, just on the lake," she replied.

Paula's face spelt impressed. "Very nice," she said, before tapping Sally's arm. "You've done well, kid."

"There's nothing—"

"—I know, going on. You're just friends. Yadda yadda yadda."

At that moment, a woman walked in with long flowing blonde hair, dressed in jeans, a checkered shirt, and cowboy boots. Paula's face lit up when she saw her, and the hug they exchanged lasted a few seconds longer than necessary.

"Jolene, meet my niece Sally and her *friend*, Harriet," Paula said, punctuating the word "friend" with wide eyes and air quotes.

Sally sighed. She really was the epitome of an embarrassing aunt.

Paula stood up, indicating with her head to Jolene they were on the move.

"I'll leave you kids to it, don't do anything I wouldn't do." She gave Sally a wink. "I'll email you next week about bank details, okay?"

Sally nodded. "Okay."

"Great to meet you, Harriet!" Paula said, before joining Jolene at a table by the far wall, engaging the waiter in more chat.

They both waited a few beats before they dared to look at each other, Sally shaking her head as their eyes met.

"I don't really know what to say about what just happened," she said. "So that's Paula, and she's a bit of a character."

Harriet's body shook as she laughed. "Understatement of the year."

Chapter Seventeen

The evening flew by, with Harriet regaling Sally with stories of her life, her business, and Joanna, leaving out the bits about how she really wanted to find someone to share it all with. She hadn't been thinking that before Sally walked back into her life this week, but now, those thoughts were meandering through her mind like an uninvited guest, waving their arms just to make sure she was sitting up and taking notice.

But for now, Sally only needed to know the ups of Harriet's life, not the downs, because tonight was a performance, wasn't it? If Sally was staying in Harriet's life, if there was any possibility of that, maybe then Harriet might open up a little more. But she lived in New York, so the chances were slim. A Facebook friend, maybe; a new Instagram follower.

Even if tonight had only reinforced the fact that Harriet would like it to be so much more, that the feelings were still there.

They'd skirted around too much emotional stuff, around too many references to their past, because what was the point? They'd both moved on with their lives, they were both in different places now. Their meeting had been a great nostalgia trip, a chance to mend old wounds. But it was coming to a close now, which is why Harriet had suggested another drink after dinner.

Sally had hesitated, her eyes alight with emotion, before finally agreeing.

So now, here they were, ensconced in a cocktail bar just off Michigan Street, Old-Fashioneds in front of them, Harriet not wanting to touch hers. Because every sip meant she was one sip closer to losing Sally again, and that thought sent an avalanche of despair tumbling through her system.

However, she did what she always did, in true Locke-family style: she pushed it away.

Inside, though, she was quietly falling apart.

"Exciting times for you, then?" Harriet said, running her index finger up and down her glass. "Investment in your business and a crazy aunt back in your life. Has Chicago lived up to your expectations?" Harriet was hoping it had exceeded them, hoping *she'd* exceeded them.

Sally held her gaze for a beat longer than necessary, before nodding, her eyes dropping to Harriet's mouth before she looked away. "It's been a whirlwind few days, that's for sure — seeing my dad, my aunt, and my mom tomorrow. I can't even believe I only left New York 48 hours ago. So much has happened since, I barely know what to think. My life's been turned upside down by my aunt, and even though she says she's going to be a silent partner, somehow the words silent and Paula don't really go together, do they?"

Harriet shook her head. "Not really."

Sally tilted hers. "Plus, meeting you again has been an unexpected bonus."

"It has?"

Sally nodded. "I sometimes imagined meeting you again, and what I might say to you, how I might act. In my visions, somehow you'd always become this hotshot attorney, like something from Netflix's latest box office drama."

"Jeez — am I a disappointment?"

"You could never be a disappointment to me," Sally replied.

Harriet's breathing shifted at those words, her tongue snaking along her bottom lip as she processed what Sally had just said. She wasn't sure she agreed, not when it came to Sally.

"I'm glad to hear you say that," she said. "But I'm not sure I deserve it." She paused, her eyes searching Sally's, looking for what she wasn't sure. Permission? Desire? A combination of both?

"You know, we could finish these and go back to my place for a nightcap if you like? I have a great view over the lake, and I'd love to show you it." Did that sound like a line? She'd be the first to admit she'd used it before, but it had never meant so much.

Because this wasn't just anybody.

This was Sally.

Sally's gaze flicked down to her glass, before reaching back up to Harriet. She narrowed her eyes as she gently shook her head. "You know, there was a time when I would have jumped at that opportunity, when I was in mourning for you. But then I chose to go the other way and marry a man."

"Don't do that again," Harriet said, reaching out for Sally's hand across the table. Sally watched intently as Harriet intertwined their fingers. Just the touch of Sally's hand was enough to make Harriet's heart falter, but she tried not to think about it. Tried not to think how this could all be over again before it had even begun.

"I'm not planning to," Sally said, with a smile. "But if we go back to your place, we both know where it's going. And these days, I'm protective of my heart — it's just the way things are."

"What about what your aunt said earlier?"

Harriet's heart was thumping in her chest. She desperately wanted Sally to come back to her apartment — surely she could feel the heat between them, too?

Sally sat up at that, eyeing Harriet like she'd gone mad. "You're really bringing Paula into this conversation?"

"Okay, bad choice," Harriet replied, giving her a wry smile. "But her sentiment was right — the one about taking chances, taking the bull by the horns."

Sally pursed her lips but didn't reply.

"The point is, I think she was right when she said there was something here. There *is* something here." Harriet paused. "If there's not, why are we sitting in a low-lit booth holding hands at 11pm — it's not something I do with most of my friends."

"It's not?" Sally said, her voice innocent. "Me and my friends do this all the time."

They locked eyes again and Harriet gulped. Their eyes were doing the Argentine tango, yet their bodies were still, like the water at the lake house in the dead of night.

"But you get what I'm saying. There's always been more to us, Sally, you know that."

Sally let out a low sigh. "I do, but what's the point? Like I say, I'm protective of my heart. And if we go home tonight and sleep together, it's probably going to be great."

"At least we're agreed on that." Of that, Harriet had no doubt.

"But then what?" Sally pulled her hand away and Harriet looked down, desolate. "Don't give me that look," Sally continued. "We sleep together, I wake up, I go back to New York and I'm fucked up. And then it's you again, floating through my system, but you don't live nearby and I can't do anything about it.

"I can't do that again, I *don't want* to do that again. I want something that's real next time I start with someone, something that can work. And that begins with at least living in the same city."

Harriet sat back, sighing. "Can I rewind to the bit

where you said we could spend the night together and it'd be great?"

"And what happens after?" Sally threw her hands up in the air. "Do you never think one step ahead? I'm sure you have to do it for business."

Harriet looked away, pursing her lips. "This isn't business, though, is it?" she said, sitting up straight.

"No, it's our lives, which is an even bigger deal."

But Harriet couldn't leave it at that. This wasn't rational after all, it wasn't something that could be worked out over a drink. This was something inside, something she was feeling. It was alive, vibrant, real. Harriet didn't want to turn her back on it again.

She'd already made that mistake once before, assuming their lives couldn't ever gel.

And on that point, she'd been so, *so* wrong.

"But what about if we try long distance?" She reached over for Sally's hand again, but this time, there was a slight resistance. Still, Harriet didn't let go. "Plenty of people do it every day, don't they?"

Sally scrunched her eyebrows together, momentarily lost for words. It didn't last long. "Are you seriously suggesting that, after what happened with us before?" she said, her eyes wide.

Harriet winced, dipping her head, feeling like she'd been slapped in the face.

"I can't even believe you'd bring it up. Absence makes the heart break way more than it makes it grow fonder."

Sally paused, shaking her head, her cheeks turning red as she spoke. "You remember what happened when we were kids, or would you like me to remind you? We got together, you went to college, we tried long distance, and then you bailed. Is that the way the story went or did I get it wrong?"

Harriet shook her head as quietly as she could manage. It felt like Sally had been shouting at her, but when she glanced around, nobody was looking their way. Perhaps the volume had just been in her mind.

"No, that's exactly what happened, everything you say is spot-on." Harriet dared to look at Sally again, her deep blue eyes watery, her face older and wiser than before. Harriet knew at that second she'd never stopped loving her, and that she desperately wanted to again.

"I guess not all the slate can ever be wiped clean, can it?"

"I guess not." Sally took a large slug of her cocktail before she continued, wiping her mouth with the back of her hand, before pulling out a tissue to blow her nose. "If you want a relationship to work, you have to be present: *physically present*. And we can't be. Long distance killed my parents' marriage, and it killed us before — and it took me *years* to recover from both. I can't put myself through that again, especially not with you. *Particularly not with you*."

Harriet sat back, taking a pull on her cocktail: if she was honest, she felt like drinking the whole damn thing.

Sally saw no way back for them, and she couldn't say she blamed her. Everything she was saying was true.

But if that was the case, why did Harriet's body still light up every time Sally touched her, or even looked her way? Why had her world gone into the biggest tailspin of her life ever since they'd met again just two days ago?

"I guess we could say our timing's always been off, hasn't it?" Sally added, her face layered with emotion.

Harriet wracked her brain for a solution, but none came. She had to concede, didn't she? "You could definitely say that," she said, her shoulders sagging, her spirit out for the count.

"But we can keep in touch, on social media, email. And I can meet you for dinner when you come to New York next." But Sally's tone held no conviction, her eyes searching Harriet's face, almost like she was begging to be rescued. Was that true? Harriet just didn't know, and that was killing her.

"You're saying all or nothing? We can't even try?" Harriet desperately wanted Sally to see it from her side.

Sally closed her eyes. "I don't see how this can work when we live in different places. So let's just call it a night and keep in touch." She paused, squeezing Harriet's hand. "We were getting on just fine before we met each other again, weren't we? Can't we just be friends?"

As Sally stared into her eyes, Harriet gulped, and she knew the answer.

No, they could never be friends. Not really. They

should only ever be lovers, and she'd give anything to try to be lovers on a level playing field now they were adults. No ifs and buts, no parents in the way, no college on the horizon. But it looked like Sally was shutting down that avenue before they even tried.

"That's just the thing, I'm not sure I was getting on that fine. You've shaken things up this weekend, made me see things differently. What if I want to see where that goes?"

"Don't make this harder than it has to be, H."

"I'm not trying to. I'm just trying to be honest."

Sally gulped, then her eyes dropped to Harriet's mouth, then back up again. "Honesty is way over-rated, you know that?"

Harriet grasped Sally's hand, putting it to her chest. "Just tell me you don't feel it. Tell me you don't feel this, too, and I'll leave it. But don't just walk away because it didn't work for your parents, or because you're afraid. You should only walk away if you feel nothing. And if you do, I'll respect that, of course I will."

She looked down, then brought Sally's hand up to her mouth and gave it the lightest kiss; contact with just this slightest part of Sally's body left her giddy. Harriet's mind swam; her body swooshed one way, then the other, and when she looked up, Sally's eyes were closed.

Had it affected her, too? Harriet hoped so.

"Just tell me that didn't make your heart stutter. Tell me I'm nothing, that this is nothing." Harriet drank in the sight of Sally sitting opposite her, just in case this was one of their very last times together. Her gorgeous russet hair, her pale skin, her face the shape of a heart just before it breaks.

Sally opened her eyes and gulped. Her lips glistened as she opened them to speak, and Harriet recalled all the times she'd kissed them before, how Sally always tasted of hope.

Now, all she could taste was fear.

And then Sally was shaking her head. "I can't do this to myself again, I've spent half a lifetime thinking about you, wondering where you were, how you were. And now you're sitting in front of me asking me to try again, when we live thousands of miles apart? It wouldn't work, you'd soon get bored of the endless emails, phone calls, and travel."

"There's phone sex."

Sally raised an eyebrow at that. "Exactly," she replied.

"And I wouldn't get bored."

"You *would*." Sally's voice was louder now, and the couple at the next table looked over.

Sally bent her head before she continued at a lower volume. "So you want me to say it? I'll say it." She took a deep breath and looked Harriet square in the face. "I don't feel anything for you and I don't think this can work. You might think this is what you want, but it wasn't all those years ago, and it probably isn't now." Her body shook as she spoke. "It's been really good seeing you again —

and I mean that. And yes, my heart skipped a beat, but my heart isn't the most reliable." She paused. "There will always be a part of me that wants this to work, but it can't — and deep down, you know that, too."

With that, she took another slug of her cocktail before reaching over and squeezing Harriet's hand. Then with one last final look at her ex-lover's face, Sally eased herself to her feet and walked unsteadily to the door.

Harriet's stomach lurched as she watched Sally's figure walking through the bar's black door and up the stairs, out into the waiting summer night.

She couldn't leave it like this — she *wouldn't* leave it like this.

Harriet threw $40 on the table to cover their drinks, then sprinted out of the bar and up the stairs, to where Sally was standing on the street corner, the flashing lights, people and traffic noise seeming like an intrusion into such a very personal moment.

"Sally," Harriet gasped, her heart pounding, her stomach churning. She didn't know what to say, so instead she approached Sally and just went with her gut. Went with what felt right. Went with what she'd wanted to do ever since she'd laid eyes on Sally McCall.

What she always wanted to do when it came to Sally McCall.

Harriet took her in her arms, gave her a stare of intent, and then with a car horn blaring beside them and the summer air thick with the smell of possibility, she gently lowered her lips to Sally's and closed the gap between, finally.

The gap that had existed all these years.

The gap she'd longed to close forever.

If Harriet had been hesitant about how Sally might react, she needn't have worried. Because as her lips slipped over Sally's, whispering sweet nothings into her soul, Sally whimpered, and then kissed her right back, lifting Harriet's feet high off the ground, until she was floating away.

All the thoughts she'd had before: would they fit again? Would it be a mistake going back, trying to revitalize something that was so long ago? All those thoughts were wiped away.

As soon as Harriet's lips met Sally's, her heart and soul roared with delight and all that mattered was the two of them, on this street corner, kissing again.

Before this kiss, Harriet had thought that perhaps they were fooling themselves thinking they could go back. Perhaps what she'd been thinking about was plain crazy. But now, as their lips and tongues danced the tango and her heart drummed out their own special beat, doing anything *but this* was the crazy option.

Harriet didn't know much in that moment, other than kissing Sally again made *so much sense.*

They came up for air a few seconds later, dazed, shell-shocked, like they were just coming back from some faraway place and neither of them recognized their surroundings. Then, bit by bit, reality filtered in: cars, people, lights, shops.

A man walked by Harriet and his elbow hit her arm: the jolt was jarring, bringing her back to the present, back from the magical place they'd just been.

And when she looked at Sally, she could see she felt it, too.

That is, until she watched reality dawn.

And that's when Harriet's stomach began to churn with fear, as Sally's face changed from bliss to... What? Harriet wasn't sure.

"You see, this," Sally said, breaking their embrace and taking a step backwards.

Harriet's heart almost stopped beating. Maybe this kiss had been a mistake, because she didn't think she could take what Sally was about to say. "Sorry?"

Then Sally was shaking her head more vehemently, her honeyed hair bouncing around her ears. She'd never looked more adorable.

"This," Sally said, taking a deep breath. "This is what I wanted to avoid, H, do you understand? I don't want a dynamite kiss from you, because what then?" Sally's face crumpled and she covered it with her hands.

"But that kiss was incredible. It was off-the-scale amazing. You have to admit that?" Harriet's tone was pleading, but she didn't care. Surely Sally couldn't ignore what just happened? Surely a kiss like that had to mean something?

More shaking of the head. "It doesn't matter, does it? I don't live here. There's no chance for this." She sighed.

"I've got to go." And then she looked up into Harriet's eyes, her own gaze watery but sparkling. Sparkling with a light that had just been turned on, Harriet was sure of it.

Sally reached out a trembling hand and ran her fingers down Harriet's cheek. "You always did this to me," she said. "Always." And then she turned and walked away, not looking back once.

This time, despite everything, Harriet didn't follow.

She couldn't, she was rooted to the spot, crushing disbelief almost threatening to swallow her whole.

Chapter Eighteen

Sally leaned back in her new black office chair and took a sip of her coffee, just purchased from her building's cafeteria. She glanced at her desk, neatly ordered with her notebooks, sketchpads, and her laptop. Natural light from her sixth-floor window danced around her workspace, and she could still smell the chemicals from where the cleaners had been in. She always liked the mornings: they represented a new dawn, a chance to start over.

Having a fresh start on her workday was easy: it just took a wipe of a duster and she was ready to go. It was the fresh start Harriet was asking her to consider that was causing her sleepless nights and clogging up her waking thoughts — and there was no magic wand that would make her decision any easier.

Sally had lived just fine without Harriet for so many years, but now they'd met again, could she carry on as if nothing had happened? She desperately wanted to think so, but reality was proving otherwise.

It had been three weeks since she'd returned from Chicago, from *that* kiss, and Sally still wasn't back to normal. Seeing Harriet had shaken her up like a snow globe, and the storm was still swirling in her heart.

Harriet had sent her a few texts after that night, but Sally had ignored them, because she hadn't known what to say. After a few days, the texts had stopped, but Sally was still checking her phone hourly, hoping for another.

Because while she'd done the sensible thing — the only thing she could *possibly* do by walking away — the aftershocks of that kiss and what Harriet had said were still rampaging through her, making her question every decision she'd ever made.

Harriet had wanted to try again, believing they'd bumped into each other for a reason.

Harriet was her first, the one who'd introduced her to the rest of her life, even though it had taken her some time to realize it.

And now she was back, asking Sally to put her faith in her. Asking Sally to trust her.

But that was the one thing Sally couldn't do when it came to Harriet.

She could smile at her, she could laugh with her, she could almost forget the hurt she'd caused her.

Almost.

But when Harriet had asked her to give her another chance, telling her she was an adult now and that things had changed, Sally's gut reaction had been protection: to batten down the hatches and not let Harriet in again, because what good could come from it?

There was a huge part of her that wanted to say yes to Harriet, to throw caution to the wind: just being in the same room as her ex-lover made her blood heat up, her pulse sprint.

Harriet had asked her to risk everything, to give her another chance, and Sally had gone with her head.

However, it was her heart that was making all the noise of late, clamoring for a retrial.

Because while her head remembered Harriet's faults, her heart just remembered that kiss.

And oh, what a knee-buckling, soaring kiss it had truly been.

A kiss to stop wars, apart from the one raging in her.

Sally took another sip from her coffee cup, glancing at her friend Taylor.

"So did you see the way she looked at you? She was almost undressing you with her eyes. It was kinda hot."

Taylor was talking about the new barista in their building's cafeteria, who seemed to have taken a shine to Sally. It was cute, but Sally was ignoring it.

There was enough pressure on her heart, without strangers wading into the mix, too.

Taylor smiled at her, her olive skin curling around her lips as she grinned up at her friend from the lower vantage point of Sally's yellow sofa. Sally had bought it to give her somewhere to sit and think when she was dreaming up her designs.

However, it had also turned into somewhere Taylor

sat when she was providing commentary on Sally's life, which was fairly often.

"I did see it, but I'm a bit preoccupied with other matters of the heart."

Taylor raised a single eyebrow at her through jet-black hair that hung down in front of her eyes, a tribute to her former Goth days. Taylor was over 40 now, but she still favored a mainly black wardrobe in homage.

"No, really?" she replied, her tone thick with sarcasm. "You've kept it so quiet."

Sally gave her a look.

"The point is, you haven't smiled much since you came back from Chicago — so maybe this barista could be your light relief? You didn't sleep with your ex, so no big deal, right? When I said you needed some action, I meant some full-on, hot orgasmic action. Not that you should kiss a woman from your past, run away, and then spend the next few weeks spinning out about it."

"Oh, I must have gotten the wrong end of the stick, I thought that's exactly what you told me to do," Sally replied.

Taylor rolled her eyes. "What's her name, anyway?"

"Who?"

"The barista."

"Oh. I think her name is Kristy."

"Kristy and Sally — I like it, it's got a nice ring to it."

"Oh, please," Sally said, sighing. "She's about ten years younger than me for a start. Plus, I'm in no state to be thinking about anyone else, am I?"

Sally pictured Kristy, but then she was quickly shoved out of the way by Harriet, strolling into her mind like she did with alarming frequency these days, giving her a confident wink, then standing, staring, arms crossed, expectations high.

"Fine," Taylor replied, sighing. "But if you're not going to jump on this — metaphorically speaking, of course — then could you please get in touch with the woman who appears to have run off with your heart and tell her to come and fuck you? You need to get this out of your system, pronto. And then at least you'll know, one way or the other, won't you?"

"You're such a romantic, did anyone ever tell you that?" Sally replied. "You should put that on your dating profile, sure to be a hit with the ladies."

"I've thought about it. I think the dating world would appreciate it."

"Fine, you win. I'll message her and tell her to come and fuck my brains out, shall I? Because that really matches up with how I left it. You know, the whole 'she kissed me and I ran away' scenario."

"Yes, but you've started to rethink it now, right?"

Sally shrugged, chewing on the inside of her cheek. "I don't know, I'm just so confused by the whole thing. I thought putting some distance between us would make it easier, bring me clarity. But if anything, every day things seem to get a little more muddy, a bit more blurred."

Sally wasn't going to admit the truth to Taylor,

because she'd barely admitted it to herself: that Harriet had consumed most of her waking hours since she'd got back, and had impacted her work productivity, too. When she was supposed to be coming up with new designs, she kept finding herself daydreaming, thinking about Harriet's smile, her hand on Sally's thigh, the way she'd looked at her with such searing intensity just before Sally had walked away.

That look had haunted her ever since.

If she was going to do that, maybe Sally should just meet up with her again and allow her to consume her in the flesh. It had seemed impossible three weeks ago, but perhaps it wasn't so impossible anymore.

"If I have to message Harriet, maybe it would be easier to sleep with Kristy."

Taylor held up a palm. "Oh no, you're not doing that. You'd be fucking Kristy and thinking of Harriet. Classic lesbian error." She paused, cocking her head. "You do know you're too old for that, don't you?"

"Too old to fuck up in love. Is that a thing?"

"If it's not, it should be," Taylor said, taking a sip of her coffee.

"Yeah well, if fucking up in love is a category, I win it hands-down right now."

"You and half of Queens, honey."

Sally grinned. "I'm not a special snowflake, I get it. But I need some time to think about Harriet, about what I should do. And in the meantime, I want no hassle from you.

"Plus, you and Ben have to fetch my coffee from now on. I can't face Kristy's big puppy-dog eyes every time I go to the cafeteria. Imagine if she asks me out — you know what these Millennials are like, they're far more forward than we ever were. I've got enough stress right now with Harriet and getting these card designs finished."

Ben was the other member of their design trio who also worked at the collective space. Together, they supported each other's dreams, and had spent many evenings at the local bars brainstorming ideas and discussing their futures, all of which were falling into place now — the business parts at least.

Taylor clapped her hands together. "But the work stress is exciting, right? Was it a big order?"

"Not initially," Sally said, leaning back in her chair. "But if the cards sell, they've got ten stores around New York, so who knows?" She twirled a black pen in her hand. "They might want stationery and bags too if the cards take off, so it could be big. And did I tell you my aunt's flying in this weekend to see where she's putting her money?"

"The crazy drunk?" Taylor said, rubbing her hands together.

"I'm not sure she'd be thrilled with that description. Let's go with my maverick aunt, shall we? Although I can't call her aunt, she hates it."

"My aunt is named Susan and she favors knitwear, even in the summer. Trust me, there are worse things to be than the crazy drunk."

"Paula is one of a kind," Sally said. "She's only 15 years older than me for a start, and she's a lesbian. I mean, a cool lesbian at that." She paused, sweeping her hand around the room. "What's she going to think of this set-up? It's hardly grand."

"She's going to love it! And with this new avenue opening up, this time next year, you might be the owner of an empire, and I can say I knew you once," Taylor replied. "You will remember to buy all your wallpaper from me when that happens, right? Because I assume when it does, you're going to have a massive house with many walls to cover."

Taylor's designs were the toast of Manhattan, being featured in *Elle Decor* at the turn of the year. Since that article, orders had been flooding in and Taylor had just completed a major one for a large hotel chain.

"Every wall in my future castle will be draped with your coverings, okay?" Sally said, moving over to her design desk, cluttered with bits of gold and silver wire, along with some popular stamps she'd just received yesterday. "And now I have to kick you out so I can drink my coffee and come up with my next best-seller."

"You should design a card to send to Harriet, you know," Taylor told her, getting up. "Something to work it out of your system. Something like 'Thanks for kissing my face off, can you come back and fuck me now please'." She grinned again, waiting for Sally's comeback.

She didn't have to wait long. "Taylor?" Sally said, ushering her out the door.

"Yes?"

"Fuck off."

Taylor held up both palms, backing out of Sally's studio. "You love me, really." Then she paused. "And this aunt, is she single?"

Sally raised an eyebrow. "She is. Why?"

Taylor shrugged, looking bashful. "Well if she's only 15 years older than you, that makes her only six years older than me."

"Oh no," Sally said, folding her arms across her chest. "You're not hitting on Paula."

"Why not? You said yourself she's single and cool." Taylor put a finger to her chest. "I'm single and cool, we could be a match made in heaven."

"Bye, Taylor," Sally said, closing the door on her. "I don't want to think about this right now."

Taylor raised a single eyebrow. "Just because you're hell-bent on not getting laid, doesn't mean the rest of us have to abide by your rules." She laughed as Sally gave her a look. "Okay, I'm going," she said, giving her a wink before walking down the corridor to her studio. "Text me or Ben if you need a coffee," she shouted.

Sally shook her head as her friend walked down the hallway, before disappearing through the double doors at the end. Sally walked back inside, shutting her studio door.

Harriet. That was the first thought that popped into her brain, as it had been for the past three weeks. Harriet was weighing on her mind. But she needed to focus on getting these cards out pronto — she just hoped she could do that today, and not be plagued by visions of Harriet's gorgeous smile, her pleading eyes.

Eyes that Sally had so wanted to give in to, but every time she focused on it, she thought her head might explode.

Was everyone else's life so complex when it came to matters of the heart?

Chapter Nineteen

Harriet stared out of her office window, her district's rooftops and balconies stretching out in front of her in the midday sun, along with the lunchtime traffic on the 606.

Joanna walked in, rubbing her hands together, giving Harriet a look.

"Who pissed in your coffee?" Joanna asked, sitting down and tapping her laptop keyboard. When Harriet didn't respond, Joanna looked up, rolling her eyes. "You know, you've had a face like that ever since that woman left town." She paused. "What was her name again?"

"Sally," Harriet replied, her body coming alive even uttering her name.

She knew it sounded ridiculous, seeing as they'd only spent two days together — but those two days were enough to convince Harriet there *was* still something there, something they should explore. Because how often did she meet women she just clicked with? Hardly ever. She and Sally might not have seen each other for a long time, but their connection was still beating bright. Plus, they were both single and attracted to each other — that much she was sure of.

If Sally were to consider them a prospect now, Harriet needed to convince her she was legit and not about to run off again. She was fast losing hope, though: it'd been four weeks with not even a text.

"Sally," Joanna repeated. "But you need to snap out of it. She's from your past, and it didn't work out back then for a reason," she said, yawning. "You only saw her a couple of times the other week, and you've been miserable ever since." Joanna stared at her. "I don't get it — you were happy before, so what's changed?"

Harriet stayed silent for a few seconds before replying, her heart slumped in her chest. "I'm not sure I am happy now I've seen her again. She's stirred me up, you know? So you telling me to get over it — it doesn't really help, Jo."

Joanna stared at her friend, moving her mouth one way, then the other. "What would you prefer I say? Fly out to New York, sweep her off her feet, move there and live happily ever after? You don't want to do that, this is your home. Plus, you like being single: being tied down isn't you, is it?"

Harriet gulped and stared at the floor. She used to think so, but lately, she wasn't so sure.

Maybe she liked being single because she hadn't found the woman she wanted to settle down with yet.

And maybe that woman might just be Sally.

"It wasn't, but who knows now? Do I really know? Look at me, Joanna. I'm 35 and what have I got to show for my life?"

Joanna gave her a disbelieving look, sweeping her arm across the office. "A thriving business, a gorgeous apartment, friends, family." She paused. "It's really not so bad, is it?"

"But I've got nobody to share them with. When Sally was here, I was due to work that weekend. What kind of life is that?"

"One that you like, one you've worked hard for."

"Easy for you to say — you've got Viv."

Joanna blew out a long breath. "I do, but if you're looking for relationship happy talk, you've come to the wrong place."

Harriet winced: she knew this wasn't a brilliant time to be having this chat with Joanna, but she couldn't help how she was feeling. "But you fall asleep next to someone every night and you wake up with them the following morning. You've got someone to share your hopes and dreams with. I don't."

Harriet knitted her fingers together, picturing her waking up next to Sally all those years ago. It had been incredible while it lasted.

"I do when she bothers to come home."

Harriet raised an eyebrow at that. "She's not coming home?"

Joanna shrugged. "She is, most of the time."

Harriet waited a beat. "We'll come back to that," she replied. "But meeting Sally again has got me thinking, maybe that's what's missing in my life. Someone to share it with."

Joanna got up and walked to their office window, looking out at the lunchtime throng, her back to Harriet. "If you're thinking of running off to New York, I have two words for you: beach house. This is a business we're building for a reason, remember? Me, you, our clients: we've got a five-year plan, H, don't forget that. You don't know this woman, not really. You know who she *was*, not who she *is*."

Harriet sat up, shaking her head. "I'm not sure you're right — this is my first love we're talking about. We kissed, we spent time together, and I *know* there's something still there. Something I'd like to explore. But I'm not thinking of moving out there — so don't worry, your retirement plan is safe. I was just hoping for a little sympathy, is all — my heart's breaking here, and you're worried about your beach house."

Joanna shook her head, turning to face her friend. "I'm also worried about your heart and I think you pursuing this will break it for sure. She's already said she's not moving, so how can it work? Long distance only works if it's for a short time, you know that. You're destined to be star-crossed lovers, and hard as that is, you just have to accept it."

Harriet felt like the rug had been pulled from under

her feet, and she was spinning round like a crazy top, out of control. "You really believe that?" Her voice came out at a whisper.

Was Joanna right? Were they destined never to be?

Joanna shrugged. "Only you know for sure. But look at the facts, they don't make for pretty reading. You were together once, you walked away, and now this time, she's walked away. You're even now, and maybe that's good. Your life's here, H, it's not in New York, it never has been. You're a Chicago girl."

"But what if my heart's in New York?"

Joanna shook her head. "Love isn't all it's cracked up to be," she said. "But if you really think your heart's in New York, then you have to find a way of bringing it back in one piece. Only you know how to do that."

Chapter Twenty

"How's the patient?" Harriet said, popping a box of Frango Mint Chocolates on the sofa beside her dad before giving him an awkward hug. However, that wasn't what her dad accepted these days, instead pulling her in for a proper hug.

Daniel had warned her, but it was still odd.

"The patient is good," he said, giving her a cheeky grin. "And even better now you've brought me some of my favorite chocolates. Have I ever told you how we only used to have these on special occasions as a kid?"

"You might have," Harriet said, sitting down on the sand-colored sofa opposite, having heard that story *every* time she brought her dad Frango chocolates.

The living room had a polished wooden floor with thick patterned rugs under the two sofas that faced each other in its center, a fireplace the same height as Harriet to her right, a log burner installed for the city's notoriously bad winters. That fireplace had always seemed huge when she was a kid. Behind the sofa her dad was sitting on there was a grand piano that nobody played, and a drinks cart that was used much less since her dad's troubles. He was now a monument to healthy living: her mom and their chef Robert had made sure of that.

"Now I can have Frangos anytime I want. That's progress." Her dad paused, unwrapping the box and taking one of the cubic chocolates for himself before passing the box to his daughter. "You know what else has progressed since I nearly died?"

Harriet shook her head, taking a chocolate and popping it into her mouth, loving the soothing taste of her childhood, one that always reminded her of her dad. Her mom hated mint chocolate, but when it came to Frangos, she and her dad were on the same page.

"My priorities. I've had an epiphany." He sat up straighter on the sofa, his chest cushion now at his side. Harriet assumed this meant, two months on, his pain wasn't quite so chronic, a good sign. "All those years I worked for the firm, all those clients I took out for dinner? It didn't matter."

Harriet frowned at him, standing up and grabbing another chocolate for herself. One Frango was never enough. "It didn't?" she asked through the sweetness.

"Not a bit. When I first got sick, I was worried about my clients, the cases I had, how everything would work out. And you know what? It turns out, I'm not irreplaceable. Which is a hard pill to swallow after building it up for the past 20 years."

"Or it means you're a good mentor who's taught people well."

He smiled at her. "That's what your mom said. And after taking a few days to think about it, I've decided she's right. And that really, me almost dying is clearly a sign. I should enjoy life while I can, throw myself into retirement, take your mom away, spend some time with her."

Harriet sat up, nodding. "You should," she said. "But wow, this is some turnaround. You live for that firm, for the law. Won't it be hard?"

"I thought so, but after a month and daily phone calls this week, I've had enough. I don't want to die on the job — I want to see Italy, I want to lie on a Greek island with a cigar, I want to go to Vegas and gamble on a big poker table."

Harriet couldn't quite believe what she was hearing. Her father, the king of hard work, wanted to go traveling? But even she knew it was a good thing. This blockage had been caught early, but it was a warning: he should slow down. But she never expected him to change the habit of a lifetime, take his wife away and put his well-being first.

Her dad's heart issues were going to prove life-changing not just for him, but for her mom, too. Their enduring love and support for each other was touching.

As for her, she'd still heard nothing from Sally, and she'd just about given up hope that anything would happen. She guessed Sally had been right: if they had slept together, this would have been ten times worse.

And yet, Harriet couldn't help but feel if they had

taken that next step, they'd have been forced to confront what was between them. Her heart ached as it always did when she thought about it, but at least it was a familiar ache now. It was almost a part of her.

"I think that's great, Dad, and exactly what you should be doing now. You're 60, you're fit, you're still young enough to see the world. It's time for you to do just that." She stood up and grabbed another chocolate. "But not too many of these, though. I don't want to be responsible for any more heart issues. Two a day, max, and I'll eat some just so you don't have to."

Her dad laughed at that. "You always were selfless." And then he pointed toward the sideboard where all his get-well cards had been moved to. Harriet knew her mom had tried to take them down, but Dad had insisted on keeping the newer ones. "Do you see the card on the right? You know who it's from?"

Harriet turned and squinted, not really sure where she should be looking. "Which one?"

"The hand-made card — the one on the end with the bunch of flowers made from tiny petals and a gold wire vase — very intricate."

Harriet got up and picked up the card. It was indeed intricate and beautiful. "Somebody spent a lot of money on this," she said, turning it over in her hands.

But then she saw the back: Sally McCall Designs.

Her hand shook as she held it, blood rushing to her cheeks. Sally had held this card in her hand, crafted the petals on the front — this card was a connection to her. Harriet flipped it open to read the greeting inside.

"Harriet told me you were recovering from major surgery — I hope you're feeling better. Much love, Sally McCall."

What the fuck? Sally had sent a get-well card to her dad and she hadn't even been in contact with her once since that night? What did that mean? Harriet's whole body shook at the impact, her mind reeling.

Why would Sally send her dad a get-well card?

"It's from Sally McCall, your friend from school. Isn't that lovely of her?" her dad said, as Harriet stared at the signature, which hadn't changed much since they were teenagers.

Harriet nodded. "It is." The chocolate was still coating her teeth, but Sally was even sweeter than that.

"I know you said you were back in contact — I always liked her."

Harriet replaced the card, pulling her eyes away from it and sitting back opposite her dad. She cleared her throat before she spoke, her heart still hammering in her chest, keeping her hands on her knees so they wouldn't visibly shake. "I told her you were sick, and she designs cards now."

Her dad nodded. "Well, send her my thanks, it was a lovely gesture." He paused, fixing Harriet with his emerald-green eyes, so reminiscent of her own. "She obviously thinks the world of you."

For once in her life, Harriet was lost for words. "She sent you the card," she croaked, feeling herself blush again.

Did Sally think the world of her? Was this her way of telling her? And if it was, a text message would have been far better.

Her dad smiled. "She did. But make no mistake — she sent it because of you."

Harriet smiled, knowing her dad was right.

This was the sign she'd been patiently waiting for.

Now all she had to do was act on it, and make sure she followed RuPaul's sage advice: good luck, and don't fuck it up.

Chapter Twenty-One

"I cannot believe I'm here." Sally covered her face with her hands, but when she peeked through her fingers, the semi-naked women were still there, dancing in cages all around the room. She was caught somewhere between titillation and wanting to wrap these women up in robes and send them home with a week's wages, telling them to choose a different career path. Her feminist principles were being tested, and of course, Paula was the one responsible.

Still, the place wasn't as bad as Sally had first feared. First, this strip club was women-only, run by women for women. Second, Paula knew the owner (of course she did), and had assured Sally the dancers were paid a good wage. After that, it had just been a case of plying Sally with enough alcohol to get her through the doors, and that mission had been successfully completed. Sally never even knew such a club existed in New York, but her aunt had her finger on the pulse.

Right at this moment, though, Paula had her finger tangled in a dancer's G-string, as she stuffed ten-dollar bills into the skimpy waistband, ably aided by Taylor.

Sally had asked her friend to come along for moral support, but now Sally had been abandoned for the lure of naked women. They'd been out for dinner in the East Village, and Taylor and Paula had already hit if off, turning out to be a match made in heaven. Sally was pleased, but their obvious attraction was only serving to highlight the fact she was still single.

Paula and Taylor hadn't slept together yet, but if that didn't follow tonight, she'd eat her hat.

She shook her head as the loud chart beats filled the air in the low-lit, velvet-cushioned room. Paula and Taylor were walking back to their table, high-fiving as they did, before ordering another round of drinks from their waitress. Sally raised an eyebrow at them both, but Paula was having none of it.

"Get off your high horse, Ms Prude," her aunt said, sitting down and slapping Sally's thigh. "We were just chatting to one of the dancers — her name's Orla — and we just gave her 30 bucks in tips. If that's not a feminist act, I don't know what is."

"Paula's got a point," Taylor said, leaning over and popping some salted peanuts into her mouth. "We're just doing our part for the cause, making sure these women get paid fairly."

"You're altruistic, I've always said that about you," Sally replied, rolling her eyes.

"And we're here for you, don't forget," Paula said, crossing her right leg over her left, her black patent pumps shiny under the red lights of the club. Paula was dressed for business in a suit and heels, having come straight from a meeting in Manhattan, whereas Sally and Taylor were both in jeans and shirts.

When Paula had gone to the bathroom in the restaurant earlier, Taylor had confided that her power-suit-and-heels combo made her weak. Meanwhile, Taylor's dark goth charm seemed to be working its magic on Paula, too, who was working her repertoire of flicks and stares to the max.

Sally held up her hands as the waitress deposited more Manhattans for the table, which Taylor insisting on paying for.

"I know, you're here for me. Although you're doing a very good impression of being here for you."

"Tonight was all about popping your strip-club cherry, so here's to that!" Paula held up her drink, and Sally and Taylor both clinked their glasses.

"But it was also to get you out and about again, stop you being so down in the dumps." Paula paused, giving Taylor a long stare before continuing. "Taylor was telling me you're still hung up on that woman I met in Chicago."

Sally shot Taylor the look that deserved, and Taylor cast her eyes to the floor, suitably embarrassed. She was clearly sharing some of Sally's secrets to get into Paula's good books, and Sally guessed that was something she was just going to have to get used to if this went anywhere.

It'd been seven weeks since their kiss, and Sally had gone to contact Harriet so many times, but had never known how to start her message. Instead, she'd sent a get-well card to Harriet's dad, hoping that would spur Harriet into action, because Harriet always was better at taking charge. However, Sally's effect must have worn off, because nearly a month later, she'd heard nothing.

Sally shrugged at Paula, resigned. "She sent me a load of texts after we met, but I wasn't prepared to listen then. She already broke my heart when we were young, I didn't want to give her the opportunity to do it again."

"But things have changed now?" Paula asked.

Sally shrugged again, but her heart was doing anything but. "I'd like to see her again, at least, because I can't get her out of my head. But I feel like I've left it too long now."

"You haven't, I keep telling you that — just email her, or text her," Taylor said, glancing over as the dancers were changing shift: the new dancer in the cage nearest them was a tall brunette with thighs of steel. All three of them were mesmerized for a moment, before their attention was shifted back to their conversation.

"Here's the plan," Paula said, putting her glass down on the low wooden table with a thump. "Tomorrow, just send her a text and let her know that if she comes to New York again, you'd be interested to see her. Simple as that." She gave Sally a wink. "It's a good thing I'm here to assist with your love life, isn't it?"

"I could say the same to you," Sally replied, shifting her gaze from Paula, to Taylor, and then back.

She was pleased to see they both looked away, blushing.

Chapter Twenty-Two

"What's up, sis?" Daniel gave her a kiss as he hopped up on his wooden chair, and ordered a Coke, a coffee, and a beer from the server.

Harriet gave him the look that deserved. "Thirsty?"

He nodded. "I've been gardening since five and it's now…" he checked his phone. "3pm. I'm done, and I need waking up and rehydrating. You haven't seen what I'm going to order for lunch yet."

"I dread to think."

Harriet leaned back when their drinks arrived, just a sparkling water for her. They were in Toby O'Reilly's, one of the city's many Irish bars. It was a favorite of Harriet's, being just around the corner from her work and enormous enough to get lost in. The bar was a huge square in the middle of the room, the service was slick and there were TVs showing sports as far as the eye could see. Today, the air was thick with the smell of toasted bread and beer, just like always.

It was making Harriet salivate. "So, I have a question for you."

"I assumed you would, seeing as you summoned me here."

"It's about Ava."

Daniel grinned. "One of my current favorite subjects. What about her?"

"You're still seeing her? You haven't frightened her off?"

He rolled his eyes. "Contrary to what you think of me, I do know how to keep a woman."

"Your track record would say otherwise."

"You're one to talk," Daniel replied, slurping almost half his Coke in one.

Harriet didn't respond. He had a point. She ran a finger up and down her ice-cold glass before responding.

"Anyway, I want to set up a meeting with her. I've been trying to do it for months, but her secretary keeps giving me the runaround. But now I have an in — that's you, by the way — so you think you can do it?"

Daniel pursed his lips, before nodding. "I don't see why not. She can't resist my boyish charms. Just promise me you won't sleep with her and I'll set up a meeting."

On the TVs, the Cubs hit a home run in a replay of last night's game and a group of young men in the corner cheered.

"I'll try not to, but I might slip up and fall into her pussy," Harriet replied, rolling her eyes.

Daniel gave her a look. "It's happened before."

"It's happened *once*."

"You're just lucky I'm the kind of brother who's very forgiving about these sorts of things. Plus, I can't see Ava falling for you — she's not on the sexuality spectrum, she just likes guys."

"How quaint."

"Isn't it? Whereas Sally — I wasn't in the least bit surprised." He gave her a grin. "Talking of which — how's that going?"

"Sally?"

"Uh-huh."

"It's not at the moment, but I'm in New York this week and I'm hoping to see her."

"Did you see the card she sent Dad?"

"I did."

"That card said, 'come get me'!"

"You think?" Harriet gave him an unsure smile.

"You don't send a card to somebody's parents out of the goodness of your heart."

"I hope you're right."

"I'm sure you'll be persuasive."

"I'm going to need to be, she's a tough nut to crack."

"Perhaps because you already broke her heart?"

"Thanks for reminding me," Harriet said, giving him a death stare. "So you'll talk to Ava? I think we could work well together."

"I'll talk to her," Daniel replied. "You think Sally is worth the pursuit, given she lives in New York?"

Harriet shrugged as she eyed her brother. "All I know

is I've never felt like I did when I was with her the first time, and that feeling came back all over again when I met her. I have to know if there's anything there, if she feels the same, if this could be a thing. Because if it could, it might be a game-changer."

Daniel let out a low whistle as their server arrived with their sandwiches: turkey club for Harriet, pastrami for Daniel. Daniel took a bite and chewed it before he replied.

"A game-changer?" He paused. "But it's Sally, so it's not a shock."

"It's not?"

"No. I remember you the Christmas you came home after that summer. Do you remember?"

"I've tried to block it out."

"You were miserable. You hated Harvard, you hated law, but most of all, you hated that you'd burned your bridges with Sally. She was still in your heart then."

"I don't think she ever left."

"No, I don't either," Daniel replied, raising one eyebrow. "I've seen you with plenty of women since then, and you've never looked like this or spoken like this. Would you like some brotherly advice?"

"If I say no, will you still give it to me?" Harriet asked, pushing her sandwich around the plate. She'd suddenly lost her appetite.

"Go into this honestly and with an open heart — neither of which are Locke specialities. We don't do emotion well."

He cocked his head. "Although, Mom and Dad are giving it a go lately, which is still weird."

"I know," Harriet said. "I was round there yesterday and Dad was joking, asking me stuff about my business, getting all touchy-feely about Mom."

"It's odd, but I like it," Daniel said. "But it still means we have to unlearn a lifetime of buttoned-up emotions. Just be brave and tell her what you're feeling."

"You make it sound so easy."

"It's a piece of cake."

Chapter Twenty-Three

Later that day, Sally was working on a new range of greetings cards that featured twisted wire on the front. She'd gone out at lunchtime and bought a selection of multi-colored wire from a hardware store. Now she was at her design desk, brow furrowed, teasing out the shape of sunshine with her wire cutters.

Only, she knew she wasn't getting it right, because Harriet was on her mind. More specifically, what Paula and Taylor had told her to do. Text her and ask to see her. How was something so simple so very difficult to do? She'd broken from her creative work to try to do it mid-morning, but she'd soon abandoned her task, after staring at her phone for a full 20 minutes. But she knew until she'd done it, she wasn't going to settle today. She had to get over her mental block and just send the text. It was that easy.

The beep of her phone broke her thoughts and she looked up. On her desk in front of her was a full cup of coffee she'd forgotten to drink — not for the first time, she pondered buying a microwave to heat up her forgotten drinks. She could afford one now, after all.

She got up and stretched her arms above her head, picking up her phone with her right hand. She opened her eyes wide and clicked to her messages.

It was from her mom, asking how her work was coming on now she had Paula's money. Her mom was still uncomfortable about this. She put her phone down and it beeped again. Only this time when she picked it up again, her heartbeat slowed to a crawl as she saw who the text was from.

Harriet. Was she psychic? Was she texting to ask Sally where her text was?

Adrenaline raced through Sally's body as she yelped as if she'd just been shocked with an electric prod, throwing her phone on her desk and hopping around her studio. She was glad she didn't share a workspace so nobody could see her.

When she'd calmed down a little, taking deep breaths to ground herself and get back in the moment, she picked up her phone again, holding it at arm's length.

Her finger was hovering over the message and she was almost too afraid to read it. *Almost.*

But she knew her curiosity would get the better of her, so she tapped it and held her breath.

"Hi Sally, it's me. I'm coming to New York tomorrow and I'd love to have dinner with you. I have a business proposition for you. 7pm? Let me know. x"

Sally stared at the message, trying to draw out any hidden meaning.

Harriet wanted to have dinner with her. Was it just possible she'd also been on Harriet's mind, too?

A shiver ran through the whole of Sally's body as she conjured up images of their kiss all those weeks ago on that sidewalk in Chicago.

She took a deep breath. It was just dinner, nothing more. No pressure, no expectations.

Harriet had a business proposition.

Whatever else, she could do dinner, right?

No, she couldn't — her aunt was flying in tomorrow and she was having dinner with her.

Damn it.

Could she move Paula to Saturday?

Maybe.

Sally quickly messaged Paula and asked if that was possible.

Five minutes later, Paula messaged back saying it was no problem.

Relief washed through Sally: if she hadn't been able to see Harriet tomorrow, it would have felt like the end of the world. Which was ridiculous, because the facts hadn't changed: she still lived here, and Harriet still lived in Chicago.

And yet, somehow, it felt like something had changed, like something had shifted.

What should she tell Harriet? Sally put her phone on the desk, pacing her workspace, ruffling her hair. Then she picked up her wire cutters and tried to get back to work, but when she looked down at the wire, all she saw was Harriet's face smiling back at her. She dropped her cutters and picked up her phone. She should just text and get this over with.

"Friday's fine. Shall I book somewhere nearby? Where are you staying? x"

She dropped her phone and stared at it. Where was Harriet staying? Did she expect to stay with her? Should she invite her? Was that too forward?

OH MY GOD.

She was spiraling back into her teenage self, her thoughts and emotions out of control. Endorphins were rushing about her body and she felt more alive than she had for a very long time.

Three minutes later, her phone beeped again.

"Great. I'll book a hotel, you book the restaurant. Can't wait. x"

A flood of excitement rushed through Sally as she skipped about her office, unable to quell the butterflies inside her.

She was meeting Harriet tomorrow night. Harriet who still lived in another city altogether, who she knew nothing could happen with.

If that was the case, why was her heart so light, it was almost leaping out of her body?

Chapter Twenty-Four

Sally was sitting in her favorite restaurant in Queens, A Taste Of Thailand. With around ten tables all crammed tight together, it was only a small space, but the food made it worthwhile. Run by a husband and wife team from Bangkok, it was always packed, with locals flocking through its doors for its special curries, stir-fry dishes and deliciously fragrant dumplings and soups. Sally had never been to Thailand, but coming here, she felt like she'd tasted it.

But had she done the right thing bringing Harriet here? The two of them came from very different worlds, after all. Harriet's family had a chef, and she was used to fine-dining. Sally was definitely not. This restaurant was where she felt most at home: authentic food for reasonable prices. But would Harriet feel the same?

She took a deep breath. If she didn't, then this was never going to work, was it? Sally wasn't about to start being something she wasn't, pretending for Harriet Locke.

She'd pretended for far too long that she *didn't* care. That she *could* survive without her. And she had, just about.

But that was before she'd seen her again, felt her heart beat for her again. Felt her heart beat in a way it hadn't for quite some time. She'd been arguing with her heart for so many years when it came to Harriet, tonight was its chance to break free and have its say, one way or the other.

Her phone beeped: it was a text from Paula.

'Just to let you know I've arrived. I'm staying at a hotel in Manhattan, meeting up with a friend tonight, and I'll head over to you tomorrow. Does midday work? I've asked Taylor to join us later.'

Sally smiled: Paula and Taylor had indeed slept together after the strip club, and were now tentatively seeing each other, long distance — an irony that wasn't lost on her. Taylor had plans tonight, but she knew Paula was staying with her from tomorrow till Tuesday.

'Sure, look forward to it. You've got my address?'

'I do — see you tomorrow. I'm off to terrorize Manhattan!'

Sally laughed at that. Was Manhattan ready, that was the question?

"Glad to see you're smiling." Sally's heart swelled as the familiar voice wrapped itself around her in a warm embrace. She glanced up, then stood, giving Harriet her full attention, laying on her best smile. The way Harriet looked tonight, with her almond hair and her Hollywood dimple, she deserved it.

Blood rushed to Sally's cheeks as her mind threw up

familiar scenarios to contemplate, most of them involving Harriet naked. She shook her head and widened her smile that little bit more.

"Just a text from Paula."

"Aunt Paula?"

Sally nodded. "That's the one. She's in town this weekend and we're meeting tomorrow."

"Coming to check up on her investment."

"Or just to be nosey, I haven't quite decided." Sally steadied her breathing. "The good thing is, she's seeing one of my best friends now, so she won't be so up in my grill when she's here." Sally paused. "You found it okay?"

She wasn't sure whether to pull Harriet into a hug or give her a kiss. When their last contact had been such a scorching kiss, anything else seemed like a cop-out.

"I did," Harriet said. "Your directions were perfect."

She could see Harriet was unsure of her actions, too, so Sally took the lead, leaning over and giving her a chaste peck on the cheek. Then they stared at each other for a moment too long, and Sally's body shook. If she'd had any doubt in her mind about how this evening would go, they were all banished now.

Her wavering stance and her thudding heartbeat were telling her she wanted Harriet Locke, and it was all she could do not to blurt it out there and then.

Harriet's cheeks flushed red as she sat down in the chair opposite — was she flummoxed, too? Sally would love to know. Harriet was dressed in black jeans and a light blue chambray shirt that was clearly new, judging by the fold marks still showing across her chest. Somehow, the thought of Harriet buying a new shirt for tonight made Sally smile.

Sally glanced around the restaurant, now filling up as people finished work. On the table beside them, a young woman was explaining to an older man opposite about her college course and he was nodding as he ate what looked like a pad thai. Next to them, two older Asian women were sharing a pot of Jasmine tea and eating Thai dumplings with soy sauce. The air was coated with the aromas of lemongrass, chili, garlic, and coconut, all included in Sally's recipe for a perfect meal.

"This place is cute," Harriet said. "And Thai — my favorite."

"It's one of my favorite restaurants."

"It's one of mine, too."

"You've been here before?"

Harriet shook her head. "No, but you're here, so that makes it a favorite now."

Sally couldn't help the smile that crept onto her face. "Are you always this cheesy, or is this a new thing?"

"You bring it out in me," Harriet replied. "But thanks for meeting me."

Sally sucked on the inside of her cheek, relieved this wasn't as awkward as she'd thought it might be. "You said you had a business proposition, and I'm a businesswoman."

"That's what I was counting on," Harriet replied. "But seriously, I wasn't sure if you would say yes, after how we left it last time." She paused. "And after you never replied to any of my texts."

Sally exhaled before she spoke, trying to place her thoughts. She wasn't sure how to put into words all the emotions and feelings that had flowed through her in the past couple of months, but she was going to try her best.

She fingered her cheap white paper napkin nervously before she spoke. "Two months ago, when we last saw each other, I was pretty sure that was it, that we were a thing of the past. But I've had time to think since then, and you've been on my mind a lot. So when you got in touch, it seemed like the right thing to say yes to dinner with you." She paused, swallowing down her nerves, currently bunched in her throat. "Actually, not so much the right thing, more the *only* thing. So here we are."

There was a beat as they stared at each other again, before a waitress appeared. "You ready to order?" she said, putting two wine glasses on the table.

Sally looked at the waitress like she was speaking a whole new language. Then she computed the words in her brain and stared at Harriet, who had her face buried in her menu, but didn't look like she was reading it.

"Would you like me to order a few things and we can share?" Sally asked.

"That sounds perfect," Harriet said, relief washing over her face.

And that was when Sally knew for sure Harriet was just as flummoxed as her because she wasn't taking control like she usually did.

Sally ordered a mix of appetizers and entrées, and then busied herself pouring the wine. Above the chatter of other diners and the traffic noise as the door was opened and closed, all she could clearly make out was her heart thudding against her chest.

Harriet raised her glass to Sally's, before giving her a smile that pierced her heart.

Resistance was going to be harder than Sally thought.

"Here's to you," Harriet said, not taking her gaze from Sally.

Sally clinked her glass, unsure of how to reply.

"So, you had business here this week?"

Harriet hesitated, then nodded. "Yep, new day, new designers. The amount of talent out there always amazes me." She paused. "And I still want to see your designs, too. Any chance I could this trip?"

Sally shifted in her seat. "Sure, we could check out my studio after this — it's just around the corner."

"Cool." Harriet took a sip of her wine. "And if I can help you with anything business-like, it would mean I'm not here on false pretences. I'm used to helping small businesses navigate commercial waters."

"I'll bear it in mind."

Harriet gave her a studied look before she continued. "How have you been? Since we last saw each other, I mean."

Sally shook her head, a wry smile on her lips. She wasn't going to sugar-coat it, there didn't seem to be any point.

"Honestly? A mess."

Harriet beamed. "Me, too."

"Really?" It wasn't just her. *Thank fuck for that.* "You've confused me. Like I said, I'd written you off as my past, and I was happy with that."

"Ouch," Harriet replied.

"You know what I mean," Sally said, giving her a look. "And now, here you are and I feel… on edge, like I'm not sure what's going to happen. And I always know what's going to happen, I'm usually in control of my emotions."

"I'm glad I've thrown them off."

"It's no big surprise," Sally said. "I just know that for the past couple of months, I've been distracted, and it's not going away." She stared at Harriet, until Harriet looked away, flustered. "What about you?"

"Me?" Harriet said, regaining her composure. "Well, let's see." Harriet counted on her fingers. "First, I've been so distracted I've thrown myself into my work, but I haven't been doing a good job — my business partner told me that."

"She did?"

"Uh-huh. And then when I told her I was coming out here, she got mad at me — she thinks I'm going to up sticks and leave her high and dry, and she's got a very clear business plan that we committed to for the next five years." Harriet shrugged. "So, she's not happy with me, and even Daniel's giving me pep talks, so things must be bad."

"Anybody else? How's your dad?"

"He's recovering well — and thank you for sending him that card, by the way. That was really sweet of you."

"You know about that?" Sally said, feeling a rush inside. It was the way Harriet was looking at her, with such gratitude and... something else she couldn't quite pinpoint. "I sent it ages ago and I heard nothing."

"You could have just called me, you know." Harriet raised an eyebrow at her.

Sally blushed, biting her top lip. "I know, but sending your dad a card seemed easier."

"Well, you made my dad happy. He keeps asking about you, which was inopportune when you'd kissed me and flown out of the state, never to return. It seems he's harbored a crush on you all these years and I never knew until we got back in touch."

"Your dad does *not* have a crush on me," Sally said, giggling.

"I think he might."

Sally shook her head, smiling. "So even with all these people on your case, you still texted. Does that mean you missed me?"

"I guess it must," Harriet replied, sighing. "I wish this was easier, but it's not. But I can't ignore what every sinew of my body is telling me — that I shouldn't walk away from this without seeing you again. I couldn't leave it on that kiss."

"Not without doing it one more time, just to see if the fireworks were a fluke first time around?" Sally said, covering Harriet's hand with hers. And just like that, her own personal firework party lit up her heart, although she kept it under wraps, taking a gulp of her wine instead.

Harriet smiled. "I was hoping for that, but I wasn't counting my chickens."

"This isn't easy, it never was — but I'm glad you're here."

"Me, too."

Their appetizers of chicken wings stuffed with crabmeat, pork and chicken dumplings, and pork pancakes with chili arrived, all served on a platter with carrots carved into the shape of flowers.

"Wow, these look amazing. Just like you, by the way," Harriet told her.

Sally held up a hand, even though Harriet's comments had made her stomach do cartwheels. Not ideal when she was just about to eat. "Can we halt the charm offensive and eat first? Then, I promise you, you can lay it on as thick as you like."

"You're definitely one of the most interesting dates I've had in a while, you know that?"

"This is a date?" Sally asked, her eyes wide, a smile tugging on the edges of her mouth. She hoped it was, even though that scared her to death.

"It is now," Harriet replied.

Chapter Twenty-Five

Sally unlocked the door to her work-space, putting her finger to her lips, even though she had no idea why. There was nobody here to disturb, and she was allowed to be here, their building having 24-hour access. She snapped on her office lights and watched Harriet's face as she took it all in.

"So this is where the magic happens," she said, running a hand along Sally's work desk, before stopping in front of her creative desk. It was a mess of wire cutters, material, paint sticks, and ink stamps, along with fine art pencils and beads. All the basics of a card designer's day, which now to Sally appeared messy and somewhat childlike. She hoped Harriet didn't see it that way. Sometimes she still marveled this was how she made her living.

However, it was the range of cards lining the wall behind her creative desk that Harriet was drawn to, Sally watching her body language as her eyes roamed her selection, some of which were still to be finished. Did she like them?

Sally hoped so, because this was her heart and soul on display.

"Wow, these are incredible, really," Harriet said, pulling her chin with her thumb and forefinger. "I mean, look at the detail on these, they're immense." She pointed at one Sally was particularly proud of: a lesbian wedding card with a flash of golden velvet, on top of which two women were sketched in charcoal, the pair holding up a love heart hand-crafted in gold wire. "I love this one in particular," she said, turning to Sally.

"I did that after equal marriage was passed into law, as a celebration. I've got a whole slew of them, but that's my favorite. It sells well, too."

"I bet," Harriet said, stepping back. "These are so you, so intricate and done with so much love." She turned to Sally. "I always knew you were talented when we were kids, but to make a living from your art is something else. It's way beyond anything I do."

Sally shook her head, thrilled that Harriet was impressed with her work. If she hadn't been, she might have cried.

"Don't be too sure of that," Sally said. "Business is a talent, a skill. You've got people skills, and that's something most artists should learn." She grinned. "Although I've got better as time's gone on, and Taylor, my buddy here — well, she's the opposite of most artists, a social whirlwind. Which is probably why we get along so well, opposites attract and all that."

"They should have something like this in Chicago — an artist collective. Is there one?"

Sally shook her head. "I've no idea, I've never looked into it."

Harriet didn't say anything, just held Sally's gaze, before looking away. She ran a hand over the wedding card before turning back to Sally. "It even feels expensive."

"That's because it is," Sally laughed. And then every hair on the back of her neck stood up as the air in the room thickened with sexual tension. It was as if someone had got hold of the gauge and turned it higher than usual, like they were trying to see how far they could push it.

Sally gulped, staring at Harriet, not sure whether to act on it or run screaming out of here. Her eyes flicked to her office sofa, then back to Harriet.

A drink would settle her nerves.

Movement would settle her nerves.

"Shall we go back to my place? I have a nice bottle of Jack there."

Sally's heart was thumping in her chest, and Harriet's gaze was fully on her, the heat almost unbearable.

Harriet gave a hurried nod, one that said a definite yes.

"Then let's go."

Chapter Twenty-Six

The thick metal elevator doors slid shut and they were sealed in, the air close, Harriet's smile fixed as she leaned back against the cool mirrored wall.

She caught Sally giving her a quick glance, her eyes not moving further north than her breasts, then she looked at the elevator panel before pressing the ground-floor button. It began its descent, the possibility in the air so palpable, Harriet could taste it, sweet and tangy on her tongue.

Just like she imagined Sally would be.

That thought sent a zap of desire to between her legs and she cleared her throat in case Sally could read her mind, allowing her eyelids to flutter shut for a second.

Harriet was just about to say something, when there was a bang, then a shudder, then the lights went out and the elevator came to a crunching halt.

"What the actual fuck?" Sally said, glancing at the lit-up elevator panel, then at Harriet. They were both silent, holding their breath, waiting for something else to happen.

When nothing did, Harriet pressed the help button, but there was nobody there.

"Anything?" Sally asked, wincing.

Harriet shook her head. She pulled her cell from her pocket, but the signal was non-existent, as she expected. "I'd say we're stuck until someone realizes we're here."

"That could take forever — it's Friday night!"

"Unless there's another artist type in the building, chasing their muse and wanting to get out of the building sometime soon."

Sally nodded slowly. "We're going to have to hope for that, aren't we?" Then she started banging on the door, shouting loudly. "Help! Is anybody there! We're trapped in the elevator!" She carried on for a few seconds, then fell silent, waiting for any response.

None came. Sally used her phone light to scour the elevator panel, flicking a switch: the emergency light. A weak off-yellow glow filled the space, which they both augmented with their phone lights.

"This is not how I intended to spend Friday night," Sally said, sliding to sit on the floor, her back to the wall. "At least the cleaners have been in — it smells like glass cleaner in here."

Harriet grinned, sliding down next to Sally. "And nothing turns me on more than glass cleaner," she said, inhaling deeply, wafting the smell into her nose. "If it's any consolation, I'd imagined us in a fancy cocktail bar by now."

"You would." Sally nudged her with her elbow.

"What's that supposed to mean?"

Sally shrugged. "You know – you're the sort of person who goes to cocktail bars."

"And what are you?"

"I go to beer bars."

"We could totally have gone to a beer bar, too. I drink beer."

"Yes, but that's not what you imagined. You imagined cocktails, low lights, velvet cushions, touching knees."

Harriet raised a single eyebrow as she moved her knee to touch Sally's. "I'm the one imagining this, am I? Because that sounded suspiciously like your scenario, not mine."

Sally coughed, covering her mouth with her hand. "Okay, busted. But I was imagining that at a beer bar, naturally."

"Naturally," Harriet replied, moving her hips closer to Sally so their thighs were touching, too.

Adrenaline pulsed through her like someone had just given her a high-speed dose of a Class A drug. But she knew full well what her drug of choice was: Sally. It had always been Sally.

"But let's look at the evidence," Harriet said, turning to Sally, waving her arm through the air beside them. "We've got touching knees and low lights."

"Agreed."

"So you just have to imagine the drinks, okay?"

Sally nodded. "Okay — what drinks did you have in mind?" She turned her head to Harriet. "And if you say a Slow, Comfortable Screw, you lose major points."

Harriet let out a howl of laughter. "What about Sex On The Beach?"

"From where we are now, Sex On The Beach sounds a good alternative," Sally said, before her breath stilled.

"What about a Kiss In The Elevator?" Harriet asked, eyes trained on Sally's lips, her teeth a bright white landing strip in the drooping light.

"Is that a new type of cocktail?" Sally whispered, moving her head toward Harriet.

"It is now," Harriet replied, leaning forward, not stopping to overthink it, and pressing her lips to Sally's.

And just like the night in Chicago, 17 years of nothing were erased, and they were back in Harriet's bed, back on the speedboat, back in her parents' downstairs bathroom, Sally's legs spread, Harriet pushing her up against the magnolia wall.

She'd never forgotten that memory, the taste of Sally's mouth, the heat of her skin. And now Sally's tongue was pushing back into hers, Harriet's brain kicked back, poured itself a cocktail and turned up the volume *everywhere*. Harriet's whole body was pulsing as she turned into Sally, pulling back from her mouth for a second.

"Oh, Harriet," Sally said, her eyes ablaze, before crushing her lips to hers again.

Harriet knew what she meant. Even after all those

years, she knew the language of Sally. The language of them. Harriet was kissing her first love again, and this time, Sally couldn't run away — and Harriet hoped she didn't want to. Because Sally was back in Harriet's arms, where she belonged.

The heat was rising inside Harriet as Sally fumbled with the buttons on her shirt, squeezing her breast gently, her fingers connecting with Harriet's nipple through the material. Harriet let out a moan.

Those hands: Harriet remembered those hands.

"I..." Sally began, pulling back, her hair pushed to one side.

She'd never looked more beautiful.

"Is this okay? Should we wait?"

"Do you want to?" Harriet asked, her chest heaving up and down, pressing her lips back to Sally's again in a wet, sticky, sexy mess.

She didn't want to wait another minute, another second.

Every part of her body was pulsing to be touched, and she didn't care they were stuck in an elevator.

If anything, being stuck in an elevator was making it all the more erotic.

Sally paused before shaking her head. "I don't think I can, I need to feel you. It feels like we've been teasing each other all night," she said, pushing Harriet down on the floor, ripping her shirt open, and smothering her semi-naked torso in kisses.

Harriet's brain wobbled, along with her whole body.

So this was how Sally played it these days: rough and proactive. She could *so* get used to it.

And she had to agree with her: they had been eye-fucking all night.

Now, it was time to go further — and that thought made Harriet's whole body groan with longing, wetness pooling between her legs. She couldn't wait to be touched or to touch: she wasn't quite sure which she wanted more, but she wanted them soon.

Sally wasn't wasting any time. She knew this wasn't the moment for sweet nothings in Harriet's ear; this was a moment for action.

That's when Harriet heard a zip coming down, and Sally's fingers slip inside her underwear. She moved her hips so Sally could pull her jeans down and then Sally was spreading her legs, peppering Harriet's neck with kisses as she loomed over her, her eyes dark in the liquid light.

Before Harriet could process any thoughts at all, Sally's hand was hot over her very core, before she slipped one finger into her liquid heat.

Harriet bucked her hips in response, crying out as she did.

Oh fuck, she even remembered what Sally felt like, how she added another finger, *like now*.

How she fucked her, *like now*.

This was going to be messy in *so many ways*. Gloriously, deliciously messy.

Messy in a way that had been missing in Harriet's life for nearly two decades.

Harriet reached up and pulled Sally down for a kiss as she fucked her, slowly at first, before she increased her speed. Harriet spread her legs as far as her jeans allowed her, feeling how wet she was, as Sally groaned on top of her.

"I can't believe this is happening," Sally said, crushing her mouth to Harriet's again.

Harriet didn't answer: she didn't need to. She was too busy kissing Sally's lips, too busy feeling her muscles tighten, feeling a flash of lightning at her very core, then its aftermath begin to rumble through her like thunder.

Suddenly, Harriet's world became brighter, bolder, the blurred edges crystallising once more. This was what she'd been waiting for — the missing piece in her life puzzle. And when Sally swiped her thumb over Harriet's clit, Harriet collapsed with desire, hanging onto Sally with everything she had.

Harriet had fucked a number of women in the intervening years since Sally, but not one of them had felt like this. Not one of them had made her heart pulse anew, as if it had just had a jump-start.

Seconds later, when the lightning struck again, it rattled through Harriet at speed, as she came undone at Sally's hand, just like always, like nothing had changed. And as Harriet cried out, thanking the stars for realigning and the thunder for returning, Sally pressed her lips to hers, sunk her fingers into her, and she didn't think life could get much better as her head fell back, thudding against the floor.

In her current state, Harriet didn't feel a thing.

Moments later, Sally withdrew her hand and the only sound in the elevator was their breathing, the smell of sex heavy in the air.

"You know," Harriet said, squinting up at Sally, her breath still scattered. "Lying on this floor reminds me of making love to you on the speedboat — it wasn't exactly comfortable, but it was thrilling, just like this."

Sally smiled down at her, giving her another kiss before pulling back. "You think we're exhibitionists? I've never been like this with anyone else."

"Me either. We bring it out in each other, clearly."

"Maybe you're right," Sally replied, staring at Harriet with such intensity. "I've been thinking about—" she began, but the elevator jolting broke the moment, and Harriet sat up, shielding her eyes as the lights came back on.

"Shit!" Harriet said, her orgasm pushed aside, her heart suddenly in her throat. Were the elevator doors about to open with her semi-naked? Not if she could help it.

Harriet pushed herself onto the balls of her feet and scrambled to pull her jeans up — but only succeeded in losing her footing and falling forward, tripping on her jeans and smacking her chin on the ground with a resounding thud. Her bottom teeth sunk into her top lip on impact, her mouth filling with the bitter, metallic taste of her own blood. She licked her lips, sucking it in, wanting to howl in pain — but there was no time to feel sorry for herself.

Her head still throbbing, her clit still pulsing, Harriet pushed herself up onto all fours just as the elevator juddered again, then began its descent. She looked up and saw the panic in Sally's eyes. But it wasn't Sally who was half-naked, was it?

"Take my arm!" Sally said, as Harriet did just that, staggering to her feet, gingerly feeling her mouth with her fingers. They came away covered in blood. Oh my god, she might faint. But she didn't have time to faint.

"Let me help," Sally said, leaning forward, her hands shaking as she went to do up the button on Harriet's shirt.

But Harriet flicked her hand away: she still needed to pull her jeans up.

She was still doing that when the elevator reached its destination, the robotic voice saying, "Ground Floor!"

Ohmyfuckinggod.

The door slid open just as Harriet jumped in an attempt to pull her jeans up fully, framed in mid-air when their audience was revealed: a man in overalls she assumed was the janitor, along with an attractive dark-haired twentysomething with a nose ring. Harriet landed with a thud as she secured her top button, smiling even though she was aware there was probably blood oozing from her mouth.

"Trent! Kristy!" Sally said, her voice about five octaves too high.

Harriet's heart sank: Sally knew these people? Wonderful, just wonderful.

"Thank god you're here — we wondered if we'd be in there all night," Sally said, moving to cover Harriet as she did up her shirt.

"Looks like you found something to keep you occupied," Kristy replied, a smirk very evident in her voice.

How long till this was all round Sally's building? Harriet smoothed her shirt down, now fully dressed, and took a deep breath, fishing in her jeans' pocket for a tissue.

She wouldn't want to be Sally on Monday morning.

Chapter Twenty-Seven

"Remember when we were at the lake house that summer?" Harriet was lying with Sally in her double bed, her thin summer gray-and-yellow duvet kicked off, the sweat from their love-making still fresh on her body. She was holding Sally's hand tight, never wanting to let her go, a haze of lust spritzed into the air around them. Sally had her bedside lamp on mid-glow, as if they were starring in a French independent movie.

"Of course, how could I forget that?" Sally replied.

Harriet took Sally's hand and kissed it, smelling herself on her.

"I remember the smell of sunscreen on you, when you were lying out flat on the speed boat in that bikini." Sally paused. "You knew what you were doing in that bikini, didn't you?"

"Not really, I was only 18, but it was all I had at the time. I wasn't sure how to respond having read those few lines of your journal — but it was enough to make me think you were what I wanted." She paused. "I should have held onto you, shouldn't I?"

Harriet's mind wandered back to the two of them, back to their young, supple bodies. Back to the years of lost opportunity. But it was no good dwelling on that now, because it was done. She couldn't change the past, that much she knew. The only thing she could do was accept the past and embrace the future. Grasp it with both hands. Take this second chance at face value and run with it.

"We were young, we didn't know," Sally replied. "I remember thinking back then I wished I was older, because then I'd know what to do, how to feel, how to make a move on you."

"Ha! The myth of with age comes wisdom?"

"Something like that," Sally replied, kissing Harriet's hand back.

"And what do you think now?"

"I think when it comes to you, I'm always confused, mixed up. You play with my emotions, it's just what you do."

"And has having sex for the past three hours made things any clearer?"

"What do you think?" Sally said, nudging her with her elbow.

"It doesn't have to be confusing, though. We could try to make this work, you know that. We could do long distance, only it's not that long if I'm traveling here all the time for work, is it?"

Sally tensed up. "You know what I think about long distance." She pursed her lips. "It's hard work, it's a lot of missing the other person, and it's lonely."

"But just think of the amazing sex we'll have when we meet up again." Harriet gave her a wink, before placing a kiss on Sally's warm, wet lips. God, this woman was gorgeous, and Harriet was leaving today. But she wasn't going until this was sorted out.

And by *this*, she meant *them*.

"My point is I'm not some random person asking you to do long distance — it's *me*, and I've been in your life almost forever. And if you think about it, we've been doing long distance for 17 years already, we just didn't know it and we weren't in touch."

"It didn't work out very well, you see my point?"

"It can now we *know* we're doing it. I have business in New York; you could easily come and see me more often, too, and I promise to stay in touch, to be there for you, to give this a go."

Sally grimaced just like Harriet knew she would. "But where would it go in the long run? I can't do it indefinitely, and neither of us are teenagers anymore, are we?"

Harriet moved her top lip one way, her bottom lip the other. No, they weren't teenagers, and she knew what Sally was saying: what was the point in going into something at her age if she didn't think it was going to work?

But Harriet wasn't having it. "You're coming at it from a glass-half-empty perspective — whereas I am very much a glass-half-full kinda gal. We'll work it out, and you know why?"

"Tell me."

"Because we want to, and because we're worth it. And if it means I have to move to New York, then so be it."

"You can't move to New York, your whole life and family and friends are in Chicago."

Harriet paused. "Then I have to work on you to move back to Chicago, be nearer your family as they get older."

"There's a reason I moved to New York."

Harriet laughed at that. "I know. Then I guess I have to give you a solid reason to move back, don't I?" She paused, running a finger down the side of Sally's face.

Sally sighed, closing her eyes on contact.

"What do you say, will you give it a go? Not just for me, for *you*. Because despite your misgivings, I think you owe yourself some happiness and I think I'm the person who can give it to you."

"Bold claims."

"I'm a bold kinda woman, haven't you noticed that yet?"

"I just did, a few minutes ago."

"I'm not letting you wriggle out of this one," Harriet said. "Say yes, give us a chance? I know it didn't work before and I know I was at fault, but I'm a different person now and this is truly what I want. If you say yes, I'm all in." Were her words sinking in? Sally seemed to be listening, her eyes fixed on Harriet's face the whole time she spoke.

"It's going to be on you more than me to travel, you know that, right?" Sally replied. "I mean, when we met was the first time I've traveled in ages for work. I'm a lowly designer. You're the one with the expense account." She paused. "Which is eerily reminiscent of our teenage years when you think about it, isn't it? Harriet with the money and the swagger, and penniless me."

Sally sighed, looking up to the ceiling.

Harriet reached out an arm and rolled Sally to face her, ignoring the petulant look on her face.

"Listen to me," Harriet said, her gaze fixed on Sally's face and not allowing her to look away, no matter how hard she tried. "Stop making excuses. Yes, I travel more for work, but that's good where we're concerned. And if I've got more money right now, so what? Money doesn't mean a thing if you don't have the right person to spend it with. I know this from first-hand experience. So please, don't use money as an excuse not to do this. I want to do this, and I think you do, too. And I don't care how much it costs."

Sally sighed. "I can't deny what this makes me feel and what *you* make me feel. But I also can't ignore my feelings on long distance love — it doesn't work, and that hasn't changed just because you've grabbed hold of my heart again."

"I've grabbed hold of your heart?" If Harriet's heart had a tail, it would be thumping on the floor right now.

"You have, which makes it problematic."

"How about if we don't call it long distance? We just chat when we want to, and when I'm in New York, I'll come and see you. No pressure, no labels. We'll start off casual — but exclusive — and see how it works."

Sally narrowed her eyes at that. "Casual but exclusive?"

Harriet nodded. "Just see how it goes." She could see the cogs working in Sally's brain. Was she going to say yes? Harriet felt like her entire life was resting on the tip of Sally's tongue.

"Is that a yes? We can put a deadline on it if it makes you feel better. We can, say, date till Christmas, and if it's not working out we can call it quits."

"I'm not putting a deadline on it, that makes it sound like a business deal. This is not a business deal."

"Glad to hear it," Harriet said, staring into Sally's eyes once more. "But it is a deal? One you agree to?" She bit her lip and took Sally's hands. "You know, sometimes the only transportation you need is a leap of faith."

"When did you get so poetic?"

"I've been working on it," Harriet said, with a wink.

Sally smiled at her, and then, slowly but very surely, nodded.

Harriet beamed, happiness flooding her system: it was as if Sally had just thrown back her heart shutters and finally let the light in, the light that had been missing for half a lifetime.

"Was that a yes? Did the great Sally McCall just say she'd try casually seeing me once every few weeks?"

Sally slapped her on the arm, her laughter filling the air. "It's a yes, you idiot, just to make you shut up."

Harriet kissed her and the contact made her head swim. When they came up for air, Sally took hold of her chin to make sure her words sank in.

"But if you let me down or make me regret this decision, there will be hell to pay, got it?"

"Hell is a terrible debt collector, so I hear you loud and clear." Harriet paused, gathering every ounce of sincerity she had and sprinkling it on her words. "I already let you down once. I don't plan on making the same mistake twice."

Chapter Twenty-Eight

Sally was woken up by a banging on the door. She cracked open an eyelid and took a moment to realize she wasn't alone. Harriet had her back to her, but she was starting to roll over when Sally opened her other eye. The banging stopped, then started again. Sunlight was trying to slither into her bedroom, but her blackout blinds were doing their job well.

"What's that noise?" Harriet mumbled, rolling over and squinting at Sally. "You don't have a girlfriend, do you? Am I about to get beaten up by a jealous lover?"

Sally smiled, giving Harriet a kiss on the lips. She tasted like sour candy. "Not that I remember. But then, I am forgetful." She jumped out of bed and grabbed some underwear from her chest of drawers. She could feel Harriet's gaze on her, and when she glanced back, even in the hazy light, there was a languid smile on her lover's face.

"Stop looking at me," Sally said, suddenly self-conscious. Although after last night when Harriet had tasted every inch of her, she had no idea why.

"I can't help it," Harriet said, as the banging continued.

"Alright, I'm coming!" Sally yelled, pulling on a blue T-shirt and then grabbing her denim shorts. "Let me go handle this."

"Okay," Harriet mumbled, rolling over.

Sally opened her bedroom door and scooted past her mustard sofa, nearly tripping on her sheepskin rug as usual, getting to the front door just as the banging began again. She yanked it open and standing there was her aunt, a wide grin on her face, her shiny copper hair up in a bun.

Sally frowned at her, going to check her watch before realizing she didn't have it on. "What are you doing here? We did say midday, right?"

"Charming," Paula replied, almost yelling her reply. "Aren't you going to invite me in?"

Panic slithered through Sally, but there wasn't much else she could do. "Come in," she said, stepping aside and closing her eyes. This wasn't going to go well, was it?

Paula stepped past her, giving her a kiss on the cheek, looking enormous in her living room — or perhaps that's just how Sally perceived her. She assessed the sofa, the TV crouched on the small wooden table, Sally's painting of Chicago hung on the far wall. Paula stood in front of it and gave a whistle: the painting depicted a view of the main stem of the Chicago River, with the famous Wrigley Building and Tribune Tower.

"This is amazing — you should commission these, too. They'd sell like hot cakes at home."

But Sally, still half asleep, just nodded. She'd heard that from her family for a while now, but she only painted for herself.

"But we did say midday, right?" she blurted out again, scratching her head and yawning. She really hadn't had much sleep.

Paula nodded. "We did, but I was up early, so I thought I'd come early and you could show me your neighborhood."

"Right," Sally said.

"Are you going to come back and get naked with me anytime soon?" Harriet shouted from the bedroom.

Every hair on Sally's body stood up as she closed her eyes, shaking her head. She didn't need a mirror to know her cheeks were the color of beetroot — she could feel it.

If Paula had been grinning before, her mouth was now wider than ever as she clamped her hand over her mouth. "Well, well, you sly dog!" her aunt said, starting to laugh. "You've got a woman in your bed! Sorry, I thought you said you weren't seeing anyone, so I didn't think I'd be interrupting."

"I wasn't till last night," Sally said. "And now I kinda am." She paused. "Actually, it's Harriet."

Paula put a hand on her hip, a furrow in her brow. "Harriet from Chicago, Harriet?"

"Uh-huh."

"Harriet who you're not talking to and nothing's going on?"

"That's the one," Sally said, smiling.

The one who fucked my brains out earlier. The one I was hoping might get to do the same this morning.

"McCall!" Harriet shouted again. "Get your butt in here!"

Sally put her index finger in the air. "You mind if I just go and shut her up, then we can carry on this conversation?"

Paula laughed, rubbing her hands together. "By all means. Better yet — how about I go get us some coffee and pastries from that café on the corner, give you two time to recover. Unless I'm interrupting something *right now*?" Paula added, raising an eyebrow.

Sally spluttered, shaking her head. "No! We just woke up, you're not interrupting. A coffee would be lovely."

"Okay," her aunt said. "You've got 15 minutes to make yourselves presentable, and then I'm coming back. Does that work?"

Sally nodded. "Perfect. Thanks, Paula." She walked her to the door. "And promise me one thing?"

"What's that?"

"No messaging Dad to tell him what just happened. This is something between us. Lesbian bonding and all that."

"My lips are sealed," Paula said, giving her a wink. "What happens in Queens, stays in Queens."

Sally closed the door and took a deep breath, then walked back through to the bedroom, where Harriet was laying on top of the covers, legs spread, naked. She wiggled an eyebrow and crooked a finger in Sally's direction.

"What took you so long?"

"My aunt being at the door and hearing you calling me to come back in and get naked." Sally waited for her words to sink in.

Harriet's eyes got bigger as she sat up. "Your aunt was here? Just now?"

"Uh-huh."

Harriet covered her face with her hands. "Oh, shit," she said, laughing. "I guess she doesn't think we're just friends anymore."

Sally crawled onto the gray-and-yellow bedding on her hands and knees, kissing Harriet's lips before laying down, her head on Harriet's shoulder. She flicked her gaze upwards and stared at her. "Friends with benefits, maybe."

"Did I mention I like these new benefits?"

"I think you had your mouth full last night," Sally replied, smiling. Then she remembered Harriet was flying home today. She closed her eyes and sighed.

"Hey," Harriet said, stroking her hair back from her face. "Why the big sigh?"

"You know," Sally said. "We just had a fabulous night, and now my aunt's here and you have to go today." She sighed again. "This is why I've never done long distance, too. I'm not good with goodbyes."

"I know," Harriet replied. "But remember, we're not long distance, we're casual-exclusive."

Sally laughed. "Then I have issues with casual-exclusive, too."

"Don't get down, not when I'm still here. Let's just

make the most of the time we have." Harriet paused, a grin crossing her face. "How long till your aunt gets back?"

"Not long enough for you to have an orgasm."

"What about you?"

"I don't want my last time with you interrupted by my aunt banging on the door again."

"Good point."

Harriet trailed a finger up Sally's arm, then down it, before kissing her forehead. "I don't want to leave either. But we'll make this work, okay?"

"If you say so," Sally said, every sinew of her body willing it to be true. "How's your lip today?"

Harriet put a hand to her mouth. "I'll live — I think you kissed it better enough last night." She gave Sally a satisfied smile. "I had a great time last night."

"Me, too."

"I'm already slotting you into my diary for a repeat performance, okay?"

"Slot away," Sally replied.

"Talk dirty to me, baby."

Sally laughed, grabbing her phone from her bedside table. "You know, maybe I can ask Taylor to come round and take her girlfriend off our hands for the morning — then we could say goodbye properly, like I thought we would this morning." Sally sat up, jabbing her phone and smiling at the screen.

"That sounds like the perfect plan."

Two minutes later, she had her answer, a grin lighting

up her face. "Awesome, Taylor's in — and I know Paula will be."

"I can think of a thing or two they could do to fill the time."

Sally threw her phone down on the bed and crawled back over to Harriet, one eyebrow raised, matching Harriet's own.

"Can you really?" she said, straddling Harriet. "Might it be something like this?" Sally reached behind her and pressed her hand over Harriet's pussy.

Harriet let out a strangled sound and closed her eyes, nodding her head at the same time. "Along those lines," she said, catching her breath.

When Sally's phone beeped again, she slung an arm to her right and felt for it on the duvet, before reading the message and putting a hand to her mouth.

Harriet scrunched her brows together. "What's wrong?"

Sally shook her head. "Nothing — just a message from Taylor asking if I've had any adventures in elevators lately."

"She knows?"

Sally nodded. "Looks like it — good news travels fast."

Harriet shook her head, beginning to laugh. "At least there were no security cameras, let's look on the bright side."

Sally's stomach dropped. "That we know of," she replied.

"If there were cameras, rest assured: you were magnificent."

Chapter Twenty-Nine

Harriet pulled up at her parents' house later that week, a skip in her step: that's what being back with Sally was doing for her, despite the fact she was missing her so much. She was still amazed at how life could spin in an instant: one lost suitcase, two months of heartache, but now she couldn't get her thoughts in order because of Sally McCall.

Joanna had informed her she was acting "out of character". But perhaps it was the other way around? Perhaps this *was* her character, she'd always been this way and she'd been hiding behind her well-manicured persona for too long. Now Sally was in the picture, she was bringing out the true Harriet.

She pushed open the heavy front door, which was slightly ajar — she was going to have to have words with her parents about security — and crossed the hallway, going to the heart of the kitchen where, from the aromas of meat, tomatoes, and spices, she expected to find Robert preparing the evening meal. The chef had been with her parents for the past 20 years, and he was one of the key reasons Harriet had kept coming home when their relationship went through a rocky patch when she first came out. Robert's lasagna, along with his cherry pie, had been a constant in the storm of emotions, and they were still here today.

However, instead of Robert, she was faced with her mother holding an avocado and looking perplexed. She had her blue shirt sleeves rolled up, and the radio on low, Fleetwood Mac's "Dreams" spilling out of its speakers. On the stove a pan of tomato-based sauce was bubbling, and the kitchen looked like a tornado had blown through, with food detritus and packaging covering most surfaces.

Her mom was sucking on her bottom lip when she looked up and caught sight of Harriet. Despite being very much out of her element, there was a light in her eyes Harriet only ever usually saw when she was under the hood of her car. She was wearing a white apron over her shirt and jeans — at least, it had been white before she started cooking.

"You are just the person I need," her mom said, giving her a wide grin. "Avocados — I'm a bit scared to peel it. I saw a show on TV the other day and it said there were more avocado injuries in the ER than most other things." She gave the offending produce a concerned glance. "Can a vegetable really be that dangerous?"

Harriet shook her head, walking over to her mom. "They're not known for their attacking properties: I've peeled one many times and I'm here to tell the tale."

"Google it, it's scary." Her mom pointed to her iPad, set on the kitchen bench.

"Never look up medical symptoms or how to peel an avocado, it's bound to be bad news." Harriet stood beside her mom, grabbing the avocado. "And it's a fruit, not a vegetable, by the way," she said. "Actually, a single-seeded berry, but that seems to be taking things a little too far."

Her mom scoffed. "A berry? I wasn't born yesterday." She watched closely as Harriet ran a knife around the center of the fruit, before twisting. The fruit came apart easily and her mom nodded her appreciation. Harriet removed the stone with her fingers, then peeled the skin slowly, the fruit perfectly ripe so it came away easily.

"What are you making?" Harriet asked as she washed her hands of avocado under the faucet.

"I'm doing a black bean chipotle chili and I read about an avocado salad to go with it."

Harriet dried her hands on a yellow dishcloth hung up on the oven, eyeing her mother as if she'd had a body takeover. Which, judging by the fact she was in the kitchen, she kinda had. "Things are changing around here — you're in the kitchen?"

Her mom shrugged. "Robert's wife had a health scare — she's recovering, though — so I gave him a month off to be there for her."

Harriet managed to stop her jaw dropping wide open in the nick of time.

Her mom continued. "I thought about getting someone

in to cover for him, but then I thought with your dad home now, I have someone to eat meals with, which is unusual but not unwelcome. He was always out or away on business, so I had no need to learn how to cook. But now I have the time, I've decided to give it a try." She pointed toward the fridge. "Robert emailed me his lasagna recipe and his cherry pie with step-by-step instructions, so I'm giving that a try this weekend."

Harriet folded her arms, shaking her head in amazement. "What's happened to my mother and who are you?" she asked, giving her mom a grin. "My mom doesn't cook or plan meals."

"Mock all you like, but I'm finding it quite therapeutic, actually. It's not that dissimilar to working on a car — it takes practice and patience, and while the end result might be worth it, you're going to get messy in the process." She held up her hands and looked down at her splattered apron to drive home the point.

"And you and Dad are enjoying being home together?" Harriet had wondered how that was going to go, seeing as her mom was used to ruling the roost.

"We are," her mom replied, running a hand through her auburn hair. "It's like getting to know each other all over again, now both our lives are standing still for a moment. I've put off all my appointments, and your dad has had to put off all of his. And far from being difficult, as I'd feared, we're enjoying each other's company." She shrugged her shoulders. "When you get a partner, you'll understand."

A double whammy: her parents were getting lovey-dovey and her mom had mentioned the prospect of her having a partner. Dad's illness had waved a magic wand and this household was now a more relaxed one. Harriet could have given a little cheer if she wasn't so shocked.

"Speaking of that," she said, grinding her teeth a little before forcing herself to stop. "I'm kinda seeing someone, so I kinda do have a partner now. Sort of. And you know her. You remember Sally McCall?"

Her mom frowned slightly, before nodding at Harriet. "I remember Sally McCall very well," she said. "She sent your dad a lovely card, it was very thoughtful. So I assumed something must be going on." Her mom paused. "She was your first girlfriend."

Harriet felt her cheeks blush: her mom had known more than she let on. Perhaps they weren't as discreet as they thought they'd been back then. "You knew?"

Her mom smiled. "I knew far more than you ever thought." Then she cast her gaze down to the avocado, picking up the knife, before taking a deep breath and putting it down. "You know, I've had a lot of time to think since your dad's episode," she said, before looking over at Harriet. "Is it my fault?"

"Is what your fault?" Harriet asked, frowning.

Her mom paused, twisting her hands together tightly. "It's just… I'm not a girly girl. I play with cars, I'm not good with emotions. Is that why you're gay, do you think? Is it my fault?"

Harriet put her hands in her pockets, shaking her head, her whole face a question mark. "It's nobody's fault, Mom, it just is. This is how I am — just like Daniel's a terrible flirt."

Her mom smiled at that. "He is, isn't he? Although he seems taken with this new woman."

"And I'm pretty taken with my not-so-new woman." Harriet paused. "But seriously, being gay is just a part of me, just like I'm ambitious like Dad, and tenacious like you."

"Who are you gay like?"

Harriet pointed at her chest. "Like me," she replied.

"And Sally McCall? You haven't mentioned her in a very long time."

"I hadn't seen her in a long time — we ran into each other by accident, and we've decided to try again."

"Even after it didn't work last time?"

"That was my fault," Harriet said, shrugging like it was nothing. "I was going off to college, she was staying here, and I wasn't mature enough to persevere."

"You better not mess it up this time, then, if she's giving you another chance."

Harriet was well aware. "Thanks for the vote of confidence," she replied.

"She's back here now, though, I take it?"

Harriet swallowed, shaking her head. "She's not — she lives in New York."

Her mom raised both eyebrows. "So you're doing long distance? After what happened before?"

"We are, but I'm hoping to convince her to come home. Or else I might move there, who knows. It's not perfect, but it's the best I've got right now."

Her mom held Harriet's gaze, studying her intently. "She must still have a hold of your heart if you're thinking about moving."

Harriet shrugged, stabbing the floor with the tip of her shoe. "I'm not getting any younger and meeting her again has been amazing." A ball of emotion worked its way up her windpipe, but she swallowed it down. "I just want what everyone wants, something like you and Dad, to be happy." She gave her mom a resigned smile. "And I would love to be happily cooking for Sally in 30 years, just like this. For that to happen, I need to give it a shot at least. I can't walk away again, not when it was such a mistake the first time. Not when I lost the love of my life."

Her mom took a step back at that. "The love of your life?"

Harriet nodded, standing up tall. "I think so," she said. But there wasn't any "think" in that sentence, she knew that. "No, I know so. I don't regret much, but I do regret losing her."

"But if she won't move?"

"I'll cross that bridge when we come to it."

Her mom considered her again as if for the first time. "I've never seen you like this about a woman."

"That's because you've never really taken the time."

Her mom looked like Harriet had just slapped her, and Harriet winced, reaching out and rubbing her arm.

"Sorry, that came out harsher than I intended. We've just never really had a conversation like this, have we?"

Her mom shook her head. "No, and I'm sorry. I'm going to try to do better from now on. Life's short, after all, isn't it?"

Harriet's heart was pounding in her chest as she nodded at her mom. "I'll try to do better, too."

"If Sally is the one for you, bring her over. I might even whip up something delicious, miracles do happen. Plus, it would be lovely to meet her properly this time, not as a timid teenager." She paused, hesitating before speaking. "Were you in love with her back then, that summer at the lake house?"

Harriet chewed on her cheek, thinking back to that summer on the boat.

Yes, she'd always been in love with her.

"I was," she replied simply.

"Then you better convince her to move back to Chicago."

Chapter Thirty

"Oh my god, I cannot believe it. Harriet's negotiating worked — well, my negotiating with Harriet's guidance. Luxury Gifts has agreed that order for that price! Now I have to fucking fulfil it, don't I?"

Sally sat forward on her stained white wooden chair, her elbows drilling into the wooden table, clutching her phone in one hand, her heart in the other.

The smells of coffee and freshly baked quiche filled the air, as Sally spied Kristy looking over at their table, but she ignored her. All of a sudden, being back in the cafeteria for the first time after the elevator incident was the least of her worries, because her phone had just brought *big news*.

She needed to call Harriet and let her know, but her hand was shaking from shock. This was all Harriet's doing, pushing her to put herself out there. It'd been a month since they agreed to give their relationship a go, and it was working out just like Sally predicted: she missed her like crazy. Harriet had come over for a single weekend in that time, but it wasn't enough. Something had to give and Sally had been pondering just what that might be last night.

She had yet to come to a satisfactory conclusion.

Sally stared at Taylor and Ben, then put her head in her hands. Ever since her aunt and Harriet had sailed into her life, things had lurched from one extreme to another. From having a trickle of orders — enough to keep her going — all of a sudden she was now being handed an order for ten stores, and it was all a little overwhelming. Luxury Gifts wanted her greetings cards, but she was going to have to create them in quantities she'd never done before. She was equal measures excited and terrified.

Taylor beamed at her across the table, getting up and giving her a hug. "That's great news!"

Sally began to shake her head. "I've never produced in this number before — they want 1,000, not 100 like normal. It's one thing saying you can do it, it's another thing to *actually* do it. Shit!"

Ben put a hand on Sally's arm, while Taylor took the other. Ben was always the calmest of the three of them, softly spoken, assured. His web design business had quietly taken off last year and Ben had taken it all in his stride. Unlike Taylor, who'd completely flipped when she was first featured in the pages of *Elle Decor* and her website had crashed from the level of interest.

Sally stared at her two friends, fear in her eyes. "I can't do this!" she said, adrenaline pulsing through her. "This is worse than having no orders at all."

"Take a deep breath, Sally, in through the nose, out through the mouth," Ben replied, his bronzed beard perfectly groomed just like always. "You can absolutely do this, and we'll all help if you need us, won't we?" Ben looked at Taylor as he spoke, who nodded.

"Absolutely. Whatever we can do to help, we will."

Sally could have kissed Taylor right then, but thought better of it. She'd already been caught having sex in the elevator, after all.

"You'd do that?" Sally said, relief washing through her. Maybe, with the help of her friends, this might work out.

"Of course — remember when this happened to me? It's what we do here, we help. It's a collective, Sally, don't forget," Taylor said.

"What are we helping who with?" Kristy appeared at Sally's left, collecting their lunch plates. She still smiled extra-hard when she saw Sally, even though her interest had cooled since Harriet had come on the scene.

"Sally," Taylor replied. "She's got a big order and the deadline is tight." Taylor cocked her head. "You did a fine arts degree, didn't you?"

Kristy nodded.

"Fancy helping out, too?" Taylor asked.

Kristy was nodding her head before she even knew what she was agreeing to. "Always — it would be great on my portfolio and I'm always happy to help Sally."

Sally gave her a pained smile. "Thanks, that's very

kind," she said, blushing. She still wasn't sure where they stood after the elevator incident, but if Kristy had the skills, she was in need.

"There you go — three helpers already and I'm sure we could rustle up a few more. If we put in time over the weekends, you'll be flying."

"I can't put this on you at such short notice, it's not fair."

Taylor held up her hands. "We wouldn't offer if we weren't free and happy to do it. Would we?"

Ben and Kristy shook their heads.

"There you go. You need help, you've got a big order, plus you're paying us, right?"

Sally nodded — trust Taylor. "Absolutely. Time and a half."

Taylor laughed. "Don't spend all your money right away. We can work overnight if you provide pizza too, whatever it takes. We're going to get this order done, okay?"

Sally sighed, happiness welling up inside her. This was her big break, Taylor was right, and she didn't want to fuck it up. And the fact her friends were willing to drop everything and come to her aid was incredible, something she wouldn't be able to replicate anywhere else. Especially not in Chicago.

Which made her close her eyes all over again. Meeting Harriet again had muddled her life completely. She missed her so much, and talking and texting weren't filling the gap of personal contact at all. But if she moved to Chicago, she'd have to find a new tribe, and would they be prepared to drop everything to save her skin? This bunch were her true friends, prepared to put their lives on hold when she really, truly needed them.

It was all too much for Sally to take in. She stood up, knocking over her coffee cup as she did, spilling the remainder on the floor.

Kristy was by her side in seconds with a mop and bucket.

"Sorry," Sally muttered, as Kristy shook her head.

"Not a problem at all," she said, fixing Sally with her crystal blue eyes. "And Sally?"

Sally looked up into her gaze, gulping as she did. "Yes?"

"Congrats, you deserve this. I love your designs and if I can help, I mean it, I'd like to."

"Thank you," Sally said, and she meant it more than ever. "I'm going back to my office to make an action plan. See you all there at 5.30 and I'll assign jobs?"

"I love it when you get all bossy," Taylor said, giving her a wink. She stood up and followed her out the door, hands in pockets, looking down at the floor. "By the way, I can help you this weekend and next, that's not a problem, but I can't do Labor Day weekend: Paula's flying in and we've got plans." She gave her a shy smile. "Sorry, but this is important. I really like her."

Sally shook her head. "I think it's great you guys are giving it a go. It might mellow her a bit, you never know."

"She's more mellow in private."

Sally gave Taylor a look, somehow sensing the same was true for her, too. She had wondered if putting them together might drive them insane, but the opposite had happened, according to Taylor: they'd taken the edge off each other, which was truly remarkable.

"Who knew she had that side, but I'm glad you're starting to bring it out of her. I knew she couldn't be that hyper 24/7." Sally paused. "I've got to go to Chicago that weekend, too — it's my mom's birthday and she won't take no for an answer. Which means I'm going to be up to my ears for the next two weeks trying to get as much done as possible. Harriet and I were hoping we could do this weekend, but I'm going to have to put her off. The deadline for this order is before Labor Day, so at least that will be done."

Taylor held up both hands. "This week, I'm all yours." She paused. "And did I tell you that Paula is talking about investing in me, too? She wants lesbian designers to take over the world."

Sally grinned. "She mentioned she might even before you kissed, so I thought it might be a done deal, now."

Taylor blushed, which made Sally grin a little more. "I like this side of you, seeing you all flustered. It's so cute."

"I don't mind it, either," Taylor replied. "And will you be seeing Harriet in Chicago, too?"

"I better, it's been two weeks already since she was here. I knew this would be hard, but it's been crazy.

We agreed to keep it casual, but every time she has to leave, so does a piece of my heart."

Sally had missed Harriet so much over the past two weeks, it reminded her of 17 years ago, when Harriet had left then, too, to go to college. Remembering how that had ended didn't make the modern version any easier to take, because she knew the first time around, those feelings had been futile. Now she was putting her trust in Harriet all over again; she had to hope this time had a different ending.

"You'll get the order done, mind over matter," Taylor said. "Plus, you've got a crack team of helpers on the case — and if you need some more, I can make some calls."

"I hope you're right," Sally said. "Because if I don't make it, my mom will kill me." She gave Taylor a slow smile. "Also, now I've had sex again, I'd really like it to continue."

Taylor mirrored Sally's smile right back. "Me, too."

Chapter Thirty-One

"So how's the order coming?" Harriet asked over the phone.

Sally sipped her coffee from her favorite red mug and leaned back in her chair. Her office had been her home for the past week, and it wasn't showing any sign of letting up, with her order due to her client next week.

"It's coming. Kristy has been a massive help, would you believe, working with me every evening this week, along with her friend Sara. And Kristy's so talented — I think I'm going to take her on part-time if things work out. We've already discussed it and she's more than happy to."

"Even though she's seen you in the worst of circumstances?"

Sally gave her a throaty laugh for that. "It could have been so much worse. Imagine if the elevator had righted itself five minutes earlier? You do remember the position we were in and just where my hand was?" A zap of desire hurtled down Sally as she recalled the exact position, up to her elbows in Harriet. She wriggled in her seat as Harriet's embarrassed laugh rumbled down the phone.

"That particular scene is etched in my brain and has kept me going through all the long nights without you, of which there have been 19 so far," Harriet replied. "Not that I'm counting. Much."

"I'm sorry I had to cancel on you this weekend, but you understand — this is a big deal and I had to get it right."

"It's fine, I understand. We both run our own businesses, they have to come first. I'm glad I was able to help you out, and who knows, they might come back with an even bigger order after you sent those newer terms back, right?"

"That's the hope, but it's a lot to think about."

"I'll help you," Harriet said. "You'll be fine."

"Yes, but this is one of the snags of living so far apart: if we were in the same city, at least you could have crawled into my bed last night."

"That's the best offer I've had all week."

"I hope so," Sally replied. "But Labor Day weekend, I'm all yours. Well, yours and my family's." If there was one thing she was certain of today, it was that. It had been five weeks since they'd decided to give their casual-but-exclusive relationship a go, and so far, it was proving eerily similar to long distance.

"Okay. And you might want to let your mom know, by the way."

"My mom?"

"Yes, I ran into her at the grocery store. She didn't even know we were back in touch, let alone that you were coming home for the weekend. Seeing as it's her birthday and you're planning to see her, probably best to call her."

"I've been too busy, it slipped my mind. I always come home, I thought she'd assume."

"Do it this week. And if you could put in a word for me, too, that would be great. The look she gave me in the store was less than savory."

"She still blames you for breaking my heart at 17."

"Wow, we have a lot to make up for to our families. Did I tell you my mom thinks she made me gay because she likes cars?"

Sally laughed down the phone. "But you don't like cars."

"Don't question mother logic," Harriet replied. "Anyway, I told her we were seeing each other and she said to invite you over for dinner. This is a first by the way, my mom inviting one of my girlfriends over for dinner."

"I'm honored," Sally replied. "But it's not your mom I'm dying to see, it's you. Not seeing you sucks."

"I agree. So when are you moving to Chicago?"

"Don't start, Locke," Sally replied. It wasn't like she hadn't thought about that question every day of late.

"Just make sure you get on the damn plane this time, okay? I hated not seeing you last weekend."

"I promise."

"And I meant it about getting you new contacts in Chicago. I've been speaking to Dan's girlfriend, Ava, for instance, and she's a buyer for Whole Foods. I could easily ask her to put you on her books."

"Didn't you say she only deals with bigger clients? I don't want you to compromise your business for me."

"I'd compromise myself for you any day."

"That wasn't my worry," Sally said, laughing. "I've seen you in action, remember."

"Let me ask her, see what she says. I'm sure she'd love your designs."

"We'll see — let's take it one step at a time." She didn't want to get in over her head — this step up was stressing her out enough already.

"And how are the elevator jokes — still painful?"

Sally smiled. "It's done, everyone's moved on. Everyone except Taylor, of course, who still insists on singing Aerosmith's "Love In An Elevator" whenever she gets a chance."

"Tell Taylor to get back in her box — after all, you found her a girlfriend. She totally owes you."

When they'd finished chatting and Sally had hung up, she leaned back to the furthest point her chair would allow, staring at her office's white ceiling, the black mark that had been there since she began renting the space still staring down at her.

Should she move back to Chicago? All she knew was long distance was hard. It would mean moving closer to her family and Harriet, which were both pluses.

However, Casey was back in Chicago; Casey who'd

run off, just like Harriet had all those years ago. It was a conundrum that hurt Sally's head way more than she was comfortable with.

When she and Casey had imploded all those years ago, she'd fled the city and moved to New York, thinking she could outrun her heart and make a new life for herself here, with fresh options, new work, new women. But she'd just run into the same trouble all over again until she'd freed herself and found this co-op space in Queens. She'd more or less given up on women because that seemed to be the easiest route to take.

Could she go back, retrace her steps and her life? Her mom would be pleased, she had no doubt about that. Her dad would be thrilled, too. Even her aunt had told her she'd help her buy a place, an offer she wasn't about to take up in a hurry. Her aunt had already helped her out enough.

There was no shame in going back, she knew that. Plenty of people did it every day, moved home to be with their family. But she'd never wanted to do that. And when she seriously thought about it, it made her jaw ache, her muscles tense.

She'd always been fiercely independent, always wanted to do things her way. But had that way worked out exactly as she'd wanted? Not exactly. The thought of her home city flooded her tastebuds with tomato and cheese, with mozzarella sticks, with all the food of her youth. All the food she didn't eat anymore in New York.

And then there was Harriet. Who was as beautiful as

ever, even more so than Sally remembered. And Harriet wanted to be with her, which Sally was coming round to. But she also wanted her to move back, so they could be together properly, as a couple.

Was it admitting defeat to go home? She'd always thought if she did, it would be triumphant, when she'd won at business, when she could show everyone that the working-class girl made good. She was on the brink: another year and she might be able to ride her horse home in victory. She had her collective and Kristy was a great addition — moving back now was bad timing for her work and her ego, but what about for her life?

She guessed she'd have to work out which was more important: her pride or the chance for love.

Chapter Thirty-Two

It'd been a brutal week, but with Sally and Kristy pulling a few all-nighters — and Taylor helping out where she could — the cards were done and delivered, two days ahead of schedule. All 1,000 of them — ten stores, 100 cards per store, and that was just for starters. If they took off, she was going to have to do it all again, but there were worse things that could happen. Sally knew this was just a toe in the water, to see if her designs sold. If they did, the sky was the limit.

And honestly, she couldn't have done it without Kristy. She was beyond grateful she hadn't slept with her, otherwise it could have been *very awkward*.

Sally had used today to catch up on all her usual orders, and she was just about to start on another batch when the ping of her laptop told her an email had arrived. It was from Luxury Gifts — and when she read it, adrenaline swept through her. She read it through once, twice, and then a third time. And every time she did, the words were the same.

Her cards were flying off the shelves, and they wanted

more for the Labor Day weekend: could she supply them by Friday?

Sally messaged Kristy and Sara, and they were both on-board. Then she emailed Luxury Gifts to say she could fulfil the order, before sitting back and calculating what it would mean. She assessed her normal orders, but she knew she could switch them up, their supply was good, they could wait.

But what it did mean was she wasn't going to be able to make it to Chicago. Again. For the fourth weekend in a row, she wasn't going to see Harriet. She'd almost forgotten what she looked like, how her lips felt. Almost.

Plus, she wasn't going to make her mom's birthday for the first time ever. But this was her dream, and she knew she had to make sacrifices. Her mom was the call she had to make first.

She took a deep breath and pressed the button.

"Hey, sweetie," her mom said, sounding buoyant.

"Hey, Mom."

"You don't sound happy."

"How can you tell?" Sally was always flummoxed by that — she'd even tried her best to put on her most upbeat voice.

"A mother knows these things," her mom replied. "Is it to do with this weekend?"

Was she psychic? "It is. I'm really sorry, but my orders have gone crazy and I'm not going to be able to make it." She let out a breath, wincing as she did. She felt like she was letting down everyone important in her life at the moment: Harriet and her mom.

"Your orders have gone crazy?"

"They have. But the catch is, they want them for the weekend. I managed to extend the deadline to Saturday, but it's going to be touch and go."

"I think that's wonderful," her mom replied.

Sally frowned. "You do? But it means I won't be there for your birthday, for the first time ever."

"I'll survive — but this is your dream coming true. You're making cards and people are loving them! That's the best birthday present for a proud mom." She paused. "So long as you send me one, of course."

"Of course," Sally replied. "I really am sorry I won't make it, though."

"You won't be the only one. I think Harriet might be sad, too," her mom replied. "Why didn't you tell me you were seeing her?"

Sally was silent for a moment: she hadn't been crowing about it because she wasn't sure where it was going herself. "Because we're not seeing each other very often," she replied. And then a wave of melancholy swept through her. She wanted to see Harriet more often, she knew that, but she just wasn't prepared to admit what that meant quite yet.

"We're doing long distance, which means we've seen each other once in five weeks. It's not ideal and I'm not sure how to change it."

"From what I saw of Harriet in the store, she seemed very positive. Some things are just meant to be. But you might have to give it a helping hand, too."

"How do you mean?"

"You could move home."

Sally might have known it would come back to that. "But my business is just taking off in New York — I can't just walk away."

"You could still do business in New York, just from Chicago. We're living in the 21st century, not the 1960s."

"Easier said than done," Sally said. But then she stopped. Did her mom have a point? "Did Harriet have a word with you?"

Her mom laughed. "She didn't need to — she had the same face she had all those years ago when she spoke about you. Her whole face lit up. Doesn't she want you to move home?"

"Of course she does, but she's not pushing it."

"I'm not either, but just think about it. It makes sense. And I know you worry about your workmates and losing them, but your family are here, Harriet would help you, and you'd meet new designers and artists. New York isn't the only place to fulfil your dreams. Just think about that." Her mom paused. "If you really want to give me the ultimate birthday gift, come home. And I know Harriet would say the same."

Chapter Thirty-Three

Harriet was late into the office. When she walked in, Joanna's face spelt thunder — and it was about to boom.

"About time you turned up," she said, pacing their brightly lit space, narrowing her eyes at her partner.

"I'm ten minutes late, take a chill pill," Harriet said, turning on her laptop and frowning at Joanna. "What's bitten your ass this morning?"

"Funny you should ask, lover girl," Joanna replied.

Harriet sat down with a thump, holding up her right hand. "Slow down, please, and tell me what this is all about. 'Lover girl'? What the hell does that mean?"

"It means you're letting your teenage crush affect your work judgement, and I want this business more than I want to help out your little girlfriend."

Whoa: where was this coming from? Why was Joanna attacking her all of sudden? She felt like she was going into battle but she had no idea why. "I'm not sure why you're bringing this up, but I don't like your tone. *At all*. My teenage crush? I assume you're talking about Sally, the woman I've been in love with for half my life."

Joanna scoffed at that. "You haven't seen her for god knows how long — half your life, actually! And then you swan in here and ask our newest client — who hasn't even signed on the dotted line yet — to make an exception for her. I can't believe you'd do that, jeopardize the contract before we've signed."

"I just thought I'd give them a heads-up, I'm trying to be proactive and give the customers what they want."

"Bullshit! You're letting your libido cloud your judgement on this one, Harriet. We've been in business for five years and never once before have I had to question you, but this time, I do. You know our criteria for business, you know we have minimum units. And you also know that we only give contracts to clients who we know can fulfil them, who have a proven track record. Yet you are now prepared to risk our reputation and put your girlfriend up for some business she may or may not be able to fulfil."

"She'll fulfil it if they give her the order," Harriet said, trying to keep calm. "I think you're overreacting."

She'd purely mentioned Sally's stuff to Ava, Dan's girlfriend, for future consideration. Plus, she'd been more than upfront about the fact Sally was just ramping up her operation and that Ava might have to give her some time to adjust. Yes, she probably wouldn't have done it with any other client, but Sally *wasn't* any other client.

"When was the last time you saw her?" Joanna asked, folding her arms across her chest, her lips pursed.

"Five weeks ago."

"But she was meant to come three weeks ago, and this Labor Day weekend, right?"

Harriet nodded her head slowly, her skin prickling with heat. "I don't see what you're getting at." She was lying, but Joanna was pissing her off.

"I'm getting at the fact she had to cancel because she couldn't cope with the order she had, and that was from a much smaller client, do you see my point?" Joanna threw her arms up in the air. "If Ava loves her work, that order will be even bigger. You won't see her, she won't be able to cope, our name will be damaged. We've always had a solid, professional relationship with all our major retailers, so why would you ask for this so early? If you're going to, at least let Sally get set up on her own properly first. Let's supply Ava with some rock-solid clients who can deliver no problem, so she knows we're not in this for a laugh."

"She knows that anyway."

"Not if you break all the rules and your girlfriend fucks it up for us. We live and die by our designers being business-savvy, *as well* as being good at what they do." She pointed a finger. "And like it or not, your girlfriend doesn't meet that criteria. This is one of the biggest deals of the past five years, and you're jeopardizing it."

"I got us this deal in the first place! I set it up!"

"Because your brother's banging her." Joanna rolled her eyes at Harriet with such contempt, Harriet gasped.

"I got the deal, that's all that matters."

"It's not signed yet."

"It will be. And what if they love Sally's stuff and Sally finds the means to produce more? What then?" Harriet was on her feet now, crossing the space between them, stopping at the edge of Jo's desk. She picked up one of her sharpened pencils, then put it down: no sharp objects nearby was best right now.

"I'd rather we had a solid run rate with them before we risk fucking up, and you would usually agree with me. But Sally is clouding your judgement."

Harriet stood there, not believing what was coming out of Joanna's mouth. Five years they'd worked together and never had a cross word. They shared the workload, they went forward together. But now it seemed like Joanna had lost the plot.

Introducing Sally at such an early stage wasn't something she'd normally do, but didn't businesses do this all the time? Sally was her girlfriend, surely that gave her some perks? And if Joanna really thought about it hard, she'd know Harriet would move hell and high water to make sure Sally could deliver.

"Look, I agree it's a little early, a bit unorthodox," Harriet said, holding Jo's gaze. "But I'll guarantee the delivery of her work. And it hasn't even happened yet, so don't jump the gun." She took a deep breath, giving Joanna the benefit of the doubt. "What's really going on here? Why are you so bothered about this?"

Joanna held up both hands and let out an exasperated yelp. "Because you're committing the cardinal sin — mixing business with pleasure. What happens when you and her blow up? What then? Do I have to deal with her solely because you can barely look at her? You're in the early stages of your relationship and you're already not seeing each other. You really think this is going to work out?"

If Harriet had tried staying calm before, it wasn't going to work now.

"What the fuck, Jo? Why are you laying into us? If you want to know the truth, I hope Ava takes Sally on and I think she will, because she's that good. And you know what? If she does, that's a huge contract for her in Chicago — a reason for her to move. And a reason why we could then work as a couple, because like you say, long distance isn't easy.

"So excuse me for being a little forward, but I didn't think you'd mind, because if I'm happy and Sally's here, I work better — and you know that's true." Harriet took a deep breath and put her hands on her hips. She hadn't even said that to herself out loud in her own head yet, but it was the truth.

"You're pinning all your hopes on love, but love doesn't last, believe me." Joanna paused, narrowing her eyes at Harriet. "And have you thought about what might happen if she doesn't come to Chicago? What then?"

"Then I move to New York, but that's a last resort." It wasn't anything Harriet had truly considered yet, but it was at the back of her mind. If Sally wouldn't move back here, going to her *had* to be another option. Because Sally was worth it, and doing long distance was making Harriet see that.

Joanna took an audible intake of breath. "You'd leave the business and everything we've worked to achieve for love, for a woman you've only just rekindled everything with?"

"It's nothing concrete yet, but yes, I might." Harriet gulped as she said it. She hadn't even said this to Sally yet, and she hoped she'd back her up. Because Sally had already made an imprint on her heart, she made her feel like the woman she always wanted to be. She made her feel fearless because when you know there's someone there to catch you, being fearless is the easiest thing in the world.

"And if I do, we'll work something out — you and I don't have to be in the same city to work together. But for me and Sally to give this a proper go, the opposite is true. We *need* to be in the same city — Sally was right all along. We just have to work out how that's going to happen. I'm not going to jeopardize our company, but I'm also not going to throw away my chance at love. There are other things in life."

"You're a fool, you know that?" Joanna said, walking to the edge of her desk, getting so close that Harriet could feel her breath on her face, see her bloodshot eyes. Had she been crying? "A damn fool. Love never works, take it from someone who knows."

Chapter Thirty-Four

Joanna didn't come into work the following day, calling in sick. Harriet wasn't going to question it. There was clearly something else going on with her, but Joanna wasn't answering her calls or texts. Harriet decided to get on: she had work to do today, and her suitcase was already by her side and ready to fly to New York to see Sally tonight. After six weeks, Harriet's heart and soul were already searching for Sally, feeling around in the dark to find their source of illumination.

These past 17 years, she'd been groping around in the dark, in clubs, in bars, in groups, trying to find Ms Right. But all along, Sally had been the yardstick they'd had to measure up to, and now it turned out the only person who could measure up in any way was Sally.

Over the past few months, her life had blown up; her carefully constructed rut had been firebombed, leaving Harriet exposed in a way she hadn't been in years. Now, all her nerves and heart wires were frayed from the emotional strain of their long-distance relationship, but if this was the only way she could have it, that was better than nothing.

Harriet's phone rang and she picked it up, reviewing an email to one of her key independent stationery stores to check she had their latest order correct. She was pretty sure she did, but she should run over the numbers one more time before she sent it off. She pulled her eyes away to see it was Joanna calling: so she *was* still talking to her.

"Hey, Jo," Harriet said, her eyes still scanning the email. She spotted a typo and held the phone between her neck and shoulder as she fixed it, waiting for Jo to start talking.

Only, Joanna didn't start talking; instead, she began to wail.

"Jo?" Harriet said, her friend now having her full attention. "What's going on, why are you crying?"

"She's… left… me…" Joanna finally managed to croak out between sobs.

Harriet sat up in her chair: she had her attention now. "Viv?" she said, knowing the answer already.

"Who else? She says I'm no fun. That all I want to do is work and save for my retirement. But I was doing it for us," Joanna said, collapsing again on the end of the phone. "I don't know what to do," she said. "I can't be single, it's not in my life plan. And I'm fucking fun when I want to be."

Harriet inhaled slowly and made a snap decision. "Take a deep breath, make yourself a coffee and I'll be there in an hour. Just let me send this email, and I'll jump in a cab. Do you have any whiskey?"

Joanna sighed heavily before replying. "Whiskey? Yes. Why?"

"Because all good sob stories need whiskey, it's the law. Has she left already?"

"Last night," Joanna replied.

"Okay, sit tight, the cavalry's coming."

"Thanks," she said, sniffing loudly in Harriet's ear. "And, H?"

"Yeah?"

"I said a lot of things yesterday that might have been coming from this, nothing to do with you and Sally. I'm sorry."

"No problem. I'll see you soon."

Harriet hung up the phone and blew out a massive raspberry, making sure to make the sound. Because now she had to make two more phone calls: one to the airline to change her flight, and one to Sally. She wasn't looking forward to making either, but she didn't have a choice.

Joanna needed her, and Joanna was her friend.

She clicked the call button and Sally answered in two rings.

"Hey, hot stuff," she said.

Harriet relaxed just hearing her voice, like honey down the line.

"Hey," she said.

"That's not the tone of voice that's going to say something happy to me today, is it?"

"It's not."

"What's up?"

"Viv's left Joanna and she's a mess. I'm going to have to fly in the morning, I'm so sorry. But I can't leave her tonight, she's too distraught."

Sally sighed before she answered, which made Harriet's heart weep.

She didn't want to be the cause of Sally sighing, but this couldn't be helped.

"I get it, it's no problem. Well, it's a long-distance problem, but this stuff happens."

"It's not a long-distance problem, it's a casual-exclusive problem."

Sally laughed at that. "It's long distance," she replied. "But you should absolutely go to your friend. It's just I had a whole dinner planned tonight before I seduced you."

"You did?" Harriet's mind went to its go-to image of Sally, naked, straddling her. And just like always, her body heated up instantly, a throbbing between her legs telling her where she felt it most.

God, she missed her.

"I did," Sally replied, bringing Harriet back to the present.

"What were we going to have?"

"For appetizers, crab ravioli. For entrée, me."

"I like the sound of that," Harriet said, licking her lips, the video still playing in her mind. "I'm really sorry."

"Can't be helped. I'll just spend the night working instead. It's what my life has become anyway." Sally gave another sigh. "Are you going to make it out at all this weekend?"

"Absolutely, I have to see you — you're not the only one who had plans that involved us naked."

"Glad to hear it," Sally replied.

"I'll call the airline now and rebook for tomorrow, I'll text you the time." Harriet paused. "Will the food keep?"

"No, but I will."

Chapter Thirty-Five

Taylor dragged Sally out that night with her and Paula — she wouldn't take no for an answer. They ended up at their favorite neighborhood bar just five minutes away from their arts collective in Queens, where everybody knew their names.

And yes, of course, that meant even Paula, not that Sally was surprised. She'd only visited twice before with Taylor, yet the bar staff were already greeting her more warmly than they ever had Sally in the past three years. She guessed it was the size of Paula's tips that gave her the edge, along with her booming presence.

The bar was called The Scoundrel, and Sally had brought Harriet for brunch after the infamous elevator incident. The same bartender was serving, wearing what looked like the same plaid shirt; the same beat was pulsing through the speakers; and the same ceiling fans were whirring overhead, spinning warm air around the dimly-lit bar. The only thing different was there was no Harriet.

Paula and Taylor were all smiles as they took their seats at the same table Sally had been perched at with

Harriet, the dark wood roughly polished under Sally's fingertips as she sat down.

She was still sad about Harriet canceling, even though she knew the reason was a good one: her friend needed her. But dammit, Sally needed her, too. And it was just another nail in the long-distance coffin, which was providing even rougher terrain for her heart.

Something had to give, she knew that.

"Okay, you need a drink, otherwise your face might stick like that and Harriet will blame us for making it so. Beer always cheers people up, doesn't it?" Paula said, slapping Sally on the back and making her cough. The woman didn't know her own strength.

"Especially on a Friday night," Taylor added, sweeping back her dyed black bangs that were so lustrous, they were almost purple. "Beer and Friday nights were made for each other." She pointed a finger at Sally. "And women who mope over other women are so unattractive."

"Thanks for the support, guys," Sally said, as the waiter took their order, Paula throwing her head back to laugh at the joke she'd just shared with him as he left.

"I'll be fine, I'm just sad she's not here tonight. I had plans."

Paula waved a hand. "She's coming in tomorrow, right?"

Sally nodded, a relieved smile infiltrating her face: that was the one thing she was happy about. This weekend wasn't a total bust, she would get to see Harriet at least.

"So you can fuck her then," Paula said with a thick grin. "Tonight though, you can get a little messy with us before I take this one home and do exactly that to her."

Taylor beamed at Paula. "Talk dirty to me, please."

Now it was Sally's turn to hold up a hand and clear her throat. "If you two continue, I'm leaving."

Paula got up to give Sally a hug. "We're on our best behavior from now on, my prudish niece," she said, holding her at arm's length. "Can I get a smile?"

Sally gave her one, hating herself as she did. Paula was still a menace.

Their drinks arrived and Sally eyed her aunt across the table. "So how are things with the two of you? Are you still thanking your lucky stars I introduced you?"

The look of lust Paula and Taylor exchanged was enough to make Sally blush: as it traveled across the table, steam rose from the surface.

"It's going well," Paula said, an unexpected hesitancy in her voice. "Wouldn't you say?" she asked Taylor.

Taylor nodded, brushing Paula's hand with the tip of her middle finger.

Paula flickered her lashes in response, and her cheeks colored.

Sally gave a little smile: underneath all that bravado, she was just like everyone else: nervous, unsure, hopeful that this woman liked her enough, at least for now.

"I'd say it's going great," Taylor said. "Although like

you, the distance is a pain in the butt. But we might be solving that soon."

"Really?" Sally said. "How so?"

Taylor shrugged, like the next thing that tumbled out of her mouth was the most natural thing in the world to say. "I'm thinking of moving to Chicago."

Sally's mouth dropped open.

Actually dropped open.

"You're moving to Chicago? You never said anything to me! When did you decide this?"

She shrugged. "I've been thinking about it for a while."

"But you've only been together two months!" Sally said. She couldn't believe her ears: Taylor was moving to Chicago just like that, as if it were the easiest thing in the world.

Which made her stop and think: was it?

"Nine weeks, actually," Taylor said, shrugging. "And you know, I'm not getting any younger and this feels… right. It feels like I've known Paula forever, and there's no reason to hold back. You only live once and we might all die tomorrow."

"That's what first attracted me to Taylor — her optimism," Paula said, letting out a bark of laughter with the obligatory head throw.

Was Taylor saying this was it for her and Paula? They were going to live happily ever after? Sally wasn't sure if she was just incredulous at the pace of their decisions, or just jealous she couldn't make them herself. Taylor was naturally decisive, unlike her: when Taylor saw an opportunity, she went for it. It's the reason her wallpaper business had taken off, whereas other designers had fallen by the wayside.

Paula reached over then, laying a hand on Sally's arm, pushing her beer in front of her. "Take a sip and a breath. You've heard of people moving cities before, right?"

Sally took a slug of beer: she needed it. "I have, but this is kinda sudden, isn't it?"

Taylor shrugged. "I can work from wherever, I'm not tied to a city. And if I need to come back to New York, it's just a plane ride." She glanced at Paula now, stroking her hand again. "And the past few weeks have opened my eyes, I guess. You don't meet people you want to be with that often, so when you do, I think it's worth pursuing."

"As do I," Paula agreed, taking Taylor's hand and kissing it gently.

Well, well. This was not the way Sally had thought this evening would pan out. "Congratulations," she said, looking between them. "I just wish I could be so decisive."

"You can — just make a decision and do it." Paula snapped her fingers to illustrate her point. "It really is that easy."

"It is?"

"Yes," Paula said. "What's holding you here?"

Sally hesitated. "Work — I can't just pick up and leave. Plus I have friends here, and my apartment's here."

"But one of your friends is moving to Chicago."

"I only just found that out."

"But that's another reason to move. And I can't believe it's just work that's holding you back. That doesn't make sense — you can work wherever you want to." Paula paused, cocking her head. "Why did you leave Chicago in the first place?"

Sally fixed her gaze on the wall behind Paula, which was advertising a beer festival in the bar next month. "I guess to spread my wings, get away from Chicago. I went back after graduation, but it got stifling after a while."

Taylor cleared her throat. "Bullshit."

"Taaaaaylor," Sally said, a warning note in her voice. But then she blew out a long breath as she realized lying to her aunt was futile in this situation, when one of her best friends was sitting next to her, who knew everything about her. She was going to have to tell the truth, wasn't she?

"Okay," Sally said. "I moved to get away from my ex, Casey, who'd just dumped me. And to spread my wings — I always wanted to try New York, and thought I'd have more opportunity to start a business here."

"And did it pay off?" Paula asked, sipping her drink.

"I've done okay."

"But Chicago might work, too."

Sally nodded. "It might." She'd often wondered if she'd made the right move, coming to New York, where there were more options, but also more competition. Would being a bigger fish in a smaller pond be better?

"So the real reason you left was to get away from your ex. Which was how long ago?"

"Three and a half years."

"And you're over her?"

Sally scrunched up her face. "Absolutely — I was over her the moment she walked out the door."

"So you've stopped running?"

"I wasn't running," Sally replied, her voice deadpan.

"You were running, don't kid yourself," Paula said, raising an eyebrow as she spoke. "But you have to stop running at some point. Even I've decided it's time to try the settling thing. Settling down, not *settling*. And if you're not running from Casey anymore, you should do that, too. Unless Casey is still dictating your life?"

Sally shook her head decisively. If there was one thing she was sure of, it was that. "Casey's my past," she said.

"And what's Harriet?"

"My future." And as she said the words, a glow rattled through her, a surety of how true those words were.

"Do you need more of a reason than that?" Paula replied, giving Sally a look. "Just think about it — and if you're worried about work, moving might open up new pathways, rather than close them. Especially with me and Harriet on your side."

"It's not what you know, it's who you know," Sally said, a ruffle of her old socialist principles sliding down her body. She didn't want any special favors, she wanted to make it on her own. However, she had to admit, getting help was a welcome change.

Paula grinned at Sally, slapping her on the arm again.

"Talk about it with Harriet when she comes tomorrow." She paused. "In between all the fucking, of course."

Sally rolled her eyes at her aunt.

Paula roared with laughter. "You're so easy, just like your dad," she said, giving Sally a wink. "Plus, I'm just buying some apartments near where I am, so you could rent one of those from me. And I might have another proposal for you, too, if you decide to move."

"What's that?"

"Say you'll move to Chicago and I'll let you know."

"I'm not deciding now."

"Spoilsport," Taylor said. "We could have decided together."

"I need to talk it over with Harriet first. And in the meantime, I need another drink. All this talking is thirsty work."

"So it seems," Paula replied, flagging down the waiter like he was an old friend.

Sally glanced at Taylor, who gave her a wink.

"You're really just going? Just like that?" She was still having trouble getting her head around Taylor's plan.

But Taylor just nodded. "Sometimes, you have to bite the bullet and just go for it. When it comes to you and Harriet, what have you got to lose?"

Chapter Thirty-Six

Sally woke up the next morning feeling like her head had been burgled. Her brain rattled in her skull when she moved, rolling slowly with her movements, like a marble in a children's boardgame. Damn Paula and Taylor: by the end of the night, tequila shots were in place as they toasted to their new lives in Chicago. Hang on, had she agreed to move to Chicago without telling Harriet first? She had no idea.

She made it out to her kitchen and stood glugging water straight from the bottle, the cool liquid soothing her dry shell. She should go for a run to shake this hangover, because she didn't want to be broken for Harriet. She'd learned at university that exercise was the best cure for her hangovers, so before she could talk herself out of it, she ate an overripe banana from her fruit bowl, then pulled on her shorts, T-shirt and sneakers, and headed out.

At only 9:30, the streets of Queens were quiet. Harriet wasn't due in till 1pm, which meant she had plenty of time to have a shower, tidy the apartment and get ready. The steady rhythm of her feet pounding the sidewalk and her headache pounding in her skull matched up perfectly as her feet took her past her local Jewish deli with its excellent bread, past the florist, past the thrift shop she'd got her perfect jeans in, and into the local park.

Overhead, the sky was a brilliant blue and cloudless, like nothing could break the spell it had over the city. The Bald Cypress trees at the park gate were bulging with ferns, and in the distance, a dog barked continuously. Straight ahead, the melting gray pathway was clear, save for a lone woman sitting on one of the red benches, reading a James Patterson novel.

Would she miss this park? This city? Maybe a little, but she knew the seeds of discontent had been scattered.

What Paula had said last night made sense. There was nothing holding her in New York but herself and her own fears. Was she really worried that Harriet would walk again like last time? If she was honest, she was hiding behind that excuse. They were different people now; things had moved on. Plus, Taylor was moving to Chicago having known Paula for five seconds, so what was Sally waiting for?

She looked up the tree-lined path back to the park entrance and took a deep breath. Which was exactly what she needed to do when it came to making a decision and moving to New York. She had to take a deep breath, put one foot in front of the other and run down the path. Make the leap, and hope a net appeared.

Deep down inside, she knew the net was named Harriet.

She got home 15 minutes later, gasping for breath, her cell ringing when she got in the door. She ran into her bedroom, picking up the call before it went to voicemail. It was Harriet.

"Hey," Sally said, leaning over, still catching her breath.

"You sound like you're going to die," Harriet replied.

"No, just got in from a run." Still wheezing.

"Okay, just listen, I'll talk."

She didn't like the wince she could hear in Harriet's tone, but she was too breathless to respond.

"I'm not coming today because Dad's had a relapse." Harriet paused, sounding like she was collecting herself. "I'm in the car, on the way to the hospital now, so I don't know much more. But what I do know is that I can't make it again and I'm so sorry."

"Fucking hell," Sally wheezed, fear gripping her whole. "You don't know anything?"

"Only that he was fine yesterday, but there's been some kind of complication with the internal stitches, I don't know any more than that. Mom says they're going to need to operate, but apart from that, I'm in the dark."

"Shit." Sally paused. "What can I do? Can I do anything?" She felt so helpless. She wanted to be there for Harriet, but yet, she was stuck in New York. It was beginning to be a somewhat recurring theme, wasn't it?

Harriet sighed. "I'd like a hug, but doing that over the phone is a little hard, isn't it?"

"Especially when you're driving," she said, wanting nothing more than to do just that. "But leave it with me, I'll see what I can do."

Silence on the other end of the line.

"Harriet," Sally said.

"Yes?" Harriet's voice wobbled when she replied.

"I'm so sorry, and I'm going to be there for you, okay?" The steady beat of her blood in her veins was like a soundtrack to this moment.

More silence, followed by a sniffle at the other end. "I know you will mentally, but I wish you could be here physically, too. Just to squeeze my hand and tell me he's going to be okay."

Sally's heart lurched for a second time. "Call me when you get to the hospital and give me an update," she said. "And he's going to be okay."

Sally rang off, then immediately ran to the living room, fired up her tablet and began looking at flights to Chicago.

Harriet needed her and she was going to be by her side as soon as she possibly could.

Chapter Thirty-Seven

Her mom was pacing the corridor when Harriet arrived. When she saw her daughter, she fell into her outstretched arms in a heap. This was not normal mother behavior, but then, this was no normal day, was it?

"Mom?" Harriet said, over her shoulder to thin air. Her mom was still clinging to her back, her fingers gripping Harriet through her shirt. "Let's go and sit down and you can tell me everything the doctor has said so far."

She pulled her mom over to two vacant white plastic chairs, nailed to the floor in the striplight-studded corridor. They sat side by side, her mom still holding one of her hands, squeezing it before she spoke. A small girl walked by, her hair limp, a dark-haired doll hanging from her hand. She was clutching the hand of a teenage boy whose face was ghostly white. Harriet wondered what nightmare they were currently living through, too.

"He was fine when he went to bed, but then he woke up in the middle of the night with some pain. He thought it was indigestion, so he went back to sleep, but then it came again and he just got worse. Eventually, I called a doctor, they called an ambulance, and here we are. He's being taken in for emergency surgery — they think something's got infected and it's causing a blockage."

She gave a crumpled wail before sitting forward, her head over her knees in the brace position. "I thought he was out of the woods, I thought we could start living our lives again soon. I can't lose him, Harriet," she added, her voice tiny, the size of a pea. "Not when we've just fallen in love all over again."

Harriet curled an arm around her mom and pulled her close. "You're not going to lose him, he's a fighter. Plus, he's young, he's got at least another 20 years." She almost convinced herself as she kissed the top of her mom's head. And they'd just fallen in love all over again? Her dad's heart had to recover, otherwise her mom's would be broken for good.

"Where's Daniel?" she asked as her mom pulled away, straightening up and sitting back in her chair.

"He's on his way — he was staying over at Ava's lake house last night, so he's got a bit further to travel." She paused. "Weren't you supposed to be seeing Sally this weekend?"

Harriet nodded, closing her eyes. "Yes, but it doesn't matter. I called her, she understands."

Her mom stared straight ahead. "Sorry for messing up your plans, but it's your father's fault."

"I'll remember to tell him off if he pulls through."

"If?" Her mom turned in her seat.

"*When* he pulls through." Harriet let her mouth curl into a smile to try to lighten the situation. "How long is the surgery?"

"About five hours. Apparently when they open you up again, it takes time."

"I imagine," Harriet replied. "But it's going to be okay — he'll just take a little longer to recover, that's all."

Harriet's phone beeped: she got it out of her pocket and checked it, and when she saw the message, she couldn't help the grin that spread across her face.

"Is that from Sally?" her mom asked.

Harriet nodded.

"I thought so. You have that look about you. It reminds me of when I met your father all those years ago."

Harriet's bottom lip trembled when she heard that, but she held it together. Her mom was comparing their relationship to her own, and that meant *so* much. It meant that finally, after all these years, they were connecting about what mattered most in the world to Harriet, and her mom was valuing it just as much as Harriet.

Her mom reached for her hand again, and Harriet decided to stop thinking it was weird.

"I know I haven't always been supportive of you and your girlfriends, and I'm sorry. I should have been, it was just… different and a little hard. It's not that I disapprove, it's more I wasn't brought up that way. We didn't talk about our sex lives, our partners. In my day, you just had a boyfriend and got married, because it was what you did. You didn't think about having a girlfriend because it wasn't an option." She paused. "Not that I ever wanted one."

"If this is you coming out to me, it's a very weird time to do it," Harriet said, a wry smile on her face.

"You know what I mean," her mom said, with a smile. "I just never expected to have a gay daughter, that's all. You surprised me. But if Sally makes you happy — and I think she does — then I'm fully behind you. Life's too short not to be happy, isn't it?" She put a hand on Harriet's face then, gazing at her with love in her watery eyes. "I love you, Harriet. I hope you know that."

Fucking hell, today was just too much. A tear trickled down Harriet's face as a wave of love crashed through her, putting her arm around her mom. "I love you, too," she whispered into her hair.

After a few moments, her mom pulled back, rolling her shoulders, sitting up. She looked perplexed, as if she couldn't believe she'd just been so emotional.

"What did Sally say on her text?" her mom asked.

"She's getting on a plane this afternoon, and she's coming straight here." The grin that had started in Harriet's heart made its way onto her face. She'd told Sally she wished she were here, and Sally had made her dream come true.

Now, her dad just had to pull through.

"That's good, she should be here, because she's part of

the family now," her mom said, letting out an enormous sigh. "I just hope your dad will still be here by the time she arrives, too."

"You and me both."

Chapter Thirty-Eight

Sally dragged her suitcase up the hospital ramp and nearly ran straight into a gurney with a patient on it. She turned sideways just in time, slamming into the doorway as she did. With pain coursing through her left arm, she took a deep breath. This wasn't a time to injure herself: she needed to be strong for Harriet.

She arrived at the coronary unit five minutes later, and saw Harriet first, deep in conversation with her mom. Mrs Locke, who Sally hadn't seen since *that* summer. Suddenly, she felt like a teenager again, diminished in Mrs Locke's presence, just like always.

But when Harriet looked up at her, that stopped. Because perhaps before, she'd felt insecure around both of them: Mrs Locke for her abrupt manner and her wealth, Harriet for her confidence and ease with the world around her. Plus, back then, she hadn't thought she was good enough for Harriet Locke.

She didn't believe that anymore. Harriet's eyes shone, radiating something — dare she say love? — across the room as she strode toward Sally, taking her in her arms and kissing her earlobe when her lips landed there.

Harriet fell into the warmth her arms provided. "You came," she said, a hitch in her voice when she spoke.

"Of course I came," Sally replied, pulling her close. When she opened her eyes, Harriet's mom was walking toward her, a gentle smile on her face, one Sally didn't recognize. In fact, in all the time she knew her before, Sally didn't think she'd ever seen Mrs Locke smile.

"Sally, so good of you to come, I know Harriet was thrilled," she said, as Harriet let Sally go. "And it's lovely to see you, too, after so many years."

Sally held out a hand, but Mrs Locke bypassed it and pulled her into a firm hug. Sally was pretty sure that wasn't Mrs Locke behavior, either.

"I'm sorry to hear about Mr Locke — how is he?"

"He made it through surgery, now we just have to wait."

"I'm sure he'll pull through."

"He better, there are a ton of people out here waiting on him," Harriet replied. She turned and grabbed Sally's suitcase, the orange ribbon still attached. She gave Sally a golden smile. "You still keep that on? After everything?"

Sally gave her a grin. "I kinda think of it as my good luck charm now, so it's going nowhere. It led me back to you, didn't it?" she said, whispering the final bit in Harriet's ear as Mrs Locke walked back to her chair.

"And please," Harriet's mom said over her shoulder,

"call me Judy. Mrs Locke sounds like an old lady and I hope I'm not quite there yet."

"Judy it is," Sally replied.

"Sally McCall, you sly dog, sneaking up and stealing my sister's heart for a second time!" The voice that spoke those words was deep, and Sally knew just who it belonged to: Daniel. In all the commotion of getting her flight and being here for Harriet, she'd forgotten that today would involve Daniel, too.

Sally took a breath, getting her bearings, pushing aside the old Sally in favor of the new. The Locke family were going to be in her future, so she'd better get used to being around them.

"It's good to see you, Dan," Sally said, as a third member of the Locke clan took her in his arms and gave her a squeeze.

"I didn't expect to see you here," Daniel added. "Not that it's not a lovely surprise."

Sally smiled. "Harriet was supposed to come to New York, but your dad changed our plans."

Daniel introduced his girlfriend, Ava, the one Harriet had told Sally about.

Sally made sure to put on her best smile to greet the woman, who turned out to be a blonde bombshell, her hair streaked with sunshine. Daniel had done well.

Ava shook her hand enthusiastically. "Sally — you're the card designer, right?"

Sally nodded her head with confidence. "That's me."

"I love your designs. I know Harriet has told me you might take a little time to get set up, but I'd love to trial some of your cards in our shops. But we'll talk about it another time, this isn't ideal," she said, dropping Sally's hand. "Just to let you know."

Sally was awestruck: this woman wanted her designs and she was a buyer for a major store. "I'd love to do you some samples. But yes, let's talk another time."

"Excellent," Ava replied, smiling.

"Now you're here, you sit with Mom and we'll go and get some coffees," Harriet said to Daniel and Ava, guiding them over to her mother, who they both greeted with hugs and kisses. "We'll be back."

Harriet moved Sally's suitcase next to her mom, then took her hand in hers, and Sally could only smile.

"So he's out of surgery?" Sally asked, as her feet squeaked on the cream linoleum underfoot, two nurses walking by in blue scrubs, one of them laughing at whatever the other had just said. The hospital smelt of disinfectant and death, just like Sally remembered when she came to visit her granddad before he died.

Harriet nodded. "He is. Now we just have to wait for him to wake up and see how the surgery has gone."

"They won't know till then?"

Harriet shook her head. "It's a waiting game, but they came out smiling, so we have to assume that's a good thing. They do this every day, right?"

They turned a corner and walked into a small cafeteria

with around 20 white tables and chairs bunched together, as if conferring. Harriet ordered coffee and five doughnuts, which they took to a corner seat and sat down.

"Thanks for coming, it really does mean a lot," she said, taking Sally's hand over the table. "This weekend has been bad enough without not seeing you, too."

"I agree," Sally said. Seeing Harriet's face was making everything better. "How was Joanna yesterday?"

Harriet exhaled. "A mess. I think she's going to need some time off, although she's insisting she doesn't. But by the time I left, she was calmer. She actually said that seeing me so happy had made her rethink her relationship anyway. In the end, she was just pissed she hadn't been the one to end it. So she's in shock and she's got hurt pride, which is never a good look."

"So her girlfriend just up and left?"

"Uh-huh. Apparently got a better offer from someone else after four years together. Just goes to show you never know what's around the corner. If this weekend has taught me anything, it's that."

"I know what you mean," Sally said, taking the lid off her coffee cup and blowing. It was still too hot to drink. "It's also taught me that long-distance relationships don't work, for one thing."

Harriet's face fell, the color draining from it swiftly. "If you're breaking up with me, this is a really inopportune time."

Sally smiled, giving a short laugh. "Yes, I fly all the way out here to break up with you. That's my style."

Harriet still didn't look convinced. "I hope not."

Sally leaned over the table and pressed her lips to Harriet's. The world stopped for a couple of seconds as their lips reconnected, before Sally eased herself back into her seat, light-headed from the contact.

That was what you didn't get over a phone line.

"I've missed you so much." Sally brought Harriet's hand to her lips and kissed it. "Which is why this can't go on. I went out last night with Paula and Taylor, and we talked. About us, about this," she said, moving her finger back and forth.

Harriet nodded. "I've been doing a lot of thinking, too."

Sally held up a hand. "Let me finish. I went for a run this morning and it all became crystal clear. And this happening has only made it more so."

"You're not making any sense, by the way."

"Sorry," Sally said, laughing. "What I'm trying to say is, I'm moving back home, to be with you." She brought Harriet's fingers to her mouth again, kissing them gently.

"I love you, it's that simple. I always have and I don't want to waste any more time fighting it." The words slipped out with ease, and an all-encompassing fire spread through Sally, one that was always there where Harriet was concerned.

Harriet bit her lip, her face breaking into a widescreen, dimple-led smile. "You love me?"

Sally thought her heart might burst with love as she nodded. "I really do — you're under my skin." Sally reached over and kissed her again, sighing as she sat down. "You always have been."

"And you're moving?" Harriet's mouth dropped open now, as if she'd only just realized what Sally had said.

Sally nodded again.

"But I was going to move to New York," Harriet said, shaking her head. "It was one of the possibilities Jo and I talked about last night. She's rethinking her whole life strategy after Viv and can't decide whether she wants to take the beach house now and work remotely, or carry on with our plan. But for me, it's become increasingly clear over the past couple of months that you're where I want to be. And if that means moving, I'd handle it. You're more important than anything else."

Sally grinned, happiness filling her to the brim. "That's sweet, but it makes no sense for you to move there — everything you have is here. And most of what I love is here, too, including you. And situations like today make me realize I need to be close by, to be able to be with you in stressful times. It's what girlfriends do."

Harriet nodded. "Girlfriend. I don't think I've heard you say that before." She paused, searching for something in Sally's eyes. "And by the way, I love you, too."

Sally breathed out a sigh of relief, laughing at the same time. "Thank god for that, otherwise I just made a total fool of myself."

Harriet gave her a grin. "You're the most beautiful fool I've ever met," she said, kissing Sally's hand. "And

I can't believe we're declaring our love in a hospital cafeteria."

Sally looked around at the drab walls, the chipped tables, the scuffed plastic chairs. "It's got a certain something, hasn't it?"

"It's got you, and that's the most important thing."

Sally kissed Harriet again: now she'd started, she couldn't stop. "I can't wait to get home and be naked with you, either," she said, not able to stop blurting that out now either, because Harriet's declaration was still coursing through her like a sunbeam.

"Believe me, I can't either," Harriet said, kissing her hand again, before staring into her eyes. "Prepare yourself when we get home."

Sally shifted in her seat: Harriet's words had reached inside her, and she could almost feel Harriet's fingers doing the same, taking her completely. "I'm prepared," she replied.

But then Sally saw a cloud cross Harriet's face. "One thing, though — if you move, I don't want you to end up hating me. *You* have to want to do this, too — you can't just move here for me."

"It's not just for you. This is for me, too. My mom's going to be over the moon, as is my dad. As for Paula, she's thrilled; Taylor, too."

Harriet raised an eyebrow. "Taylor is thrilled to see you go?"

Sally grinned. "Yes, but only because she's coming, too."

"To Chicago?"

"To give her and Paula a try."

Harriet sat back. "Wow."

"That's what I said," Sally replied. "But it's not just about them — it's more about us. And the only thing holding me in New York was work, and I can do that from anywhere."

"But you love your collective, you tell me that all the time. They're your people."

"They are, and I'm going to miss them all so much. But I can make another here, I'm sure. And I need to be with you, that's the most important thing. Not work. Even though I'll probably be working all the time, just so we're clear."

Harriet smiled at that. "Totally clear."

"But even if I'm working late, I can still see you, crawl into bed with you, and wake up with you. That makes a big difference."

"A huge one," Harriet replied, taking Sally's hand in hers. "And I love the thought of waking up with you, have I said that?"

"You haven't."

"I have now." She took a deep breath. "This weekend has been so weird in so many ways — Joanna falling apart, Dad getting sick, Mom acting like a hugging machine — weird. But you telling me you love me and you're moving to Chicago?"

"Unbelievably weird?" Sally asked, laughing.

"The least weird thing in my life," Harriet said. "Thanks for bringing some happiness to the weirdness."

"You're welcome," Sally replied. "Now shall we get these coffees back to your family before they go cold?"

Chapter Thirty-Nine

Harriet drove back to her apartment ultra-fast as usual, but this time, Sally didn't complain. They'd gone for dinner with Harriet's family before heading back to the hospital, Harriet's dad groggy but awake, his progress steady.

When he'd fallen back to sleep and the nurses had told them to go home, Daniel and Ava had driven back with Harriet's mom, with Harriet and Sally agreeing to pick her up in the morning.

All of which gave them one precious night to themselves, and Sally was determined to make the most of it. She'd been waiting long enough, and she was sure this dessert would be the sweetest she'd ever tasted.

Minutes later, Harriet screeched into the parking space in her underground car park and jumped out, grabbing Sally's suitcase before locking her car. Then they were in the elevator, Harriet giving Sally an intense stare, her head leaning against the mirrored wall.

"That was some day," Harriet said, as the floors slipped by at speed.

"You can say that again." Sally stepped into Harriet's space and ran a finger down her cheek. "You're gorgeous, you know that?"

"I could say the same about you," Harriet said, leaning forward and pressing a kiss to Sally's lips.

Sally sunk into it willingly.

"You were amazing today, with your mom, too," Sally added when Harriet pulled back, her face still inches from hers. "You were really there for her."

"I think things are changing in the Locke family, and only for the better," Harriet replied, kissing Sally one more time. "Like my life in general."

When the elevator arrived at their floor, Harriet grabbed Sally's hand, pulling her down the wide gray hall. Sally had a flashback to Harriet pulling her up the stairs in her lake house, and grinned. She was always happy when her hand was in Harriet's.

Harriet dumped the suitcase as Sally walked over to the picture window and looked out over Lake Michigan, the sky a brilliant blue once more. She was standing in Harriet's apartment as if she hadn't been aching to be here for the past few hours. As if there wasn't already a pulsing between her legs. As if she didn't want Harriet to press her against the glass and take her right away.

And even though she wasn't facing Harriet, she could feel her energy, and she hoped she could read her mind.

Harriet didn't disappoint, stepping up behind Sally and nibbling the back of her neck. "I've wanted you since you stepped into the hospital and into my arms," she said, pulling at Sally's red-and-white stripey shirt and tugging it over her head.

"I know," Sally replied, as Harriet unclipped her bra, letting it fall to the floor before cupping her breasts from behind, claiming Sally as her own.

Sally had never been more happy to be claimed in her life.

"Drop your jeans, I want you naked and against the window," Harriet whispered into her ear, her breath hot.

Sally wilted, her booming desire for Harriet etched into every breath she took. She wobbled as she stepped out of her jeans and boy shorts; her heartbeat was so elevated, it was almost colliding with the stars.

Harriet pressed herself into Sally's exposed back, her hand reaching down and cupping Sally's bare butt cheeks, before moving between the legs, groaning as she connected with Sally's wet heat.

A torrent of desire rattled through Sally as Harriet pressed home her point, her hand hot and firm. Sally pressed down, wanting more, but instead Harriet swept both hands up Sally's butt and back, her skilled tongue following every step, before her teeth claimed the back of Sally's neck.

Sally let out a moan. This was what Harriet's earlier heated stare had been promising, and she was delivering with style.

And then Harriet's hand was between her legs again, cupping her, pressing, honing. She heard a hitch in Harriet's breathing as she moved a hand through Sally's silky heat, and then Sally shuddered, biting her lip as Harriet slipped one finger slowly inside her, closely followed by another.

"Oh my god," she panted, as Harriet placed her other hand on Sally's butt and then slowly began to fuck her from behind.

"The thought of doing this to you again has been tormenting me for the past few weeks," Harriet whispered in her ear. "I can't believe we're finally here."

Sally closed her eyes as she felt a gushing in between her legs, Harriet's words sending shockwaves down to her very core. She couldn't get enough of Harriet: she spread her legs, pushing her butt out, letting Harriet have the easiest access possible.

Over the past six weeks, this is what had been in her mind: Harriet taking her. So as Harriet sunk into her, Sally let herself go completely, surrendering to them, to their love, to coming home. Because in the end, this really was where she belonged: back with Harriet, back to her home.

And Sally had no doubt that this moment, *right here*, was home.

She rolled her head back as Harriet fucked her harder, letting out a loud moan as her orgasm started deep inside, starting out with a light drumbeat, before quickly progressing to a drum solo, coming to a crescendo any minute now.

Sally was close, so close. She could feel it in her bones, in her veins. She could feel it *everywhere*.

So when Harriet slipped her other hand round the front and over Sally's swollen clit, she bucked her hips, with no idea what to focus on anymore. Harriet was behind her, in front of her, in her very soul.

As Sally looked out over Lake Michigan and came in an avalanche of pleasure, she shouted out Harriet's name, wanting to light it up over the water for everyone to see, so the whole city knew how fabulous her girlfriend was.

Because she was, inside and out.

Especially when she was inside Sally.

When Harriet withdrew her fingers moments later, Sally gasped. But then, with her other arm around Sally's waist, Harriet trailed her index finger — the one that had just been inside Sally — up Sally's neck and over Sally's chin, making Sally's insides quiver. When she pressed that finger to Sally's lips, moving her head level with Sally's, Sally wilted again.

"Look at me," Harriet said, her voice soft but firm.

Sally gushed on the spot, doing as she was told.

"Take it into your mouth," Harriet said, her jaw set in determined fashion, which only sent Sally's levels of want even higher.

The erotic scent of herself was making her even wetter, and when Sally took Harriet's finger inside her mouth and moved her tongue around it, she had no idea this level of desire even existed: it was beyond anything Sally had experienced before. Harriet added another finger and Sally sucked it hungrily, her lust overflowing.

Judging from the lust pooling in Harriet's eyes, it was working for her, too.

After a few more seconds, Harriet withdrew. Then Sally watched as her fingers traveled south, Harriet plunging them back into Sally, fucking her hard, making her come all over again.

By the time Harriet had her arm around Sally's waist for a second time, Sally's mind was blank, her body only experiencing pleasure in the here and now, nothing else. Harriet had depleted her utterly, gloriously.

Sally waited a few moments to get her breath back, as Harriet kissed her shoulder blades. She eventually composed her thoughts, before sinking back into Harriet's arms. "You think we could go to your bed now? Otherwise I might collapse on the floor right here." She leaned her head back and kissed Harriet's cheek lightly.

"Your wish is my command," Harriet said, scooping Sally up into her arms and carrying her to the bedroom, making Sally's stomach churn with delight. Not only was Harriet damn sexy, she was also swoonful.

"When did you turn into my knight in shining armor?" she asked, her words slurred as if she'd been drinking. Which in a way she had: drinking in all the love Harriet had to give. She was drunk on the stuff.

But when her back hit the bed and Harriet was stripping off her black attire in front of her, revealing her tanned, toned physique and her gorgeous breasts with her nipples already erect, Sally suddenly became more alert, more awake.

How could she fail to with Harriet naked in front of her?

She held out a hand and pulled Harriet onto the bed, kneeling up beside her, running her hands over Harriet's soft, smooth skin. Sally had long ago learned to live with her milky complexion, but Harriet was something else altogether, like she was born tanned. Sally recalled Harriet telling her she had some Mediterranean blood in her background, which would explain it. Sally was transfixed, Harriet's body so different to her own.

As Sally's mouth traveled down Harriet's neck, her tongue licking a trail down to her breasts and her nipples, she breathed in the scent of her: Harriet was quickly becoming one of her favorite smells. She took her right nipple into her mouth and Harriet sucked in a breath: her nipples had always been sensitive, Sally remembered that.

And then Sally turned Harriet around and pushed her down on her back, with a sudden, overwhelming thirst for her.

Harriet groaned as Sally's polished hair caressed her stomach, her mouth traveling south, settling over Harriet's core.

"Spread your legs for me," Sally said, her voice gravelly, speaking right over Harriet's pussy, knowing her breath was right where it needed to be.

Harriet groaned again, but complied.

And when she did, Sally swelled with desire, licking her lips: she was *desperate* to taste her, to be inside her. Sally ran her tongue up the inside of Harriet's thighs, before pulling her closer to her mouth. She parted Harriet's legs further with both hands, before using them to open her lips and flick her tongue through her liquid heat, then back down. Slowly, tantalizingly.

Harriet squirmed above her, and it was taking every ounce of naked ambition Sally had not to bury herself in Harriet, to bring her to quick climax, to proclaim her undying love for this woman again and again. But she wanted to take it slow, to give Harriet the best she had.

Sally swirled her tongue around Harriet's clit with sweet, teasing precision. When she eventually pressed her tongue flat and swept it north in grand, arching strokes, as if she were painting a masterpiece on Harriet, her girlfriend cried out, her body stiffening as Sally got into her groove.

When Sally arced two fingers into her lover, still lavishing her clit with attention, Harriet tightened her grip on Sally's hair. And as Sally swept Harriet over the edge with her grandstand finish, hot, bright lights danced in Sally's soul as Harriet came all over her fingers in a hot rush of passion, studding the air around them with her cries.

Sally never wanted it to stop, never wanted *them* to stop. They had so much time to make up for, it was dizzying.

Desire drenched her body as she gave Harriet another crescendo, before her lover stilled her hand and her tongue.

Only then did Sally crawl up Harriet's body and grind into her, both of them breathing heavily.

"Kiss me," Sally panted, only vaguely aware of where she was and who she was.

Harriet brought her head up and did as she was told, with Sally plunging her tongue into Harriet's mouth, biting her lip, trying to envelop as much of her lover as humanly possible.

When she pulled back, dazed and confused, she let a languid smile stroll on to her face, kissing Harriet again. "I love you," she said, simply, staring into Harriet's now dark green eyes, her face red, her breathing sketchy. "With everything I am, I love you."

"I love you, too," Harriet replied. "I always have and I always will."

Sally crumpled at those words, her heart cartwheeling with happiness.

She was home, at last.

Chapter Forty

Six weeks later, Sally stood in her old room: 34 years old and back in her childhood bedroom, with her mom downstairs watching TV. If she closed her eyes, it was as if the intervening years had never happened. And yet, she knew they had, and she was glad — yes, even the bad ones. Because all of those years had brought her to where she was now, and today she was happier than she'd ever dreamed. Who would have thought that meant coming home again?

She was staying with her mom while she got settled and found an apartment; she hadn't wanted to move straight in with Harriet, she didn't want to move too fast when they hadn't talked about it. Her mom wanted her to move close by, but that was never going to happen: it was too far from the center and from Harriet. Sally still had to decide where she was going to live, but Paula had told her not to make any plans until she'd heard about her proposition. Sally was meeting Harriet, Paula and Taylor later, so she guessed she'd find out the big secret then.

One thing she knew: she was going to stay clear of

Avondale, the area where Casey lived. Sally knew she might still bump into her wherever she was, but she'd rather not move next door if she could help it.

Saying goodbye to the collective had been hard: she'd built a life there over the past few years, had come to see these people as her alternative family. She'd been sad, but also excited to get on with the next phase of her life: the one that came with the great unknowns of love and money.

It turned out, in the end, Sally didn't have to choose between them — both were being thrust upon her whether she liked them or not. She was still insisting Paula's money was a loan and every time she did, Paula rolled her eyes. She was getting used to her aunt's personality, but sometimes, she was still a little overwhelming.

A car horn outside broke her thoughts and she scrambled for her bag, checking her make-up in her old mirror. She was getting a huge sense of déjà-vu, but then, this whole house was a melting pot of that.

"Sally!" her mom called, as if she were deaf and hadn't heard. "Harriet's out front beeping her horn!"

Sally yanked open her bedroom door and clattered down the stairs, looking around for a hairbrush as she descended.

"It's cool," she said, opening the door and waving to Harriet. She always had been averse to leaving her car, and nothing had changed. She waved her hand, telling Harriet to come in, but she didn't move.

"Where are you going?" her mom asked, trying to make her voice as light as she could.

"I told you — we're meeting Paula and Taylor for dinner. Taylor just moved here this week, too, so it's a celebration."

"Right," her mom said. "You can tell Harriet to come in you know. She's not a teenager anymore and I don't bite."

Sally smiled. "I totally agree and I promise to work on her etiquette. But we're running late, so you mind if I run?"

Her mom shook her head. "Of course not," she said. "Will you be home later?"

Sally shook her head. "I'm staying at Harriet's tonight, so I'll see you tomorrow." She gave her mom a hug and an extra squeeze. Having her daughter back in town meant her mom wanted to spend all her time with her, but Sally was having to put her foot down. "I'll see you then, okay? Love you."

"Love you, too, sweetie."

* * *

"So what do you think?"

They were back in the Links Tap Room in Wicker Park, home to Harriet and Paula, new stomping ground for Sally and Taylor. The TV screens in the bar were showing its latest beer arrivals and a group of bearded men at the end table were studying them like they were a racing-form guide. Craft beer was now a serious business.

"Tell me again," Sally said, frowning. Ever since they'd arrived, Paula had been a blur of armography, like she was auditioning to star in a remake of Madonna's "Vogue".

"Listen this time, okay?" Paula said, getting ready with her arms.

Sally put a hand on her beer to hold it in place.

"I've seen a building that I want to turn into an artist collective, just like the one you had in Queens. I'll get someone in to project-manage the set-up, then when it's done, you and Taylor can move in, get some more artists to move in, too, and we can design it anyway you want."

Sally pursed her lips: was Paula for real? This kind of thing didn't just drop in her lap every day. Only, since she'd come back into her life, Paula had acted like her fairy godmother. Paula had led her back to Harriet, and ultimately, back home. It was almost enough to forgive her for the near-drowning incident when she was five.

Almost.

"That's what I thought you said, but I just wanted to check." Sally paused. "What's the catch?"

"There is no catch — I'm not doing this for charity. It's a business, you'd still have to pay me rent. But if there's a need — and I think there is a need, especially in an area like Andersonville, lesbian central — then let's meet the need. Set it up, build it, they will come. It'll be like Kevin Costner all over again. What do you think?"

"I think it sounds… amazing. Perfect, even. Although

the only caveat is, I will probably need a bigger workspace than I had back in Queens. What with Whole Foods wanting me now. Did I mention that?" Sally grinned as she spoke.

Harriet put her arm around her and kissed her on the cheek. "I think you might have mentioned it once or twice."

Paula was doing the arms again. "That's why you can tell me what you both want and I'll get the architect to factor it in. Think about what didn't work in the space in Queens and we can change it here. This can be a bespoke space for creatives, designed by creatives." She rubbed her hands together. "I don't know about you, but I'm excited."

"I am, too," Harriet agreed.

"Give me a minute, it's a lot to digest," Sally said, turning to Taylor. "I can't see a downside, what do you think?"

"I think it's incredible and I think my girlfriend is amazing," Taylor replied.

"Finally, someone sees my true worth," Paula said with a grin, leaning over and placing a long kiss on Taylor's lips. "Shall we drink to it, then?" she added, holding up her glass. "To the Chicago Creative Collective — or whatever you want to call it. Here's to all the dykes who flock there like moths to a flame."

They all clinked their glasses in celebration.

"One last thing," Paula said, raising a single eyebrow in Sally and Harriet's direction. "I'm leaving the elevator christening to you both, as is now tradition. Let us know when you want to do it and we'll take the stairs, won't we, Taylor?"

Paula and Taylor followed that up with screeching laughter, and soon, Sally and Harriet followed.

If you couldn't beat them, it was best to join them.

Chapter Forty-One

The clean country air was drifting through Harriet's Prius as she drove with the windows down, the AC off. Over the years, she'd got bored of her whole life being air-conditioned, controlled, and sometimes when she was in the car, she liked to drive this way, feeling the wind ruffle her arm hair, the unseasonably warm November sun heating her skin. It felt good, but not anywhere near as good as having Sally sitting beside her, hand on Harriet's thigh, a declaration of love in her heart.

Sally had moved, and now it was Harriet's turn for a grand gesture, although she was pretty sure Sally had a hunch where they might be headed, seeing as they were on the road they'd driven down many times before: the one that ended in her family's lake house, where it all began.

"You know, I remember this drive from all those years ago," Sally said, taking her hand from Harriet's leg and sweeping it through her thick hair. She'd let it grow over the past few weeks, and it was now nearly down to her shoulders. It suited her.

"What do you remember most?"

"Wondering whether or not I'd manage to kiss you. Wondering if I was a lesbian. Wondering if it was okay to kiss you after I'd kissed your brother."

"That was a little weird. I can understand you wanting to kiss me, but Daniel?"

Sally's laughter filled the car. "In my defence, he did have long hair and looked a bit like a girl. Plus, I was young, so bite me." She paused, turning her head. "Actually, I believe you did."

"Your hickey was tiny," Harriet said, turning to her, demonstrating the size of the hickey with a tiny amount of space between her thumb and index finger.

"Nevertheless, a hickey. What a predictable teenager you were."

"And what an unpredictable one you were. Thankfully. Otherwise, we wouldn't be here now, would we?"

They pulled into the old house around half an hour later, cutting a Taylor Swift track in its prime and both sitting, staring. It looked just the same, and Harriet couldn't wait to get inside to see what had changed. Her family had sold it around ten years ago, and it was now a rental — which was exactly what Harriet had taken advantage of this weekend.

"This is more than a little strange," Sally said, shivering as she got out of the car, even though the sun was still a hot yellow ball above.

Harriet didn't need to ask the reason for the shiver: being back was bringing up a torrent of emotions for her, too. "I know, I didn't think this bit through." She walked around and stood beside Sally. "I thought it would be romantic, but coming back to the place where I spent my childhood summers is making me feel like I'm a kid again."

"You've got a better haircut now, if that helps."

Harriet laughed at that, and the tension was broken. "You always know how to make me smile, you know that?"

"That's a good thing, right?" Sally said, taking her hand as Harriet unlocked the black front door, walking into the hallway, the air frosted with furniture polish and air fresheners.

"A very good thing. My mom always said to have humor in your relationship, that it was more important than anything else. But then she married my dad, so what does she know?"

Sally elbowed her in the ribs as they walked through the large, airy hallway with the same plush carpet as before. "Your dad's still recovering from major surgery, give him time before you lay into him."

When they entered the kitchen, Harriet smiled: it hadn't changed a bit, still being the stylish space Robert had remodeled all those years ago. She remembered when it was done, the mess that had driven her parents mad all summer. Harriet walked in like she still owned the place, opening the double-fronted chrome fridge and pulling out a wicker picnic basket, along with a bottle of chilled white wine.

"How did that get there?" Sally asked, her eyebrows knitting together.

"I have ways and means," Harriet said. "Plus, I bribed the owner with an obscene amount of money if they left it in the fridge, and it worked great." She paused. "I thought we could take it out to the speedboat, a picnic on deck before it gets too cold? Only this time, we don't have to smuggle the wine in your jacket."

"Which makes it not nearly as fun," Sally replied, putting an arm around Harriet's waist. "But this *is* fun, being back here."

"You're sure?" Harriet asked.

"Of course," Sally replied, holding her gaze. "This is where we fell in love. How can it not be a good thing?" She paused. "But if you think you're getting lucky on the speedboat today, I'm going to have to disappoint you. Yes, it's warm, but it's still November."

Harriet grinned. "Where's your sense of adventure?"

She took Sally's hand and led her out of the house and across the front lawn, where the leaves on the Sugar Maple trees had turned a vibrant rusty orange. The speedboat was in front of them, still tethered to the wooden jetty, her parents having sold it along with the house. Harriet offered her hand to Sally, wary of her fear of water, and she took it with a determined smile.

Once they were both on board, Harriet unfurled the picnic blanket, securing it with the picnic basket on one corner, and her bag on the other. Then they both sat down together, pulling their jackets around them, legs splayed and squinting into the fall sunshine. Harriet didn't say a word as she poured them both a glass of wine, holding hers up to Sally when they were filled.

"To us being back here, where we first kissed." She leaned forward and planted a kiss on Sally's lips. "And to kissing you feeling just as good today as it did back then."

Sally's blue eyes sparkled as she smiled at Harriet. "If anything, kissing you has only got better. But now there's so much else to think about — being an adult is terrible. Moving back, finding somewhere to live, setting up the collective space with Taylor. It's all a bit much to take in."

"And do I fit into that lifestyle change somewhere, too?"

"You're the catalyst — you and your suitcase-stealing ways," Sally said, leaning forward and kissing Harriet again. "I've always loved you, Harriet Locke. It's like the sun, shining every day. It just is."

And Harriet couldn't agree more. When you loved someone so simply, so thoroughly, it was like breathing, like air. She hadn't realized fully, but before Sally came back into her life, she'd been living in black and white, in an era before Sally. But now, the color had been switched on, the contrast set just right, and her life had never looked so rosy.

She kissed Sally once more, her world view slurring as she did, and then came up for air, focusing on Sally's beautiful face.

It had always been Sally.

"I love you, too, but I hope you know that."

Sally smiled, nodding her head. "I do."

Harriet squeezed her hand, her eyes filling with tears. Dammit, she didn't mean to get emotional, but it was like Daniel had said: once she started talking about feelings, the floodgates were open. And she had to admit; being open with her emotions was kinda freeing. She wiped her eyes before continuing.

"And you know, this collective is going to take off, I just know it. With me, you, Paula, and Taylor behind it, how can it fail?"

"I hope you're right."

"I know I am," Harriet said, bracing herself. She had been planning to build up to this question, but now they were here, it seemed as good a time as any.

"And about you finding somewhere to live. I..." She paused, glancing out at the lake, before holding Sally's gaze, locking it in. "I don't want you to. And I know Paula offered to help you out, but I don't want that either."

"You want me to turn down money? That's not like you."

Harriet smiled: she deserved that. "Sally, we've been apart way more than we've been together in our lives, and from now on, I want us to be together, always. I have a three-bedroom apartment, and it's big enough for you. And if you don't want to live there permanently, we can move to somewhere else, somewhere we've both chosen.

"But the point is, I want you to live with me. I want to wake up next to you every morning. I want to do all the ordinary things, like make toast, watch TV, read a newspaper with you by my side."

Harriet took in a lungful of air before continuing. "I should have asked you years ago. I should never have let you go. But now I've got you back, this is really important. So, will you move in with me?"

Sally looked at her with so much love in her eyes, Harriet's heart boomed. It took less than five seconds for a wide grin to break out on her face, and for her to nod her head, her eyes getting watery.

Sally put down her glass, before taking Harriet's from her fingers and wrapping her arms around her neck, Sally's warmth enveloping her like the sun.

"Of course I'll move in with you — I just wasn't sure if you'd think it was too soon."

Harriet let out a strangled laugh. "When it comes to us, nothing's too soon, is it? We've got so much lost time to catch up on."

Sally nodded. "We really do," she said. "Starting now?"

Harriet nodded. "Starting right now," she said, placing a kiss on Sally's lips.

THE END

If you've enjoyed this book and want to read more,
you can download a FREE lesbian romance
It Had To Be You *by going to:*
www.clarelydon.co.uk/it-had-to-be-you

Also by Clare

London Romance Novels
London Calling
This London Love
A Girl Called London

Other Novels
The Long Weekend
Nothing To Lose: A Lesbian Romance

The All I Want Series
All I Want For Christmas (Book 1)
All I Want For Valentine's (Book 2)
All I Want For Spring (Book 3)
All I Want For Summer (Book 4)
All I Want For Autumn (Book 5)
All I Want Forever (Book 6)

Boxsets
All I Want Series Boxset, Books 1-3
All I Want Series Boxset, Books 4-6
All I Want Series Boxset, Books 1-6

A Note From Clare

I hope you enjoyed reading the story of Harriet and Sally — I know I enjoyed writing it. I did toy with the idea of calling it *When Harriet Met Sally*, but was told that was naff. I still kinda like it, but not as much as *Twice In A Lifetime*! I never had the luck of meeting my soulmate at age 17 — I had to wait till I was 33 for that to happen — but I hope the story resonated whatever age you met yours. And if you're still waiting, I hope it gave you hope that day will come!

If you have a moment, I'd also really appreciate an honest review on the site you bought it on. Reviews are hugely important as they encourage new readers to take a chance on me — if my book's got some reviews, they're far more likely to give me a try. So if you'd like more books from me, please take a moment to leave your thoughts. And it doesn't have to be a novel — even a few lines makes a difference and every review means so much!

If you fancy getting in touch, you can do so using one of the methods below — I'm most active on Twitter, Facebook or Instagram.

Twitter: @ClareLydon
Facebook: www.facebook.com/clare.lydon
Instagram: @clarefic
Find out more at: www.clarelydon.co.uk
Contact: mail@clarelydon.co.uk

THANK YOU SO MUCH FOR READING!

Printed in Great Britain
by Amazon

J189